I am Simran

AF538696

I am Simran

S.K. Narang

No part of this publication can be reproduced, stored in a retrieval system or transmitted in any form or by any means, electronic, mechanical, photocopying, recording or otherwise, without the prior permission of the author and the publisher.

Published by
PRABHAT PAPERBACKS
An imprint of Prabhat Prakashan Pvt. Ltd.
4/19 Asaf Ali Road,
New Delhi-110002 (INDIA)
e-mail: prabhatbooks@gmail.com

ISBN 978-93-90900-14-5
I AM SIMRAN
by Shri S.K. Narang

Edition
First, 2021

Price
₹ 300.00 (Rupees Three Hundred only)

© Reserved

Printed at
R-Tech Offset Printers, Delhi

To

Simran,

Lost somewhere,

In the mist of

TIME.

1

The sweltering combatant summer was extremely hot in Jaipur and appeared to smash all old records. There was no option but to bear the fury of sun-god. The fans had also thrown their hands up and sweat was running down the body like a stream of hot water. Four-hour official power cut and two-hour unofficial, had further added to the woes of the poor. Situation in rural Rajasthan was worse, where women with long-drawn veils had to battle miles of barefooted walk in sizzling sand and blazing sun, to bring water in few pitchers smartly balanced on their heads. Even a few hours' current was a luxury there. The unbearable heat of the day was fortunately compensated by little cooler nights. Conditions in over-populated metros like Delhi were no better. Here, besides the furious summer, over two million vehicles out of total five million registered ones were every time running on the roads, further multiplying heat and pollution levels.

On one such blistering night in Delhi, she got down from the bus, hurriedly tried to cross the road, stumbling at places while repeatedly looking back, and headed straight towards the nearest platform of the railway station. Head covered with *dupatta* to avoid easy recognition, she was trying to locate a telephone booth. Fortunately, she soon spotted one. With trembling hands and prayer on her terrified lips, she picked up the receiver, dialled a number and inserted a one-rupee coin in the slot. Fortune favoured her and the call got connected.

Hiding her face from the mad jostling crowd with eyes looking through the corners to see if the devils were still chasing her, she covered the side of the receiver with her hand to ensure secrecy of talk.

Puris had just finished their dinner and Pooja, Ramesh Puri's wife, was in the kitchen when the phone bell rang. Popping her head out of the kitchen and wiping hands with *dupatta*, she said, "It must be Dolly's phone. Just talk to her. I will join in a few minutes."

Dolly was their daughter, now living in America and she normally gave a call every Saturday night. Pooja always anxiously awaited her call and their talk would usually last an hour. She would sit comfortably on the sofa with crossed legs and go on non-stop with her daughter, whom she intensely loved though she loved her son Rohit with equal warmth. Topics could be anything under the sun, and normally ranged from kitchen to clothes and maid to kin, while poor weather was generally cursed, though sparingly appreciated. Ramesh was sometimes amazed at the variety of topics of discussion and the ease of switching from one subject to another. Poor father could hardly get enough time to say 'hello' to his daughter at the beginning or end of the call.

"Hello," said Ramesh in a very affectionate tone.

"Uncle." The voice on the other side was very feeble.

It was not a call from his daughter. "Who is on the line? Please speak loudly. I can't hear you."

"Uncle, I am Simran. Is it Puri uncle speaking?"

"Yes, I am Ramesh Puri. Sorry, I am unable to place you."

"Uncle, I am Simran. I worked in your home and left a few months back."

"Oh! Simmi? Your voice was shaky and you were sounding very nervous. That's why I could not recognise it. I recollect now. How are you?"

"Uncle, please do not disconnect. I am in terrible trouble. They are after my blood. They will kill me if they locate me. My life is in danger. Please come immediately to take me. I have no money. Please help me. I request you in the name of God." She said non-stop in a terrified and quivering voice.

"Who are after your blood? And where are you?"

"Uncle, I am at Old Delhi railway station. My father's two friends are out to kill me. They had kidnapped me. Somehow I have managed to get out of their clutches. Please come and save me. You are my only hope, my last hope."

"Why don't you call your Rani *maa* who is in Delhi? She will be able to take you immediately and you would be safe there. She loved you and had always been kind to you."

"Uncle, I don't want to go there. They will immediately trace me and then take me with them. If I resist, they will kill me. Only you can save me. I will tell you everything. Please come as early as possible. I request you with folded hands. I am calling from an STD booth and the line may get disconnected any time. I may not be able to call you again."

Ramesh Puri was utterly confused. Helping someone in distress is a noble deed but may land him in some unwanted trouble. There was no time to consult his wife, as Simran may not be able to call him again. Decision had to be taken immediately. He maintained his calm under pressure. Reflecting on all aspects of the problem, he acted on his instinct and immediately replied, "Simmi, you do one thing. Stay there. It will take me about four hours to come by taxi." To make sure that she was listening, he asked, "Are you getting me?"

"Yes uncle, I am on the line. Please tell me."

Safety of Simran was the prime concern. At the spur of the moment, an idea clicked his mind. "Since someone is chasing you, staying at the railway station will not be safe as they will immediately think of railway stations and bus terminals. Do one thing. There is *Gurudwara Sis Ganj* near the station. You come out of the station and turn left. Go straight and turn right at the next turning. You will see the *Gurudwara*. It will take hardly ten minutes on foot. Have courage and don't be panicky. It is 9.30 now. I will take a taxi immediately and shall be there in about four hours. At 2 o'clock, you meet me at the gate of the *Gurudwara*. Till then, stay inside the *Gurudwara* and pray. I am leaving Jaipur now. Have you got everything?"

"Yes uncle. I have understood your instructions. Thank you very much. I will wait for you at the gate of the *Gurudwara*. But please do come, else I may be no more. I cannot talk now."

"God bless you. Go to the *Gurudwara* and pray."

Call was disconnected. The pleasant conversation immediately brought a flicker of hope and joy on the deeply distressed face of Simran.

Meanwhile, Pooja joined her husband. She had some patchy indication of the discussion, but could not guess the context.

"Whose call was that and whom were you telling to go to the *Gurudwara*?"

Ramesh narrated details of the whole conversation to his wife. She had always been very supportive in life and Ramesh did not expect any divergent opinion from her. By nature, she had been helpful to the poor, particularly the girls. Fortunately for him, she immediately appreciated and endorsed his decision of helping Simran. She had loved her as her own daughter and had never treated her as a maid, when she worked in their home for about four years.

"The poor girl must be in great trouble, otherwise she would have not called you at this time of night. You have taken a very sensible decision to immediately go to Delhi and bring her. Change your night suit. Meanwhile, I will call the taxi. You leave for Delhi immediately. Keep me informed on the way. I will pray for her safety."

Ramesh was mighty relieved at the favourable response of his wife, though he was sure that she would reciprocate his decision to bring Simran and save her from any life-threatening danger. She gave him a bag containing a bottle of ice-cold water, some fruits, a hand towel and a comb. She also gave detailed instructions to him regarding the care and safety of the poor girl in distress. Out of sheer anxiety, she repeated them to ensure that her forgetful husband had grasped them properly.

Ramesh Puri had retired as Deputy Director from the Department of Education, Government of Delhi. He had two children, a son and a daughter. Rohit had done his B.Tech. from Delhi Engineering College and was now working as a software engineer in a company in America. Dolly, ten years younger to her brother, did her MBA from Jaipur and was also well-settled in America. Ramesh was an enterprising and ambitious man and was keen to establish his own school. While in service, he had applied for a plot in Delhi, Haryana and Rajasthan. Fortunately, he got one at Jaipur for a Kindergarten school. It was primarily on the insistence of his wife, that he decided to move to Jaipur to start a KG school, where girls of poor parents, who could not afford fatty tuition fees were preferred and provided free education. They bought a two-bedroom flat at Jaipur. In a flat in another society, bought in the name of Rohit with his earnings, they started a Paying Guest accommodation for college girls. During her earlier stay, Simran also worked in the school and because of her affectionate and adorable nature, had endeared herself with the staff and was loved by all. Much against her wish, she had to leave Jaipur because of the stubbornness of her father.

On way to Delhi, Ramesh kept on praying for the safety of Simran. His anxiety was all the more intense on account of his inability to talk to her again. A wide array of thoughts kept on crossing his mind and tormenting him as normally happens with all, under such scary circumstances. Puris did not know much about Simran except that she was born in a small village near Patiala in Punjab. Her father, Daljeet Singh, was a mechanical engineer and had shifted to Delhi after the death of his wife. He started living with Suman, whose elder sister, Rani, was working as a maid in their flat at Delhi. It was with her that Simran, about five years old, occasionally used to come. She was a beautiful, fair-complexioned girl with dimpled cheeks and bright prospects of growing into a tall and fair Punjabi young girl. Her long and lusty jet black hair further added to her charms. She hardly uttered a word, and was extremely shy and reserved. At times, she carried a very innocent smile on her comely cheeks, but a sense of some strange fear was always discernible on her face.

Her childhood, as briefly disclosed by Rani, had been full of horrifying tragedies and she had survived merely because of good luck and care of Rani, who loved her as her own daughter. She was about thirteen, when Rani brought her to Jaipur to pull her out of the dusty, dingy and unhealthy slums of Delhi, and she worked in the home of Puris for about four years. Extremely disciplined, obedient and hard-working, she was loved by all in the family. Dolly loved her most and always motivated her to study. It was because of her persuasion and inspiration that Simran passed X class with good marks and had to appear in XII class, when her father took her back to Delhi. Her welfare after she left them was always a cause of grave concern to them. Daljeet did not maintain any communication and Puris were ignorant of the fate of the young girl. Deeply drowned in these recollections of the past, Ramesh Puri reached Delhi.

Simran meticulously followed the instructions of her

uncle. Looking around with worrying looks, toe profusely bleeding, she reached the desired destination and thanked God for her safety. Depositing *chappals* at the designated place, she washed her feet at the entrance of the *Gurudwara* as was customary before entering the abode of *Guru*. To recharge her mind with greater confidence, she folded her hands and began to recite *Japuji Sahib* that her grandmother had made her remember by heart. Awfully fatigued physically and mentally, she dozed off intermittently but her eyes remained transfixed at the gate with every devotee appearing to be her kidnapper. Ghosts seemed to be following her to catch her, drag her on the road, and confine her to the veritable hell. Mind wandered over the painful past and hopeful future. She prayed for her woes to end. Some deeply disturbing fear of future was violently churning her heart.

Terrified, Simran was hardly able to concentrate on her prayers. Forgetting and jumping from line to line, she sat with her head buried in hands. She would often keep eyes closed like the pigeon, who believes that the cat is also not able to see him, or the ostrich, who buries his head in sand with the hope that the hunter has gone. In distress, time appears to stand still or moves at snail's pace, while in happiness, it seems to take wings. She did not realise that time does not run on one's direction, but moves at its own pace. It is our perception that makes it slow or fast. By going out, time would have passed perhaps more easily, but that was fraught with grave danger. Caught again, suicide would be her only option. Being optimistic, she wanted to live, and some voice within impelled her to survive for some better cause in life. Time passed in hope and fear, and finally lost race. Smaller hand of the clock reached the digit of two. Bowing down and thanking God for her survival so far, she got up with hands still folded in prayer. She hurried towards the gate of the *Gurudwara* in the hope of meeting her uncle.

With taxi parked, Ramesh reached the *Gurudwara*. Looking anxiously in all directions, the two hearts were beating fast, with hope in mind and prayer on lips. Anxious to find their respective target, both were moving swiftly and looking at the devotees at the gate. Finally, the momentous moment arrived and Simran was first to spot her uncle. Mighty relieved, her fear substantially disappeared at his sight. Her heart began to beat faster, and, in excitement, she shouted, "Uncle!"

Ramesh looked around. His eyes wandered all over. Simran came closer to him and said, "Uncle, I am here. Perhaps you did not recognise me." Immensely excited, she momentarily forgot all her past woes.

Ramesh repeatedly looked at her from head to toe and was absolutely stunned. It would have been almost impossible for him to recognise her if he had met her somewhere by chance. Her dress was awfully shabby, body totally soaked in sweat, hair dishevelled, eyes dreary and deeply sunken, and face gone miserably pale. All natural glow of the once stunningly charming young girl had woefully withered. Perhaps hungry for days, she looked more like a moving skeleton.

Holding her hand, Ramesh said, "Simran, let us move quickly from this place." At the parking lot, he handed over the bottle of water to her. "Drink some water and wash your face." Giving her the comb, he asked her to set her hair properly. On asking about dinner, she told him that she had taken *langar* at the *Gurudwara*. Waiting for a moment, he resumed, "Simmi, be careful. Do not talk about any problem on the way and try to behave absolutely normal. You are the daughter of my cousin and a part of my family. All this is essential to dispel any suspicion from the mind of the driver or any other person." He repeated all that his wife had directed him to say.

Simran nodded in affirmation and did as directed. To make sure that it was a reality and not a dream, she pinched herself. A sense of confidence was discernible on her face and hope of safety and better future had partially returned her charm. Occasionally she began to display slight smile on her lips and repeatedly looked at her saviour, perhaps to thank him inwardly for rescuing her from the clutches of merciless barbarians. Comfortably seated in the taxi, the first thing Ramesh did was to inform his wife about the safety of Simran, and that he was bringing her home. To give an idea to the driver that she was his relative, it was essential to talk about something rather than sit dumb.

"Simran, was everyone all right at home?"

Taken aback, Simran surprisingly looked at her uncle. Regaining her composure, she replied, "Yes uncle, everyone is fine at home and all remembered you and aunty." Some more fake family matters were discussed. Ramesh was surprised and wondered how quickly she had understood and grasped the motive and direction of discussion. He looked at her with a satisfying smile perhaps to thank her for her absolutely normal behaviour.

Back home, Pooja could not have a wink of sleep after the departure of her husband. Tormented by the sufferings of Simran, she was extremely restless. She kept on listening to *Hanuman Chalisa* on her mobile, and prayed for the safety of the poor girl. Though apparently satisfied after the call of her husband, she constantly talked to him to know all details of their whereabouts. While they were about half-way down, Ramesh received a call from her.

"Do not ask me anything. Just listen to me." Ramesh was surprised and waited with bated breath. "It is possible that her father, who seems to be in league with the abductors, may come here. He is a very shrewd man and may enquire from the guards of the society who know Simran, since she had earlier stayed here. Do not bring her here. For her safety, we will keep her in our other flat. We have to take all necessary precautions and think of all possible moves of her father and his associates."

With all his imagination, Ramesh could have never thought of this safe and sensible move of his intelligent and far-sighted wife. Simran had still not turned 18, and there were always legal implications of keeping a minor against the permission of her father. Once she was a major in about seven months' time, there would be no legal hassle in keeping her as per her desire. Fortunately, the other flat, earlier occupied by six college girls, was vacant, as all girls had gone home after their exams, and the new lot was expected in July only. The flat was fully furnished with all necessities of kitchen and Simran would have no problem in staying there.

Immensely satisfied with all precautions for the safety and future well-being of Simran, the two reached Jaipur. Pooja was already anxiously waiting for them. Though sure of Simran's safety, still she would have not been mentally satisfied till she had physically seen her with her own eyes. Simran folded her hands, bowed down reverently and respectfully murmured in hardly audible voice, "*Namaste* aunty."

Surprised but mighty pleased, Pooja hugged her tightly. Tears frozen in the cold eyes of Simran suddenly melted and began to flow like a stormy river. To lighten her mental fatigue, she began to weep loudly. Breath came in hitching gaps. Pooja tried to console the inconsolable girl. With some difficulty and having exhausted her present quota of tears, Simran stopped weeping, but did not relax the grip of her loving aunt's hand. Her throat was too parched to say even one word. In her mind, she was unconsciously trying to say, 'Please do not leave me. I have no one in this wild world to take care of me.' Pooja made her sit comfortably on the sofa and brought a glass of water.

Pooja had already kept tea ready in a flask that all enjoyed.

Pleasantly surprised at the warm reception, teary-eyed Simran warmly held Pooja's hand and looked affectionately into her eyes. The foundation of confluence and perfect fusion of love and reverence of mother and daughter had been laid in those few moments.

Pooja's searching eyes suddenly fell on the feet of Simran. There was some dried blood on the toe of the right foot that Ramesh had not noticed. "Why, your toe had been bleeding?"

Simran tried to cover the foot with her other foot and said. "I just stumbled against a piece of stone and hurt my toe." Pooja brought some warm water and tried to wash the foot of Simran, who immediately withdrew it.

"Aunty, I will do it."

"Stop saying anything", said Pooja with the affectionate authority of a mother. "You are so careless. It can become septic." She softly washed her toe, taking utmost care not to hurt her, applied some antiseptic ointment and bandaged it properly. With tears falling, Simran kept on looking at her. She wanted to say that this will heal soon, but the pain of the wound inflicted on the soul by the devils will last forever. Though Rani had incredible affection for her and treated her as her own daughter, nobody had ever cared for her so lovingly. She began to dream about the advent of a new dawn in her otherwise gloomy life.

Simran hugged her aunt again and thanked her. Looking around, she was surprised and suddenly said, "Aunty, have you changed the residence? I don't think this is the same flat."

"I appreciate your keen power of observation. Actually, this is our other flat. It is a paying guest accommodation for girls. We did not think it safer to keep you in the old flat as your father, I am sure, will soon come in search of you. With criminals and those of criminal mind, we have to think differently. One should move a step ahead of the adversary, and every move of the enemy must be anticipated and countered at the right time. Prevention is always better than cure and it is better to be safe than sorry. You will be absolutely safe here."

Ramesh looked at his wife. He was astonished at the affection and care that she was taking for the restoration of Simran's confidence. The physical pain and mental agony of the young girl, who had suffered at the hands of destiny and the society was inexplicable in words, and could only be felt and fathomed by a woman.

Strange are the hues of relations. Blood relations betray while strangers stay. Discarded by her very own, the unknown embraced Simran. Fortune had been playing a see-saw game with her. Tossed from one place to another, she finally landed in the safe and secure arms of Pooja and Ramesh, who came from nowhere to clasp her warmly in their arms for no craving of any return. She was now fully convinced of her sound and promising future. She looked at Pooja and silently thanked her for her far-sightedness and care for her safety.

Affectionately holding her cheeks in her hands, Pooja said, "Simran, now you relax. Take bath and get ready. I have brought one of Dolly's suits. You can wear it for the time being. I will get a few more good ones altered to your size. There are some fruits for you for breakfast. We will come after an hour or so. Do not prepare lunch today. We will do some shopping and have lunch there. You can also have a glimpse of the market, and know its difference from the mad crowds of Delhi, though Jaipur environment is not alien to you. Uncle will get the TV shifted from drawing room to one of the bedrooms. There are some good books that girls had left. In solitude, they will be your closest friends. Tonight, both of us will sleep here so that the strange new place does not haunt you. Fortunately, school is closed for summer vacation and both of us will stay here with you during the day also."

Before leaving, Ramesh Puri turned back and with a very serious and stern look, suddenly dropped a bombshell. "Simran, you are not allowed to go out and will remain imprisoned in this flat."

Simran was completely bewildered. Shocked and terrified, her face suddenly went pale. Fear of another confinement began to agonise her. She was speechless, and wondered if all the affection shown so far was sheer sham. Standing like a statue, she quizzically looked at her aunt. Seeing her state of mind, Pooja smiled and warmly hugged her. With gravely anguished looks, she turned towards her husband and said, "Why are you scaring my chicken-hearted innocent child? She is already so tense and still struggling to be normal." Embracing her tightly, Pooja continued, "My child, change your tears into cheers. Uncle is just kidding. We will lock the flat from outside. Sometimes property dealers come and ring the bell to know about the status of renting the flat. Seeing it locked, nobody will ring the bell. In the evening, we will get it disconnected. This is simply to ensure your safety."

Hugging Ramesh and looking lovingly into his eyes, she said, "Uncle, you had scared me dead. My heart virtually stopped beating and ground slipped from below my feet. All sorts of negative and destructive ideas flashed across my mind in those few chilling moments."

Coming closer to her aunt, she held her hand and said, "Aunty, I have to make one request to you. Please promise that you will not disappoint me."

"Apart from your request for leaving, you can ask anything."

With little heaviness in her heart, Simran said, "Aunty, I have no place to go to now. I will never leave you, and hope, you will not throw me out as an unwanted burden after listening to the horrific and repulsive story of the last few months of my life, when I was taken away by my father, if he deserves to be called so."

Both Pooja and Ramesh were stunned at the frankness of Simran. Her past, though suspected to be extremely tragic, was completely beyond their comprehension. To make her more comfortable and to reassure her, Pooja warmly looked into her eyes and said, "Simmi, my child, get rid of the fear of desertion. We cannot even dream of asking you to go. A daughter is never a burden. She is a gift of God to the mother. Do not scratch the memories of the bygone days. They cause nothing but pain. The timid live under the shadow of the past; the courageous always move forward."

To strengthen her confidence, Ramesh added, "Simran, never get entangled in negative thoughts. Sweep them under the carpet. Life is growth. It is never still. Remember, life is a boxing ring. You have to fight and defeat your opponent rather than moan about his existence. Dark clouds will wither one day; bright sunshine will come. Howsoever long the night, dawn will certainly break, but we have to keep our eyes open to see it."

Hugging her, Pooja said, "You are my second daughter and third child. Please tell me what you wanted to say."

Simran regained her strength, and after taking a deep breath, said with the authority of an affectionate daughter, "Aunty, from now onward, I will take over all kitchen duties. You may enter the kitchen to guide me but are not permitted to do any work."

Simran's request was beyond the imagination of both. They were also surprised at the confidence with which she had forced her request. Both looked at each other and then at Simran. Pooja said, "Simmi, I agree, though reluctantly. For the time being, you may take over the charge of the kitchen, but remember, you are our niece, daughter of uncle's cousin brother and have come here from the village for studies. Do not reveal any detail of your past life to anyone, though nobody will ask you. Try to remain little reserved but cheerful. Soon more college girls will come here as paying guests and a maid will cook for all the girls. There will be complete academic atmosphere. Uncle will bring books in a few days and you start studying. Appear in your Senior Secondary examination in March and then join the college. Live here like a normal student and study in the company of senior girls. We will provide all the physical, financial and moral support for your career. Be a noble human being and strive for your bright and prosperous future. This is not only our wish but also our command."

Simran was astonished at the love and care being extended to her by both. She had thought that she will work as a maid as in the past, but never imagined even in her wildest dreams that she would be treated as a family member. Warmly placing her head on the shoulder of her aunt and arms around her neck, she said, "Aunty, please do not give me so many privileges. I am a withered and trampled flower, and once you know my disgraced past, you may discard me as a rotten piece of linen. I had come here to work as a maid and would be quite comfortable in that position. I do not want your prestige and honour to be dented on account of my shameful past."

"Simran, I will slap you if you say again working as a maid. You are our own dear child and we want you to lead a dignified life here. Your past, pure or impure, dirty or clean, is of least concern to us. We are interested in your present and future. We know for sure, you are a very simple girl of noble virtues. If anything has happened, we are fully convinced that you have not been responsible for the same. Even while following a righteous path, your clothes can be stained with mud for no fault of yours. You might have suffered on account of your destiny, or this unethical society. I reiterate, break free of the shackles of the past, and do not wallow in its dirt and scum. Do not lose hope of tomorrow for the tears of yesterday. It is unfortunate that we live in the pain of the past or fear of the future, but not in the pleasure of the present. Remember, yesterday is history; tomorrow is mystery. Today is a gift. Think of the future but live in the present. We want you to be a good human being and lead a noble life."

To reassure Simran, Ramesh also joined. "Look Simran, we are not cowards and in no way afraid of this wretched society. We can visualise problems of a lonely adolescent girl in modern times in a metropolitan city, particularly when she is deprived of the support of even her father. We can imagine the worst even if you do not tell us. We will certainly try to know all details from you at the appropriate time."

Assurance of Ramesh further strengthened her confidence in her safe future. She could never imagine the force with which they would support her and allow her to stay with them as a part of their family. Breathing a sigh of relief, she said, "Uncle, you are my last hope of life. Either I will stay here or go to God, who will not refuse to accept me."

"Simmi, cowards only think of ending life; courageous face it and fight. Remember, all our thoughts and actions emanate from our mental map. Positive thoughts lead to nobler deeds that change the fabric of our life. Always be optimistic. It leads to more creative thoughts though too much optimism is also dangerous and can sometimes lead to negative consequences." Ramesh waited for a while and resumed, "You are our child and we need you more than you need us. With Dolly also settled, we have no one here to look after us. You are the support of our old age." Simran was simply humbled by the gracious remarks of her uncle.

Pooja wanted to further reinforce her confidence. "Simran, in future, never talk of leaving us. I also want you to fight against this despicable and cruel society. Be a role model for all. Always think you are born for a mission. Relentlessly strive to achieve it. Create dreams, aspire to follow them, and fortify your determination to achieve them. I have an ardent belief that a bright morn awaits you."

Simran was absolutely tongue-tied. She had no words to speak. She knew that both uncle and aunt were very kind-hearted but could never imagine that they would be so nice, generous and caring. She placed her head in the lap of Pooja. Her eyes were moist. Pooja affectionately kissed her forehead and started caressing her messy dry hair. The nagging fear of desertion by the Puris completely vanished from her mind.

The flat was locked and both left. Suddenly Pooja was looking little stressed and Ramesh got worried. Sensing some nervousness on her face, he asked, "Pooja, why have you suddenly become so tense? Some worry seems to be plaguing your mind."

"My sinking fear is Daljeet. If he comes by any chance and claims the custody of Simran, she will be in great trouble and we will be helpless."

"I am also concerned about that but less worried. I pray that seven more months may pass peacefully and once she is an adult, Daljeet will have no legal right to claim her custody. My worry is up to 13th December. There is remote possibility of his tracing her before that date, but if by any chance he comes, I will consult some experienced advocate. In legal wrangles, seven months can easily pass, and then, Simran will be safe. So, bury the worry and get rid of any negative concern. Best way to deal with fear is to ignore it."

"I have a very strong apprehension that she has suffered some grave tragedies in the last few months. Fortune seems to have been unkind to her. Let us strive to restore her confidence. I am quite optimistic and hope that with our motivation and encouragement, and her hard work and determination, she will have a bright future. Fortunately, she has all the requisite qualities of a good human being."

"You try to probe into her past life. Once we know those details, we will be in a position to plan her future properly. As a girl, she may be more prone to open up with you. We have to encourage her to shake off her pain of the past. Constant hammering and encouragement will be needed."

Simran was now completely relaxed in the flat. After bath, she looked into the mirror and locked her smile with her reflection. She had not seen her face in the mirror for the last few days. She was looking stunningly charming with her long lusty locks falling merrily on her shoulders. There was joy and confidence on her face. Suddenly, the mental calm was disturbed and she began to fear some danger lurking in those moments of delight. Unpleasant memories overshadowed her happiness and started haunting her. Tragedies that had continuously chased her, began to rewind before her inward eye. What would have happened if Puri uncle had not come? With no alternative, she might have put her neck on the railway track. Death, she thought, would have been more sympathetic than the cruelty of life. She feared now that her father might come anytime to snatch her from the Puris. She, however, decided to be firm and never go back with him. With all these scary thoughts, she began to dream of her bright future and comfortable stay with her benefactors for the rest of her life. Deeply drowned in the sweet and sour memories of the past, smile intermittently returned to her face. She was oblivious of Pooja standing behind her and smiling. Her teasing cough startled her.

"Be careful. See! You don't fall in love with yourself?"

Simran blushed and immediately clung to Pooja like a baby. She could only say, "Aunty?"

After a few moments, Pooja said, "Come on, leave me now. Let us go. Uncle is waiting."

In the market, Pooja bought four suits, a pair of jeans, T-shirts, a pair of night gowns, some simple but very essential make-up material and other stuff needed by girls. Simran was amazed at the expenditure and said, "Aunty, please do not buy so many things. I don't need them. I can wear Dolly *didi's* suits. You are spending too much."

Looking at her with a sense of authority, Pooja retorted, "You don't interfere in my job. I am well aware of the needs of my daughter, even if she does not demand". Simran had no courage to react. A mobile phone of moderate cost was also bought. She was told that same was only to be in touch with them. Her safety was extremely paramount at that critical stage and even for talking to Rani, she should use only Pooja's mobile. After a sumptuous lunch, all returned to the flat for a well-deserved rest.

Though very keen and anxious, Puris were careful not to open the topic of the past with Simran on that day as her wounds would be still fresh, and scratching them could be extremely painful. Little restraint was more advisable. That night, Pooja slept with Simran on the same bed. She often got up to reassure that Simran was having a comfortable sleep and was not under any tension. She was careful to relieve her of any mental baggage, and tried her best to see that she did not slide into depression. She was aware that at that critical age of adolescence, and with her past as she could vaguely guess, Simran needed utmost mental and emotional support.

Next day, after breakfast also Puris did not think it desirable to open the topic of her past. Simran was keen to know about Dolly *didi*, who had been a source of great inspiration to her during her earlier stay at Jaipur. She loved Simran because of her affable nature and treated her as her own younger sister. It was only due to her encouragement and persuasion, that Simran started studying. She had to appear in Senior Secondary, when her father came and forcibly took her to Delhi. It was during her absence that Dolly was married, which she could not attend, even though her father had promised to bring her. In fact, he never maintained any communication with them after taking her from Jaipur.

"I could not attend *didi's* marriage, for which I was so keen. I requested papa a number of times to take me to Jaipur. Aunty, though there was no apparent reason, he hated the mention of your names. He threatened me and beat me a couple of times for praising you. Surprisingly, he hated everyone who loved me."

"To know your welfare, we also tried to contact him but he did not care to even pick up the phone. We had a deep-rooted apprehension that all was not well with you but were helpless. Rani also did not reveal anything and would only say that Simran was happy and enjoying."

"Aunty, she was also in the dark. Papa did not maintain any contact with her. She was completely ignorant about the tragic developments of that period." Simran was not keen to discuss anything about her past, and to break the seriousness of discussion, she changed the topic. "Aunty, how are *didi* and *bhayia*?"

"Both are fine and enjoying. We will tell Dolly about you after some time. She will be mighty pleased and would talk to you."

After the tasty lunch prepared by Simran, all were relaxed and it was an appropriate time to start the topic of Simran's past.

□

2

"Simran, during your telephone call and later on after your arrival, you had hinted that your life was in danger and abductors were after your blood. We did not ask you the details at that time, as we wanted you to mentally relax and regain the proper frame of mind. Please do not feel any pressure. We will not force you against your wish, though, as your well-wishers, we certainly want to know the tragedy that befell you after you left us last. This will facilitate us to know the problems of our child better and help us in your future settlement. If you are not prepared now, we can talk about this later on."

"Aunty, I have no reservations with you now. I am physically and mentally relaxed. I will open my heart and reveal even the minutest details of my past with the fond hope that after listening to me, you will not start hating me as that would be the end of my life. My fear is your reaction."

Retorting sharply, Ramesh said, "Simran, Pooja has already told you to get rid of the fear of desertion. You must have faith in us."

"I am sorry, uncle. I apologise with folded hands. The words inadvertently came on my tongue. I promise I will never repeat this again in my life."

To soften the seriousness of the situation, Pooja asked, "Now, tell us all details since you left us last and do not hide anything. A daughter is always very frank with her mother, and you should tell me everything without any hesitation."

"Aunty, my long traumatic tale is a grim sob story intricately layered with heart-bleeding and hair-raising episodes. There are many gripping details particularly of my stay in Delhi, before coming to you, that you are not aware of. Rani *maa* had intentionally not revealed all facts to you at that stage to avoid causing any pain to you. Let me start with my childhood, even though you have some vague idea. I have very faint and hazy memory of my early days. Life had never been kind to me, and my misfortunes started from the day I was born. My mother died immediately after my birth. Family is a cradle of love and happiness in childhood, but I was bereft of that. My father started hating me, thinking that I was responsible for the death of his wife, whom he intensely loved. Disowned by my father and bereft of the warmth of the lap of my mother, I was left to the care of my grandmother, who was the only one in the family, who loved me. The severely superstitious society also despised me and considered me a curse for the family. I was often addressed as *'daayan'*, an evil spirit that devoured human beings."

"Simmi, it is very common in our society. Prejudices overtake reason, and people do not realise that life and death are in the hands of God. How can a baby just born be responsible for the death of her mother? It is so sad and distressing that for our misfortunes, we seek refuge in blaming others."

"Aunty, children would not play with me or even talk to me. Ladies used to take their children away on seeing me. They believed that I would swallow their children. Their behaviour surprised me most. My grandmother was very supportive and fought with such superstitious women. I was profoundly attached to her and never left her even for a moment. Just as creepers need support to grow and climb, she was my support in childhood. She was affectionate like a mother, caring like a sister and playful like a friend. She used to say that in me, she rediscovered her motherhood, relived her childhood and enjoyed all the happiness of her life. I feel if she had not been there, I might have been buried alive by my father and relatives."

Reacting to Daljeet's hatred for Simran, Ramesh remarked, "Simran, thoughts originate in mind and give rise to our actions. One reason for negative and destructive behaviour of your father was his passionate love for your mother. He could not bear pain of her separation, and instinctively shifted all the blame for his misfortunes on you. Instead of coming to terms with realities, he decided to seek reprisal by inflicting injury on someone, and here, he chose you. You became his soft and easy target, as he could not take revenge against anyone else. As a student of psychology, Pooja will be better able to throw some more light on such a retributive and repulsive behaviour of your father."

"Simran, inside governs outside. Hatred exists in mind and not in an incident, though it is the incident that becomes its cause. Revenge is a consequence of that inner hatred and has no solid logical reason. Generally, people when deprived of something that they cherished most in life, quench their hostility by inflicting injury or harm on some other person around them. Revenge aggravates wounds caused by the original offence, and gives rise to a cycle of retaliation. The victims believe in 'eye for an eye' and do not realise that this makes everyone blind. Their will-power generally becomes weak and they find solace and satisfaction in wreaking vengeance on others, without gaining anything in return. An emotionally insecure person is always an easy prey to such negative tendencies. He can suffer for long periods and even whole life, unless some corrective mental restoration measures are taken. I am afraid, retaliation of your father may also continue his whole life."

Endorsing the strong assertions of Pooja, Simran reiterated, "Aunty, I also have strong misgiving that death of my mother was the main cause of his frustration, and his hatred for me. The result was my desertion and all the future tragedies of my distressed life. Unfortunately, this feeling of hatred also inadvertently got transferred to all those closer to me."

Heaving a deep sigh, Pooja said, "It is difficult to fathom the feelings and ambitions of a dying mother at that moment. The unfortunate lady died with lots of unexpressed hopes and aspirations in her mind. Strange are His ways. He puts us in deep dark pit to test our patience. So was the will of God, and destiny had preordained all these tribulations in your life."

To lighten the sad and gloomy mood, Simran hopped on to another topic to narrate the details of the marriage of her parents. "Aunty, the story of marriage of my parents is like a fairy tale. Papa was the only child of his parents and his father had died when he was just five years old. *Dadi* told me that papa was a very happy-go-lucky man and in the enjoyment of his youth, he always avoided the subject of marriage. He would straightaway refuse any marriage proposal put before him by *dadi* and would sidetrack the issue. All pleadings of *dadi* of growing old, and desire to see and play with grandchildren fell on deaf ears of my father.

One day, *dadi* placed before papa the proposal of Channi, daughter of her cousin brother. Papa had already met her in some village fair and both had immediately fallen in love. He often used to meet her on the outskirts of the village and in fairs. He used to take her for joyrides on his bike. Their cute romance blossomed, and they decided to marry each other. He was, of course, ignorant of the family relations. On meeting her in the home they acted as if they were meeting for the first time. Their eyes and actions did convey some intimacy, but in her innocence, *dadi* did not suspect anything. She was, of course, surprised when papa immediately accepted the proposal. The meeting resulted in matrimonial alliance.

Dadi told me that mama and papa intensely loved each other and would not tolerate separation even for a second. According to her, my mother was tall, slim, fair complexioned and very social. Everyone was particularly enchanted by her captivating smile and pearl-like sparkling teeth. She used to participate in all social functions, was a good dancer and sweet singer of folk songs. Affectionate by nature, she was loved by all, and looked after *dadi* very well. Unfortunately, the tragedy befell and she died immediately after my birth, without even having a glimpse of me."

Simran could not continue further. Her voice was completely choked. Tears rolled down her comely cheeks. Pooja wiped them and hugged her. Consoling her, she said, "It was so sad but who can defy destiny? Her death bestowed a beautiful gift to us. You seem to be her mirror-image with all her physical charms. I feel her hilariousness missing in you, mainly due to the sting of circumstances. It is unfortunate that her death devastated your childhood and turned a romantic lover into a brute."

After waiting for a while, Pooja continued, "Simran, now you understand. Intense love was the basic reason of your father's hatred. This is based on the theory of cause and effect. Cause of hatred is the impaired perception that the victim carries. Here the cause was the death of your mother, and effect was the revenge. You became a victim of his retribution. No external force could enforce love in him, as it also manifests from within. Even your tears could have not stirred compassion in your stone-hearted, emotionally feeble father. Sometimes hatred diminishes with the passage of time, but in your case, it was further aggravated and went to the extent of ruining your life."

Pooja put her arms around Simran and embraced her. She did not say anything for some time to let tears flow freely and lighten the heart of the distressed girl. After some time, she said, "Simran, you must have enjoyed your childhood with your *dadi*, who was so affectionate with you."

A gentle smile returned to the depressed face of Simran. Wiping it with *dupatta* and making her more comfortable, she said, "Aunty, you will be amused at the dreams that I used to have during my childhood. You will simply laugh at me." Regaining breath, she resumed, "In fantasy and world of make-belief, I would dream dressed as a fairy running around in snow-clad mountains with my mother. We used to run after each other and play with snowballs. Sometimes, I dreamt sitting with her on sea beach, making sand pits and enjoying ceaseless rhythm and fright of the mighty roaring waves. I often dreamt of running on green grass turf after butterflies of vibrant hues, listening to songs of birds and humming of bees. I never felt scared by those dreams."

"Are you a lover of nature by temperament?" asked Ramesh.

"I feel more relaxed in the lap of nature. For me, nature is not soulless. It never betrays and is not cruel like man. It has a rhythm that showers harmony. It indiscriminately bestows its bliss on all and gives joy, peace and solace. When I was here last time, I used to go on top of the flat every day to feed pigeons, who became my most faithful friends. The moment they saw me, they would come flying from all directions, as if they were desperately waiting for me. I used to talk to them and felt that they were listening to me. I used to hold them and narrate my past life and future dreams. They appeared to enjoy with their curling dance movements."

"It shows the tenderness of your heart and your deep love for man and animal alike."

"Aunty, *dadi* would warmly hug me on listening to my dreams. She often wondered, for I had never seen mountains or sea. She was very friendly with me. She used to make dolls of old clothes and both of us played with them. Marriage ceremonies of dolls were performed. *Dadi* used to be from the bridegroom's side, and I was from the bride's. She explained all marriage functions and ceremonies through these plays and told me how my father married my mother. I really cherish the misty memory of those days of merriment."

Continuing, Simran said, "She always tried to make me forget the pain of the loss of my mother. She used to narrate stories from epics and also of *Gurus* and always encouraged me to be bold and fight for justice. She told me to be a good human being and kind to everyone. She would also say that my father's heart was tender like that of a child and had changed only due to the death of my mother. She took a promise from me to look after him when I grow up, and to always love him in spite of his indifferent behaviour."

Ramesh was very keen to remove any negative feeling of hatred from the innocent mind of Simran. He said, "Simran, hatred of your father was primarily due to the loss of his love. He carried a conviction that if you had not been born, she would have not died. His animosity and anger were generated by the loss of his most precious thing, even though you were not the perpetrator or originator of the offence."

Waiting for a while, Ramesh resumed, "Simran, hatred is a self-created inferno and a passion stronger than love. It destroys the peace and happiness of both, one who hates and one who is hated. Its strength and duration can vary but it is very difficult to eradicate, once it enters the psyche of a person. Unfortunately, in your case, its intensity was very high and all these years, you had to bear its pain and drink its poison. With the shifting of interest and emergence of some love-bird in his life, it will certainly diminish and your father will regain his normal life. You should always heed the advice of your *dadi* and never be reactionary. Remember, hatred does not cease by hatred, it ceases by love. Bestow your love on him. After all, he is your father. He will need your care in old age. I am sure one day, he will shower all his paternal love on you."

Heaving a deep sigh, distressed Simran said, "Uncle, I pray for that day." A little pause and she resumed, "He began to hate everything and perhaps himself also. He started drinking heavily, neglected his job and would keep on sitting in a corner, deeply engrossed in the memory of my mother with her photograph in his pocket. He found refuge in seclusion. Alone, sad and dejected, he normally did not talk to anyone. This had a very deleterious effect on the life of my grandmother. Her health suddenly deteriorated and she was mostly confined to bed. There was none to take care of her, and she was living only on the mercy of God. Instead of caring for her in her old age, my father decided to shift to Delhi. He wanted to detach him from the cursed environment and was also enchanted by the charms of the metropolitan city. He was a qualified mechanical engineer, and soon got a good job in a factory. With sound financial position and change of environment, happiness partially returned to his life.

At Delhi, he came in contact with Suman and was soon lured by her advances. She was a young woman of about twenty, slim and fair complexioned. She was extremely charming and always smiling. She had great weakness for money and costly dresses. Obsessed with her make-up, she was always flashing her clothes to entice people. She often used to say, some earn through their brain and some through their body. Before my father, she had lived with a person for one year. She deserted him for his pocket failed to satisfy her insatiable appetite for her unbridled desires and requisites of her equally ambitious mother. My father now came in her life to satisfy all her physical and financial needs. Both mother and daughter discovered him to be a convenient peg to beat upon. With return of joy and satisfaction, love of my mother got transferred to Suman. His hatred for me, however, did not diminish, as I now became a thorn in the love-life of Suman."

"Did your father marry her or remained only a live-in partner?" enquired Pooja.

"He did not marry her. Such a relation suited the ambitions of Suman. Kamla, her mother, also never insisted on their marriage. Both tried to emotionally blackmail my father. Blinded by the oppressive temptation of money, they consumed his salary in shopping sprees and kitty parties. He became their note churning machine and was often dubbed as ATM. All the three enjoyed drinking regularly and would hit the bottle at the slightest excuse. Their house became a den of dance and loud music. Kamla was Suman's main life-planner, responsible for forcing her to follow a fast-paced lifestyle. They did not realise that sooner or later, such habits spell disaster. Blinded by the charms of Suman, my father fell into the trap of their glamorous life and began to merrily dance to their tunes."

Continuing, Simran said, "Kamla was a midwife by profession, and had very intimate relations even with the tough neighbourhood of slums. Hooked to the annoying habit of chewing tobacco, with one or two pouches always stuffed down her bra, she was an extremely talkative, arrogant and dominating character. Her tongue was rude and temper terrible. Her violent screaming and hustling rustic abuses silenced everyone at home and outside. In an effort to beat the age-clock, she desperately tried to conceal her age under layers of heavy make-up. Obsessed with youthful exuberance, her singular focus was to look beautiful and young as her daughter. Dresses used to be a matter of keen competition between the two and both could not abandon their passion for a luxurious life. Gripped in vanity, she had all the symptoms of a disoriented mind."

"But why did Daljeet not marry Suman if he loved her so much?" asked Ramesh.

"Uncle, I came to know about Suman's philosophy of marriage from Rani *maa*. She would often persuade Suman to marry my father, who could be her perfect life partner as he was young, well settled and financially sound. But her suggestion was always vehemently turned down. Their views are best described in their own conversation."

"*Didi*, don't force your decision down my throat. Daljeet is of course, a good man and is very keen to marry me. He intensely loves me and has repeatedly proposed for marriage. He tells me that he will only marry me, or never marry in life. But my views on marriage are different from others. I do not want to be chained to a pole like an animal. I want to fly freely like a bird from one garden to another, and enjoy the nectar of different flowers of my choice. For me, husband is like a lottery ticket; keep it if it's a winning number, else tear it, throw it and buy another. Moreover, marriage is binding, where one can get rid of the husband only through a rigorous process of divorce, after years of struggle. In live-in relations, you may discard the partner any moment without any legal or social hassle."

"Society has laid down certain norms for social relations. Any violation and crossing *Laxman Rekha* lands you in the hands of some Ravan. Marriage is a stamp of social acceptance, and it enhances your respect and prestige in society. In live-in relations, people generally look down upon you."

"That is your narrow-minded assumption. I do not care for the society. In modern days, living as partners without marrying is not a social taboo. I want to live life on my own terms and enjoy unbridled pleasure."

"And if Daljeet throws you out?"

"He is a timid hearted person, tight in my grip and enchanted by my charms. There is remote possibility of his leaving me. But if he does by any chance, there are half-a-dozen Daljeets waiting in the queue. A wink, and they will fall flat on my feet."

"You seem to have no sense of shame or remorse. Remember, man equates beauty with youth. You may enjoy so long as you are young, but what will you do in old age, when charm withers and beauty fades?"

"Firstly, my youth has no expiry date. Secondly, in old age, there is no dearth of the rich, who want a partner for company and care. They shower their wealth and there will be chances of foreign trips also."

"But wealth offers no joy after a point of comfort."

"It is your perception. For me, wealth is the perennial source of enjoyment at all times and at all places."

"Does it mean you don't want to have children?"

"Certainly not now. I want to enjoy the prime of my youth and middle age also. Children are last priority on my list. They are a burden and bone of contention in life's enjoyment. I don't want to suffer pangs of pregnancy and burden of child rearing. I may adopt a child in later life only for my care in old age."

"Strange are your views on marriage and family life. You seem to have inherited the qualities of mama. She lived and enjoyed almost a similar type of life except that she married, but never cared for our father. She never realised that relations are above money. Such a negative attitude towards the sacred social custom of marriage is condemned to be doomed."

"*Didi*, this is the age of internet and fast food. Why prepare food at home when fresh varieties are readily available from the market. Just order and the stuff are at your door step."

"I only hope you do not suffer in the vain pursuit of a cheap glamorous life."

"I am sure I will not. Even if I suffer, I would have enjoyed life to my full satisfaction."

"Suman, remember, birds fly high, but ultimately come to the ground to join their flock. Stay grounded as you will have to come to this society one day. I hope you do not repent your decision. As an elder sister, I wish for your happy and settled future, though I have all the apprehensions in my mind. You will reap tomorrow what you sow today. At present, you are seeing everything through tinted glasses and your sky-high ambitions may ruin you. I pray that wisdom may dawn on you one day. But advising you is writing sermons on water."

Reacting sharply to the theory of Suman on marriage, Pooja said, "I am shocked at the philosophy of Suman. Simran, our thoughts shape our mind and our choices are determined by our passions. People like Suman blindly follow their physical lust, unmindful of the established moral and social values. They are not concerned with the age-old norms of marriage, and peace and contentment associated with it. Their primary concern is self and not family or society. If we live like animals, life would be plunged in chaos, and jungle rule will prevail. Such people do enjoy pleasure but not happiness."

The young girl could not comprehend the difference between the two words. She inquisitively asked, "Is there any difference between pleasure and happiness?"

"Simran, pleasure is distinct from happiness. Pleasure is more a physical state, while happiness is mental and emotional. Pleasure is temporary; happiness is perpetual and infinite. Happiness is in having pride in your possessions, and not in hunger and craving for wants. Happiness is not in consuming recklessly but in giving generously. In happiness 'less is more' but in pleasure 'more is less'. You can buy pleasure with money but it does not guarantee happiness. Money can give you a cosy bed but not assure sound sleep. You will understand it better, when you grow."

To stress her point further, Pooja said, "Self-centered pleasure-seekers like Suman live only for physical needs. They have a negative social outlook and fail to see life beyond the immediate present. Needs fulfilled, they are obsessed with wants. Addiction to materialistic life ruins peace and leaves them in dust. Greed is the root cause of their miseries. It is another word for grief. It never ends; it ends life."

Ramesh became little aggressive and interrupted in a violent tone. "Desires are the forerunner of greed. If not satisfied, they fuel more desires and the cycle continues to spiral sometimes out of control. Insatiable longing for material gain or craving to acquire someone's possessions always breeds sufferings. The greedy always feel that enough is not enough. More they get, more they want. They fail to overcome temptations, and compulsive buying becomes an addiction with them."

"I am tempted to add something more", said Pooja. "In our times, needs were few, and trust and love were more. With rampant needs emerged greed, and both love and trust were crucified. Simran, if you don't feel offended, I will say that Daljeet became a sacrificial lamb in his blind love for greedy Suman. He was impulsive and an emotional fool. The two cunning ladies played with his emotions and made him dance on their fingers. Unless time changes, I am afraid all the three will have a miserable life."

"Aunty, at that time, I thought that Suman and papa were married since they were living together. I considered Suman to be my mother. However, she was highly incensed, when I addressed her as 'mother' for the first time. Eyes blazing fire and lips curled up with disdain, she hurled vulgar abuses. Holding me fiercely, she shouted while aggressively pushing me. 'Don't call me mother. I am not your father's wife. Do you understand? Never come to my room.' I fell down on the ground and started crying.

I was shivering from head to toe, when Rani came in by chance and her timely intervention saved me from further abuses and kicks of Suman. Lifting me, she said, 'Suman, why are you shouting at the innocent child? What does she know about relations? You could have politely told her all this.' Suman retorted fiercely, 'If you have so much sympathy for her, why don't you keep her with you? I do not want to see her face. She is a thorn in my flesh. She is the greatest hurdle in my enjoyment and is making our nights miserable.' Rani lifted me in her lap, brought me to her room and gave me some water. She hugged me, kissed me and made me comfortable in her arms. She explained to me that Suman was not married to my father, and they were not husband and wife. I could not fully comprehend the difference at that age. She told me not to go to Suman or call her 'mama'. 'From today, I am your mother. You can always call me *maa*. I have one son and you are my daughter now.'"

Heaving a sigh, Simran resumed, "My sobs and cries became feeble in the cosy lap of Rani *maa* and soon died. From that day, I started living with her and she became my mother. I now understand that relations don't create love; love creates relations. *Maa* began to shower her love on me but now her son, who was ten years old, started considering me his rival. He was naturally not prepared to share the love of his mother with me, and nursed a grudge against his mother for her undue love and care for me at his expense. *Maa* was intelligent enough to allay his feeling. She politely explained to him that I was too young, had no mother and so needed the love of a mother. Since then, he started behaving better and the family relations remained cordial."

"When did you come to Delhi?" enquired Pooja.

"My grandmother was getting very weak and was normally confined to bed. She insisted that papa should marry and settle down in life. He told her that he had already married Suman. *Dadi* now wanted him to take me also, as it was becoming difficult for her to look after me. Unfortunately, she died and papa brought me to Delhi. I was four years old then."

"How was Suman's mother behaving with you?"

"Her behaviour was absolutely indifferent. She was least concerned with me. With Suman, she was also a parasite feeding on my father's earnings and was always busy pampering him, as he was also the main source of her income. Always busy in her make-up and social parties, she had no time to even look at me."

Both Ramesh and Pooja were patiently and curiously listening to Simran. They were happy, for she was sincerely narrating all facts of her life. Potential relations can't be based on falsehood and all these facts were further cementing their relations and confidence in Simran.

Switching the track from Kamla to Rani, Simran resumed, "Aunty, Rani *maa*, in her early thirties, had a very distressed married life. Her husband was a farm labourer and both lived in a small village in district Jaunpur of Uttar Pradesh. After the birth of the son, her husband began to ignore her and started living with another woman in a nearby village. The strained matrimonial relations were further estranged due to the aggressive behaviour of her mother-in-law and finally completely broke down. *Maa* decided to leave amicably. She believed that broken relations and broken glass should not remain in home. They hurt one day. She moved to Delhi and started living in a room of her father's hut. Her husband came to Delhi later on and stayed with her for some time. He pleaded for reconciliation but due to trust deficit, Rani refused to go with him. Illiterate or barely literate, she could only work as a maid and worked in your home and some other homes in the society, in which you also had a flat."

Waiting for a few moments, she smiled and said, "Aunty, you will not believe the lines that *maa* had written in Hindi on charts pasted on the four walls of her room." Reflecting on the lines, she continued, "She had written, 'Do good and throw it in the river'; 'As you sow, so shall you reap'; 'Things not destined for you, your hands can't reach and those destined for you shall find you where you be' and 'This body is of dust and to dust it will return.'"

"This is really amazing. I never thought her to be so philosophical. She appeared to be absolutely illiterate."

"Rani *maa* was more mature and a woman of very simple and clean habits. She was extremely well-mannered, soft-spoken, gentle, and a picture of grace and charm. Always patient, she never lost her nerve. I had never seen a frown on her face. She was morally upright and inherited all the virtues of her father, while Suman was a carbon copy of her mother and followed in her footsteps. Both were poles apart and starkly different in behaviour, habits and lifestyle. She normally avoided intimacy with both and used to say, if relations begin to clash, it is better to change course."

Coming back to her life, Simran resumed, "Uncle, my childhood thus passed in extremely unhealthy surroundings. Totally neglected by my father, and *dadi* also gone, Rani came from heaven and bestowed motherly affection on me. In my ruined childhood, she was a silver lining. She generally kept me away from the contact of the two ladies, and the distressing slums. I remained in her protective hands and it was mainly because of her, that I did not pickup any negative quality. But for her, I would have been in hell much earlier than when I was thrown in."

Simran looked at the wall clock, suddenly got up and dashed to the kitchen. Ramesh was very punctual in his tea and meal timings, and tea had been slightly delayed as Simran was totally lost in narrating the gory tale of her childhood.

"I am surprised how much physical and mental pain the innocent girl had to suffer at that young age?" said a distressed Pooja.

"That is the tragedy of human relations. They are a source of both pleasure and pain. If healthy, they bestow all the happiness, otherwise life is a tragic hell."

"I have a grave apprehension that worst tragedy and suffering has still to follow in her life. But it is good that you brought her here, and saved her from the cruel clutches of some devils. We will keep her here, look after her studies and plan her future. I am sure our children will also support our stand."

Meanwhile, Simran brought tea and apologised for the delay. "Don't feel sorry. Even I forgot in the shocking details of your life. You may continue, while we all enjoy the nice tea."

"Uncle, I was telling you about my childhood. It was laced with intense motherly love of *dadi* and Rani *maa*, and hatred and indifference of papa, Suman and Kamla. I would not see papa for days. His unwanted burden was now off his head, and he never cared to know whether I was dead or alive. Motherly love of Rani started gaining strength, and I began to forget the hatred of my father and his keep, as it may be more appropriate to call her. His complete negligence left a very deep negative impact on my innocent life, but his happy love-life gave me immense satisfaction."

Interrupting her, Pooja shifted to another subject. "Simran, I wonder whether Daljeet's salary was sufficient to satisfy the greed and financial needs of Suman and her mother."

Taking a deep breath, Simran replied, "Aunty, it is this greed that devastated the life of my father. Suman did not appreciate that lust and greed were self-defeating. The craving for excessive desires never ends. She wanted to have the wealth of the whole world, and senseless pursuit of wealth and physical pleasures were her only concerns. She never tried to put a cap or exercised any moderation on her luxurious shopping. In greed, Kamla surpassed her daughter and was always compelling her to extract as much money from my father as possible. I came to know later on that Suman was a significant source of income of her mother right from her adolescence. The old lady would persuade her daughter to shift relations for the sake of more money. For her, money mattered more than man. Though she had perhaps other sources of income also, they squeezed my father most. The tragedy is that papa was aware of all these facts, but was too naive and kept his eyes closed for his petty physical pleasures. In the enjoyment of his life, he showered all his salary on them. He started borrowing and was always in debt. This became the prime cause of a terrible tragedy and life of my father was thrown in disarray. One night, I came to know that Suman and my father were shifting to Dehradun, and with this started his painful tale of sufferings that ruined more than ten prime years of his life."

Puris were completely astonished. Dumb for a while they looked at each other, and Ramesh asked, "Why did they decide to shift to Dehradun?"

"Some tension was simmering in the family of which I was not aware of. I was baffled to hear Suman and Rani discussing one night. They thought I had gone to sleep. Actually, I was awake and was very attentively listening. From their conversation, I gathered that papa's factory had closed due to heavy business losses and most of the staff had been laid off, papa being one of them. He tried to look for another job, but failed. Starting own workshop was not possible due to financial constraints. Due to these reasons, they decided to shift to Dehradun.

Suman told *maa* about her friend Madhu. The two were hand and glove with each other, and mutually shared all their love secrets and devious romantic relations. Though bold, Suman was always apprehensive of the caustic comments of the slum-lane rowdies. To evade their covetous glances, she frequently used Madhu's residence for her make-up and changing over to more revealing dresses for special occasions and romantic dates. These regular visits had brought the two emotionally very close to each other."

Gaining some strength, Simran continued, "Aunty, Suman discussed the dwindling financial condition with Madhu, who promised to help her. She told her that her elder brother, Vikas Pandey, was an advocate in Dehradun and was very close to some local politicians. He was coming next day to meet her, and they could discuss their problem with him. Suman was delighted. Provoking Suman light-heartedly, Madhu teased her that her brother was a lover of beautiful girls, and his youth and jingling pocket may also trap her. Very confidently, Suman reacted that she was quite experienced to deal with such love-sick birds.

Next day, Suman and papa went to Madhu's house. All details were discussed, and Vikas Pandey immediately offered to help papa and painted a rosy picture of their bright future. He also told them that he had a fully furnished flat at Dehradun that was vacant and they could stay there without paying rent, till papa was employed. He also told them that if they wanted, they could accompany him next day with their essential clothing."

Ramesh intruded. "Greedy Suman must have immediately agreed."

"Uncle, your judgement is absolutely correct. Without caring for the consent of papa, Suman immediately confirmed their departure with Vikas. Papa was rudely shocked, but she convinced him that Delhi had not proved to be lucky and it was better to shift. Papa warned her of the association with the advocate, and that they may have to lament their sudden and reckless decision. Clever Suman assured papa that she would always protect him from all problems.

Suman did not want anyone to know about their shifting to Dehradun. She also told *maa* to keep me here as she hated my sight, and did not want Vikas to know anything about me. She bluntly told *maa* that she wanted to fully enjoy her freedom at Dehradun and did not want to share her privacy with anyone."

Narrating further details of her father's shifting to Dehradun, Simran said, "Aunty, I was perturbed and utterly astonished to hear their future plan. Both were swayed by the sweet talk and great convincing power of sly Vikas. They did not heed the writing on the wall and easily fell into his trap. The decision proved to be a grave error of judgement. Suman was very assertive by nature, and completely ignored the prophetic words of papa, that indicated the onslaught of an incoming storm. On the other hand, papa was too simple and with pitiable paucity of foresight, easily fell in her line of thought. Wearing blinkers, he failed to anticipate the impending future crisis and intriguing secrecy of the pre-meditated malicious plan of Vikas. In his blind love for Suman, papa did not visualise the events more objectively and the dark and uncertain period that lay ahead."

Reacting to the decision of Suman, Ramesh said, "Simran, the tiger was stalking some prey, and it willingly fell in his lap. She appears to have been enchanted by the green pastures offered by Vikas and wanted to explore fresh avenues offered by him. Her greed and Daljeet's emotional weakness were perhaps the main reasons of their shifting to Dehradun. Suman was foolishly trying to explore fragrance in paper flowers."

"Uncle, that's the true analysis of Suman's character. She was more concerned with immediate gain and got easily trapped in the phony promises. Disaster loomed large on the horizon, but charms of the new place and new-found relations blinded her vision. *Maa* also told me that Vikas was instantly magnetised by the outrageous and irresistible charm of the sensual and sexy Suman. Expert in trapping women, he could easily judge her to be a soft target."

Waiting for a few moments, she continued, "Leaving me at Delhi did baffle me, but I was indeed blissfully happy. I did not want to go with Suman, even though I had to badly miss my father. I would also say that to a large extent, Suman was responsible for widening the gap between me and my father, though I cannot fully absolve papa." After a little pause, she resumed, "Next day, I saw them leaving. I could not resist and ran to my father, and clung to him. I asked him where he was going, and he lied that he was going to the village. I requested him to take me also, but he pushed me aside saying that he would take me next time.

In my mind, I was aware of all details and the lie that papa was telling. Deeply saddened and hurt, I did not say anything, hugged him again and ran back with tears in my eyes. Back in the room, *maa* consoled me. I wanted to know from her where papa had gone. She took a promise from me not to weep and told me the details."

"Do not tell anyone. My conscience does not permit me to hide the truth from you. Actually, they have decided to permanently shift to Dehradun. You know Daljeet has lost the job, and the brother of one of Suman's friends has promised to help him. They have gone with him in his car."

"But why have they not taken me?"

Looking at Simran with searching eyes, Rani said, "You don't want to stay here with me?"

Simran tightly hugged her. "I want to stay here and will never leave you."

"And if I don't want to keep you?"

"I will take poison or hang myself with the fan."

Rani was stunned at the sudden and shocking reply of young Simran. She immediately clasped her, kissed her several times and said, "Simmi, never say this. You are my own child and I love you as I love my son. I cannot dream of leaving you, even if your father wants to take you."

"*Maa*, I also don't want to go. I do not know about papa but Suman will cut me to pieces. She hates me and doesn't want to see my face. Please, please do not leave me." Rani tightly hugged her and kissed her again.

"Aunty, that night I could not sleep. I requested *maa* to allow me to sleep with her. She told me that at times I got up, and started sobbing and crying. I was deeply disturbed and my eyes were swollen next morning."

"Simran, we had absolutely no idea of your father's going to Dehradun. In fact, Rani also never told us,"

"Aunty, *maa* had told me not to disclose anything to anyone as the tragic tale of deception at Dehradun is depressing and highly disastrous. In life, tragedies followed papa like a shadow, but for the short span of love with Suman."

Simran suddenly became very sad. Her voice was choked and tongue failed to cooperate. Emotions got in the way of narration. Pooja realised her state of mind. She suddenly got up and brought a glass of water. Placing it lovingly before her lips, she said, "It appears that life of Daljeet at Dehradun was really very painful."

Simran was surprised at the affection of Pooja. She took some water, regained her strength and composure, and resumed. "Thank you, aunty. Let me continue the story of my father. As I said, this was the most distressing chapter of his life. He could never have peace later on. The tragedy is that he always acted on his love-instinct, and not on logic, or any set plan. Dehradun, in fact, proved to be his graveyard and the main cause of the most tragic events of my life also."

Both Ramesh and Pooja were absolutely stunned. Keen to know all details, Ramesh said, "Please tell us what happened? Did he not get a job? Did Suman or Vikas betray him?"

"Worse than that happened. I asked *maa* one day that I missed papa very much, and had a horrible dream last night. I requested her to let me talk to him. On my relentless requests, she revealed all facts more out of compulsion, as I would have not left her otherwise."

"Simran, let me tell you all details, as you must know everything about your father. After he and Suman left this place, they started residing in the flat of Vikas. Daljeet soon got a job in a factory due to his efforts, and happiness returned to the family. With money flowing in, my mother also often went to Dehradun. Vikas was an extremely shrewd man. He was happy that the prey had herself come to the hunter. He carefully crafted a plan from day one and deftly executed it. Maintaining very cordial relations with Daljeet, he simultaneously instigated Suman against him. It was like running with the hare and hunting with the hounds. Vikas began to shower more money on both Suman and my mother, and had insatiable Suman fully in his grip. Relations between Daljeet and Suman began to crack. Visits to malls and cinemas became more frequent, and the starry world of greed brought Suman emotionally closer to Vikas. Both started enjoying each other's company, and costly presents to the overtly ambitious lady further pushed her into the arms of Vikas. He managed to send Daljeet on tours, and friendship changed into very intimate physical relations. Daljeet failed to hear the wake-up call. He could not see the snake in the grass, and the dubious plot being hatched against him. A foe in friend's garb is more dangerous than even a sworn enemy. You remember, once I went to Dehradun for a few days?"

"Yes *maa*. I do remember. In fact I asked you that you were looking very tense. You scolded me and did not say anything. Next day, you suddenly left and came back after three days."

"The events had moved very swiftly, and your father called me to Dehradun. He told me that he suspected Suman having intimate relations with Vikas. He also told me that Vikas was around 45, was married, had three children and his daughter was almost of Suman's age. When he told Suman that relation with Vikas was an age-inappropriate romance, she first denied any relation, but then retorted that age was just a number in love. My mother closed her eyes at Suman's closeness with Vikas, as this also satisfied her financial needs. Daljeet also told me that for money, Suman wanted him to sell his ancestral house in the village."

"Did papa sell the house?"

"Initially he was reluctant but then to please her he agreed. He sold part of the house for ₹ 20 lakh, retaining a portion on the roadside. With that money he wanted to buy a flat at Dehradun or at some other place to separate Suman from the evil clutches of the wild beast. He thought that selling property, giving some money to Suman, leaving Dehradun, and settling down in some other place may take Suman away from crafty Vikas. I have no hesitation in saying that though Daljeet loved Suman, her relations with him were more out of physical and materialistic lust."

Reflecting on the stark contrast between the nature of the two sisters, Simran said, "*Maa*, though children of the same parents, both of you are so different in nature and habits. You are so sober and lead a very simple life, while she is so extravagant and free with everyone. You are so kind to me, but she hates me." Waiting for a while, she asked, "What did papa do with the money?"

"Suman wanted five lakh. Daljeet had planned to establish his own workshop at Delhi but to please her, gave five lakh with a promise to take it back, if needed, for the workshop. I suspect Vikas got a wind of his plan. Do you remember I suddenly went to Dehradun again, without telling anyone?"

"Yes *maa*. I was in fact shocked and annoyed with you, when you came back after three days."

"I will tell you about the traumatic tragedy that befell your father, and his present whereabouts. But you have to give me a solemn promise that you will not weep."

"I promise, *maa*. Please tell me. Is papa all right?"

Rani became very tense. Her eyes were full of tears. She hugged Simran again and made her more comfortable in her warm arms. Simran looked at her with strange searching eyes. Stopping at intervals to gain some strength and to reassure her that Simran was all right, she said, "Simmi my child, Vikas is not a man of good character. He carried an iron fist in velvet gloves. He wanted to get rid of your papa by means, fair or foul. He did not reveal his nefarious pre-meditated plan even to Suman, otherwise she might have checked him. Conflict of interest prompted him to crucify Daljeet. One night, he came to Suman, held her tightly in his arms, repeatedly kissed her, and said, 'Baby, you are my love. We are inseparable. Shadow can leave the body, but I can't leave you. You are in me, and I am in you.' With a very dejected look, he said, 'Darling, a great tragedy has befallen Daljeet.'

'What has happened?'

Vikas further tightened his grip and expressing some fake empathy, he said, 'Baby, Daljeet has been caught in a very serious case.'

Suman was astounded. Daljeet was a simple man and how could he get involved in any serious case? Vikas started painting a grim picture of the character of Daljeet. He tried to sow seeds of doubt and hatred in her mind, and showing outward sympathy for Daljeet, said, 'I never knew that he was a drug peddler.'

'What?' said the astonished Suman. 'What are you saying?'

'I was shocked, when I came to know this. He must have brought this from Punjab, which is a drug haven these days.' Your papa is now in jail because of that."

"What is that *maa*? I do not understand."

Looking into the puzzled eyes of Simran, Rani struggled for words and finally tried to explain. "Simmi, there are certain things that are banned in society and anyone selling or even possessing them is immediately imprisoned. Vikas was referring to one such drug." Taking a deep breath, she continued, "Suman was devastated to hear all this and began to cry. With all her weakness for wealth, she liked Daljeet because of his sincerity and great human qualities. Even though she had not married him, she could never stay away from him. I met Daljeet in jail and he told me that he had never dealt in drugs, and that someone had planted drug pouches in his bag. He suspected this to be the work of Vikas, who thought him to be a thorn in the path of his relations with Suman. Vice prospers in greed and to ensure that Suman does not slip out of his grip, he hatched the sinister conspiracy to create a permanent wedge between Daljeet and Suman. In the triangular love story, Daljeet became a scapegoat. Real facts of your papa's fictitious involvement, and details of the main actors in the disgraceful allegation are most intriguing and still shrouded in mystery. The tangle may never be solved."

Simran began to cry. She wondered what would be the fate of her father, who was innocent. Though he never loved her, she always prayed for his happiness and safety. She was aware of his habit of drinking, but not of any such vice. In fact, Suman also did not believe all this, but the wily advocate convinced her of the concocted activities of Daljeet.

"What happened to my father? Is he still in jail or has police released him?"

"In such cases of drug smuggling, there is no bail, and there is restricted possibility of release of the suspect till the case is finally decided in his favour and he is proved to be innocent."

"*Maa*, what will happen to my father? I love him so much. Will I not be able to meet him again?"

"Do not worry, my child. Fortune turns like a wheel, one man it lifts up, another it sets down. Today, Daljeet is down, tomorrow he will be up. Since he has not done anything wrong, I am sure he will be soon released, and then we will all go to meet him."

"I will tell him to come here or go back to the village. We don't want to live in such a wretched place, where only lie thrives and innocent are hanged." Gaining some composure, she resumed, "*Maa*, is Suman trying for his release?"

"Here again the wily wolf tried to cheat her. Vikas told Suman that bribe of ₹ 5 lakh will be needed to get Daljeet out of lock-up. Poor Suman gave him five lakh that Daljeet had given her. But the clever advocate had no intention of getting Daljeet out of prison. He kept on promising and finally told Suman, that it was too late as the case had already been filed in the court."

Ramesh Puri was shocked at the mysterious details of the life of Daljeet. "Simran, this is so touching. Innocent Daljeet had been trapped by the love-hungry advocate. What was the final verdict of the court?"

"Uncle, it is a tough pill to swallow. Papa was sentenced for ten years. I wanted to meet him but *maa* declined. Suman paid frequent visits to him and was always crying, as told to me by *maa*. My days of intense turmoil and unrest returned. I went into my shell and virtually stopped talking to anyone. I used to sit in a corner and weep at my fate. With all his failings, I loved papa from the core of my heart and always prayed for his happiness. Though given enough pain by him, I could not bear slightest scratch to him. His innocence and blind trust in others ruined his life. I cursed the day he had gone to Dehradun, but had no control over his decisions. Fate had willed it that way. I started reciting *Japuji Sahib* daily and prayed to God for his well-being. There is celestial power in prayer and this gave me some solace and peace of mind."

"Simran, this would touch the hardest of hearts. Sometimes, I wonder how could you bear all this at such a tender age? Fortune had been extremely unkind to you. But I am glad you showed immense inner strength and will-power", said Ramesh.

"Sometimes, I also wonder how I survived all those years. Perhaps ink had completely dried in His pen while writing my fortune. May be He forgot that I was also one of His beings. Fortunately, with all the sufferings, He gave me courage and strength to bear the misfortunes and the will to survive in adversity. For this, I am ever grateful to God." Heaving a deep sigh of relief and gaining some strength, she resumed, "Unfortunately, this is not the end of the story. There are graver tragedies to follow."

"What happened? Did you suffer or your father?" said the surprised Pooja.

"Both." A little pause and she resumed, "It is past midnight and both of you may be feeling sleepy. I will stop here and continue tomorrow."

"Not that we are sleepy, but want to ponder over your grave sufferings. You can also take some physical and mental rest. Pooja will sleep with you. Don't fear anything. We are with you and shall always be with you." Ramesh tried to reinforce her confidence in them.

□

3

Though sure of a safe future in the lap of Puris, Simran was extremely restless at night. Tossing from side to side, she was frequently startled in her sleep. Pooja tried her best to make her comfortable, and at times, embraced her tightly to relieve her of the nightmares that she might be experiencing. She had a wink of sleep only towards dawn. Pooja did not wake her up and went to Ramesh's bedroom. They reflected on the misfortunes of Simran and prayed for her bright future.

Simran suddenly got up and went straight to the kitchen to prepare tea. She apologised for the delay. Consoling her, Pooja said, "You need not feel sorry. You had a rather disturbed sleep last night and I did not wake you up. Let me prepare tea today. You can start your duties from tomorrow."

"No, aunty. Let me do my duty. Postponement is the genesis of laziness and an act postponed is the act denied."

Pooja was surprised at her intelligent reply. She patted her shoulder and said, "OK. I will not stop you. I know you will not allow me to do anything in the kitchen."

Both Ramesh and Pooja were quiet during tea and simply kept on occasionally looking at Simran, while sipping the tasty tea. After tea, Ramesh said, "Simran, we will go to our flat now and shall come before lunch. We will have our breakfast in our flat. You also take something, and get ready. Remember, the door will be locked from outside. In case of any difficulty, you can contact us through your new mobile."

After lunch, when all were little relaxed, Ramesh opened the topic. "Simran, we appreciate your frankness in revealing all details of your past. The intention is not to scratch the wounds and cause any pain to you, but to take care of you so that you do not suffer any more in future. If not inconvenient, please tell us what happened after your dad's imprisonment?"

"Uncle, I am also keen to tell you everything of my life. Unless I untie all knots of the past, I will have no peace. It will lighten my heart and will also give me greater courage and strength."

Pooja held her hand and said, "Joy shared is joy doubled and sorrow shared is sorrow halved. It is unfortunate that you had fallen on miserable days. Open your heart and rest assured, we will be a source of greater strength. You are a brave girl, and courage already lies in you. We want to ignite the spark and motivate you further to bear all that you have suffered and be more courageous in future. But remember, courage alone is not enough. Self-belief and determination of a woodpecker are equally essential. There is only one person who can restore your self-belief and it is *you* only."

With a glint in her eyes, Simran replied, "Aunty, I am not worried now. I have your blessings and care. My future is safe in your hands. Now my concern is to serve you to the best of my ability and strength."

"Yes Simran, we also need your care at this old age. Children are away and only you have to look after us. Please continue your story."

"Fortune had been playing hide and seek with me and life was kind and cruel in equal measures. With pain of hatred not only from my father but also from Suman and Kamla, love came from Rani *maa,* but for whom, my childhood would have been extremely miserable. She gave me all the love and affection not only of a mother but also of a friend. She used to play indoor games with me, cut jokes and always tried to keep me happy and cheerful. She looked after all my physical and emotional needs, even though she was always facing financial crisis. Her son, indifferent earlier, was normal now, but neighbours continued to look down upon me as a discarded girl."

Praising Rani, Pooja said, "By nature, Rani was an embodiment of contentment, laced with endearing modesty. She was very sober and hardly talked, when she worked in our home."

"Aunty, about nine more years passed peacefully under her benign care, but now destiny had something else in store for me. A spate of most unfortunate and miserable days of my life appeared from nowhere."

Both Pooja and Ramesh were shaken to hear this and looked at each other. Ramesh said, "Simran, misfortunes come stealthily. They never come with drumbeats."

"Uncle, the greatest weakness of Kamla was insatiable greed. Suman was now leading a more comfortable and satisfied life with Vikas. She used to send some money regularly to Kamla, but the greedy lady was always short of funds. Unending demands eclipsed relations between the two, and Kamla now wanted to explore some independent source of income. It was a cruel irony of fate, that her covetous eyes now fell on me."

"What? This is really shocking. How could you provide money to that old wild cat and satisfy her needs?" asked Pooja.

"Aunty, she was a very cunning lady. Means were not her concern so long as the end satisfied her aspirations. I was just entering my teens and in her quest for material satisfaction, the hungry fox now decided to devour me. By no stretch of imagination, you can think of the way the resourceful lady conceived her mischievous plan.

One morning, she came to me when *maa* had gone for

her work. She hugged me warmly and kissed me for the first time in my life. I was truly amazed. How could the wolf change into a sheep? I was not intelligent enough to envisage her trap. Placing her cold arm on my shoulder, she took me to her room. A stranger was sitting there. Introducing me to him, she said, 'She is Simran, my dear granddaughter.' Completely perplexed at her stress on 'dear', I looked at her. Her eyes were brimming with fake love, and there was a wily grin on her face. Continuing, she said, 'And Simran, he is my cousin brother.'

The man held my arm and made me sit by his side. He placed his arm around my waist. I sneaked a glance of his ulterior motives, and was feeling very uncomfortable. Looking at me, he said, 'I could not bring anything for you.' Saying this, he gave me a hundred rupee note. I declined to accept. Kamla insisted on my taking the money, convincing me that he was just like my father. Not taking would have delayed my escape, and I wanted to get out of the situation. Very reluctantly, I accepted."

"The cunning lady must have been having some treacherous plan up her sleeves", said Ramesh.

"Uncle, later developments are one of the most horrifying episodes of my painful life. You will be shocked to listen to the details and the real intentions of Kamla and her so-called cousin. At this stage, it may perhaps be little difficult to guess."

"Greed must have blinded her to shamelessly entrap you. I am sure, they both wanted to make you a scapegoat and put the honour and life of an innocent girl at stake. Please tell us as we must know the character of the people with whom you stayed," said the horrified Ramesh.

"The cousin kept on looking at me, complimenting my fair complexion, hair, eyes and figure. Kamla reciprocated all his comments, adding few adjectives here and there. It was highly embarrassing for me to listen to those words of praise.

He started fondling with my hair, putting them sometimes in front, sometimes at back. I was very uncomfortable, and was struggling to get out of his grip. Finally, I managed my escape.

Maa came in the afternoon, and I narrated the whole story and handed over the money to her. She became little serious, and only remarked that she was not aware of any such cousin of her mother, as described by me. She also told me that she was utterly amazed at the subtle shift in her behaviour but did not suspect the grave malicious plan conceived by her. I also could not imagine even in my wildest dreams the future that my fate held for me."

Looking at surprised Pooja and Ramesh, she continued, "Next day, Suman came from Dehradun. This time she brought for me a new fashionable dress, matching hair clips and earrings besides shampoo, cream, powder and some similar stuff. Perhaps to hoodwink Rani, she also brought dresses for her and her son. The real story starts from the next morning."

Both the Puris looked at Simran. Pooja said, "Rani also must have been shocked at the sudden change in Suman's attitude."

"She must have been, but did not say anything. In fact she became more serious. Knowing her mother and sister very well, she smelled something fishy.

To execute their already hatched wicked plan, Suman came to me the next morning, when *maa* had left for her routine work. Very affectionately, she placed her hand on my shoulder and said, 'Simmi dear, I want to go to the mall for some shopping. I don't want to go alone. You give me company. Also put on your new dress. I want you to look smart. You are growing now.'

I had no option, but to obey, as I could not seek any guidance in the absence of *maa*. As I came out, I was shocked to see Kamla also there with Suman. Both were very smartly dressed with full make-up, Kamla with the addition of kohl-rimmed eyes. The thrill of going to the mall withered and the smile suddenly vanished. I could not understand why Suman wanted my company, when her mother was with her? Things were happening so fast that I could not look beyond the obvious, and had no time to realise their real implications. On coming to the main road, I saw a car with Kamla's same cousin standing there. I was shocked and suspected that they were perhaps not heading to a mall, but to some other place. Before I could regain my strength, Suman sat on the front seat and Kamla made me sit on the rear with her. The cousin started driving. I sat helpless, unable to say or do anything. My innocence could not contemplate the despicable motives of the wicked women and their equally atrocious partner."

With a questioning look, Ramesh enquired, "Did you not ask where all were going?"

"I did ask. Kamla replied that I should not worry and would soon come to know. It is as if I was mesmerised and followed them under the spell of magic, unmindful of the dashing storm. After about half-an-hour drive, we came to a big building and inside, I saw as if some film shooting was going on. Initially a sense of excitement permeated my heart, but fear checked me to move forward. Kamla held my hand and pulled me. I had no option but to yield. I was introduced to people and a man told a lady to change my dress, and set my proper hairstyle."

Ramesh was furious and said, "Simmi, you should have shown some spine and refused."

Defending her conspicuous silence, Pooja said, "You must imagine the condition of a young, immature and helpless girl. How could she refuse? She might have been in greater trouble. Restraint was the most sensible option. It is good that she did not resist."

"Aunty, you are right. I thought of being little aggressive but all my wails and howls would have been in vain. In the company of a pack of hostile conspirators with questionable motives, and none to support me in those scary surroundings, I decided to maintain utmost normalcy and waited for the suitable moment, to get out of the hell.

A man being addressed as 'director sir' looked at me twice from top to bottom, and nodded his satisfaction. My dress and hairstyle were changed, and photographs in different poses were taken. I was repeatedly asked to smile but who could smile with the sword of Damocles hanging on the head. The director carefully and keenly watched the photographs. Happiness and satisfaction was discernible on his face. He asked me to go to the other room. Suspecting something fishy, I went but stood behind the door. I was very much tempted to hear their discussion and understand their sinister motives."

Breaking seriousness of the situation, Ramesh said, "This is more like a spy story."

"Uncle, mystery of the real drama unfolds now. The director told Kamla's cousin, 'She is a gold mine, but is too raw at present. She is very shy and reserved. Let her mix with people and shed her inhibition. She has to be more open to reveal her body, which is so essential in our industry. Unless she is free, she will not do in front of the camera what we want her to do with men. Bring her here twice a week, and we will prepare her for our job. The stuff is really valuable but has to be groomed.' Kamla intervened and said, 'Leave it to me. I am expert in this. I will prepare her for the job. Girls at this age can be easily enticed with dresses, make-up material and some jewellery. Creating greed for money and desire for fashionable dresses, will lure her for our purpose. Suitable films on mobile and laptop will further brainwash her and programme her thoughts and actions for our business.' I was shocked to hear the discussion. In a state of numbness, the ground slipped from below my feet. Now I realised that there was wisdom in my silence. Resistance would have been disastrous."

"I am utterly shocked," said Pooja. "How could a woman do all this to you? I had read that a bad woman is worse than ten bad men, but could never imagine that the old bitch could be so cunning. Though difficult to guess the exact final motive, she was certainly weaving a dirty invisible web around you. She is a blot on womanhood."

Ramesh was very forthright and said, "Pooja, such people can go to any extent. I feel they were preparing her for some dirty film. They could have even sold her to a brothel, but they did not want to kill the goose that would lay for them a golden egg every day. Mark the shameful words in which their plan and Simran's future were concealed. 'She is a gold mine...She has to be more open to reveal her body...in our industry...what we want her to do with men...Creating greed for money...brainwash her'. You have to read between the lines to correctly grasp their real intention. The motive of Kamla's sudden change in behaviour has also become evident now. She wanted to trap Simran for her sinister plan and make her a permanent and independent source of her income. She was a rotten fish of the dirty drain."

"Uncle, your analysis of the situation is absolutely correct. The incident had a stupendous impact on my future. It became the most vital turning point in my life and the reason of my coming to Jaipur."

"The whole story is now clear," reciprocated Pooja. Continuing, she said, "What happened afterwards? Did you tell everything to Rani?"

"Yes, aunty. But let me first tell you little more. On the way back, Kamla and I again sat on the rear seat. Terror-stricken, I was curiously looking at her all the time. She repeatedly hugged me and kissed me. Guilty conscience pricks the mind and to alienate any suspicion from my mind, she said 'Simran, many questions might be disturbing you. To dispel all your doubts, let me explain everything. My child, your future is going to change. My cousin is a film producer. He is always in search of new faces and fresh talent. As soon as he saw you, he told me that you have a very photogenic face. We will groom you for modelling and acting, by admitting you in the institute. For this, it is essential that you shake off your shyness.'

Pressing my breast in an inappropriate manner with no sign of shame in her cunning eyes, she kissed me on my lips. I frowned and wanted to hit her, but was helpless. She said, 'Shake off your shyness. Be bold and free with men. You are so charming, but you have to display your charm to others, as you see in movies. Soon you will move to Mumbai and will be on big hoardings on the roads. Don't forget us, when you become rich and famous. Do you understand me?' She laughed loudly and hugged me very tightly to her body. I had no option but to show a fake smile. She mistook my smile as a sign of my approval of her decision, not realising that every smile is not indicative of joy.

"Aunty, I was itching to get out of her clutches and any disapproval would have been suicidal. I looked at her and nodded my head. She was very happy. Finally, we reached home, and I heaved a sigh of relief for my safe return. When I look back, I feel that it was my good luck that Kamla brought me home. To mint immediate money, she could have done anything to my honour. Back home, I lay on the bed and started crying. *Maa* came and saw me with swollen eyes."

"Simran, what has happened? Why are you crying and how are you in this new dress?"

"I immediately hugged her tightly, and refused to leave her even on her persistence. With sobs and tears, I revealed all details to her. She kept on looking at me, but did not say anything. She appeared to be very tense and deeply engrossed."

"*Maa*, are you annoyed with me?"

"I will talk to you later," replied the grim-looking Rani.

At night also Rani did not speak at all. Simran was worried that she had perhaps lost her only well-wisher. Fearing that Rani might have been offended by her action, Simran begged forgiveness, but Rani did not utter even a single word. She had realised the looming crisis and had taken her decision. Waking up Simran early morning, she asked her to take bath and get ready. She stuffed all her clothes in a backpack and asked her to accompany her. Shaken and shivering, Simran asked. "*Maa*, where are we going?"

"Will you stop asking questions? Do as I tell you." Rani was unusually perturbed, and shouted violently at Simran for the first time. Simran was terrified, but knew there was safety in going with her. She instinctively followed her as she realised that Rani's indifferent behaviour was due to her, obsessive love for her. Rani first went to the flat, where she was working perhaps to request for leave and also some advance. They now headed straight to the Inter State Bus Terminal, and boarded a bus for Jaipur.

Simran's heart was sinking. Though sure of her safety, she was unable to understand the actual motive of Rani. Inside the bus, Rani took some water and gave to Simran also. As soon as the bus started, Simran hugged her, and with tears struggling to roll down her dry cheeks, picked up some courage and asked, "*Maa*, please tell me now at least, where are we going?"

Rani was trying hard to control the volcano of her emotions. Embracing Simran, she said with faltering tongue and trembling lips. "Simmi, my child, I am separating the pearl from the shell."

Completely shocked and confused, Simran looked into her

eyes. Meaning of the deep philosophical words was beyond her comprehension. Rani tried to dispel her fear.

"Simran, it is time for you to leave me."

"What are you saying, *maa*? Are you angry with me? What is my fault? Why are you discarding me? I have no place to go to? Please do not desert me." She said all non-stop in one breath.

Rani affectionately pressed her to her breast and said, "Though still tender, I feel time has come for you to live away from me. This is how the mother-bird teaches her young ones to fly. Mother throws the baby in the bath tub to let her struggle and learn swimming."

Perplexed, Simran asked, "*Maa*, I cannot make head or tail of what you are saying."

"You know Pooja aunty, in whose flat I used to work. She is a very kind-hearted lady and so is uncle. She used to help poor girls and always encouraged them to study. Her daughter, Dolly, also loved you, sometimes gave you chocolates and gave one beautiful dress on your birthday. They had shifted to Jaipur. We are going there."

"Yes, I remember Dolly *didi* very well. Aunty also used to love me a lot. But why are we going there?"

"Simmi, my child, I will be very frank. You are not safe now in this city of rising crimes. I am strong enough to fight the avarice of my mother and Suman, and save you from their treacherous plans, but am too weak to save you from the greed and evil eyes of the whole wicked world. You are growing now. Be bold and courageous to bravely face the world. I could not afford school education for you, but have tried my best to groom you to be a good human being and imbibe noble values." Waiting for a while, she resumed, "At every crossing of life, you will have two choices. One will be tempting and seemingly easy, but will lead to disaster. The other will be difficult, but will take you to success. Discriminate between right and wrong, and always follow the right path. I am sure you will become a good girl and look after your home properly, when you grow up. I may not be available in life to support you. Charter your own course and fly into the world of your dreams."

Rani could not control her tears now. Words failed her and her eyes communicated emotions. Simran put her arms around her waist, head on her shoulder and started crying. Short glimmer of happiness after a disastrous childhood was coming to an abrupt end. Misfortune was again knocking on the door of her life. Her whole life was suddenly shattered. Fear of the unknown began to haunt her. Puppet in the hands of unkind destiny, she had no option but to float in the river of time. Winds and waves were too strong, and she was too weak to counter their might.

Simran took little water to moist her dry throat and parched lips. "*Maa*, I can bear everything, but not your separation. Please do not desert me. Without you, I will have no option but to commit suicide. You are my only support in life."

"Never even think of ending your life. It is cowardice. Remember, life is the most precious gift of God. Only He has the right to take it back. Once you end it, everything is lost. Hope survives with life and with hope, everything else. Suffering today may turn into happiness tomorrow. You may get tomorrow what you missed yesterday. Never get dejected."

"But *maa*, I cannot live without you."

"Do you think I can? For your safety we have to bear the unbearable pain of separation, which is too trivial a sacrifice for the greater goal of life. Don't worry. Pooja aunty and uncle will look after you equally well. Both are very nice human beings. They will provide you what I could not. You can study at Jaipur. I will request them with folded hands to look after you. But do not tell them anything. I will explain in my own words. We will tell them everything at the proper time. Again, I tell you to be courageous. Birds also spread their wings one day, leave the protection of their parents and fly high. After marriage also, you would have left me. Think that you are getting married today and going to your new home."

Looking deep into the eyes of Rani, Simran suddenly shot back. "*Maa*, were you my mother in my last birth?"

"Not only in the last. I am your mother in this birth also. You have not been in my body but will always remain in my soul. Remember, relations are not a product of blood, but of heart. Blood may create relations but only heart cements them." Kissing her hand and with a little confidence in her eyes, she resumed, "Now forget the past and think about the future. Look after both uncle and aunt, and serve them as your parents. Dolly is also there and will be a great motivating force for you. Do not disgrace my upbringing or jeopardise my reputation. My prestige is now in your hands."

Simran was completely speechless. Tears refused to stop and she kept on sobbing in the lap of her mother. Problems seemed to have no end in her life. Perhaps, this was her destiny. Rani wiped her tears, patted her cheeks, repeatedly kissed her, and kept on caressing her hair. Simran suddenly looked at Rani and said, "*Maa*, why have we to suffer in life?"

"Simran, I am not intelligent enough to answer your question. I can only say, it is difficult to comprehend these unsolved mysteries of life. It is a puzzle that even great sages have failed to solve. Answers to some questions are embedded in the womb of time. You will understand better when you grow up. Explore your own answers to such unanswerable questions. But remember, pain and pleasure, loss and gain, and success and failure are integral parts of every life. We have to be bold in distress, and humble in happiness. Courage and humility reduce sufferings and give us strength to face problems. Never worry about problems. They are transient like dew drops. I also want you to give love and happiness to others, even if you have to suffer. There is eternal joy in giving. If you can't give love, at least don't hate."

Simran was too innocent and immature to realise the intricacies of life and just kept on thinking. She suddenly said, "*Maa*, will your mom not be annoyed with you?"

"She will try to adopt all possible means to take revenge from me. With the death of my father, I have lost my last support also. I can anticipate her devious plan of retaliation for the loss of her treasure. She knows that with my meager earnings, I cannot afford the rent. To make my life miserable, she will try to throw me out of the hut by means fair or foul. This is the only thing in her hands."

"*Maa*, beware of the flurry of the frustrated sly lady."

"For your sake, I am determined to fight with the whole world. Sufferings in life have taught me to be bold. Courage and fear are both products of the mind. Fear is a feeling of the timid; courage is the weapon of the brave. Once you shed fear, courage will automatically emerge. This world is a cruel place for sensitive people and you have to be thick-skinned." Looking at Simran and patting her cheek, she continued, "Do not worry about me. If needed, I will threaten her that I will report the whole matter to police. This will certainly work, as she is timid at heart. I know how to deal with her. I will be both polite and firm. Handling such serious situations is an art, and you must also learn it. It needs intelligence, the strongest weapon against all enemies. But let me remind you again. Keep everything to yourself. Do not disclose anything to uncle or aunt about your father's misfortunes or Kamla's plot. They will be highly disturbed. We will certainly reveal the complete truth, but little later. I will continue enquiring about your welfare." The bus finally reached Jaipur.

Details of arrival and stay at Jaipur flashed before Simran's eyes, as if all had happened just yesterday.

On reaching the flat, Pooja was taken by surprise to see them. "Rani, how are you here? You rang me up yesterday, but I did not know that you were coming here. It is a very pleasant surprise to see you." Waiting for a few moments and looking at Simran, she said, "This is Simran? Look at her? She has grown so tall. Girls shoot up like bamboos." Lovingly stroking her cheek, she said, "Initially, I could not recognise her. She is such a charming girl with face reflecting the same childhood smile and innocence." She hugged her warmly and kissed her. Simran blushed, folded her hands to say *Namaste* and lowered her radiant eyes.

Comfortably seated and after having a glass of water, Rani said, "Aunty, I have come here with a very special and sacred mission."

"Tell me. What can we do for you? You have been such a nice person. We will do all to be of any help to you."

"Aunty, you know Delhi and the unhealthy environment in slums. Simran is now thirteen, and in a very sensitive phase of her life. The place is not safe for young girls, and I realised that it may be better to pull her out of that rotten atmosphere. I have to be out for my work, and with my son also going to school, Simran would be all alone in the home. I had been thinking of some safe solution, and finally decided to seek your help. I request you with folded hands to please accept this motherless girl. She is honest, obedient and very hard-working. You will never have a cause of complaint. She is also an expert cook, and will serve you all. Aunty, I have said everything without mincing words. I cannot say more."

Rani's throat was completely choked. She fell at the feet of

Pooja, and began to cry. Pooja struggled to lift her. Meanwhile, Ramesh also joined them. Consoling her, he said, "Rani, I am sure Pooja will reciprocate my decision. Let Simran stay with us. She will be absolutely safe here. We will look after her as our own child. Dolly is here. She is doing her MBA, and shall be a great motivating force for her. Simran will be emotionally very comfortable in her company. We run a school. After the household duties, she may go to the school. The atmosphere here is wholly academic, and she can also start her studies. We will provide all necessary facilities, and if she takes interest and works hard, she can pass tenth class or even higher. We will prepare her to be independent and self-supporting in life."

Endorsing the decision of her husband, Pooja said, "Rani, I feel you have taken a very sensible decision for the safety and future of this innocent girl. It was essential to pull her out at the right time. She is growing, and this is the most delicate period of her life. Rogues in slums can always take advantage of her age, innocence and loneliness. She will be away from you, but that sacrifice is no price for her better future. We will certainly compensate for your love and care."

Rani thanked Pooja and Ramesh, and left for Delhi after lunch. While departing, she gave her last piece of advice, "Simran, see that you do not bring any blot on me. You should be my pride, not my shame. They are your parents and guardians. Pain of hatred has taught you to love and serve everyone, and spread joy and happiness. Look after them and serve them. Do not miss me as you are now in safer hands."

With tears in her eyes, an inconsolable Simran said with a lump in her throat, "*Maa*, please do not worry. Look after yourself. I will always follow your advice."

With all the words of advice and encouragement, Rani bid farewell to her love. She was struggling to hide her tears, but broke down, when Simran hugged her and started crying.

Tearful separation was painful, but had to be borne. There was no option. Safety and future of Simran was the topmost priority, and any sacrifice was too small for this.

Dolly came from the college in the evening, and was pleasantly surprised to see Simran. She hugged her and was happy to know the reason of her coming to Jaipur. Soon the two began to share a warm equation and became intimate friends.

One day, while cleaning the room of Dolly, Simran started looking at her books, when Dolly suddenly entered. Little embarrassed, she said, "*Didi*, these heavy books must be quite difficult."

"Nothing is difficult in life." Waiting for a moment she said, "Simran, come to me without raising your step."

Simran was surprised, looked at Dolly and said, "*Did*i, are you joking? How is that possible?"

"Exactly. Just as you cannot come to me without taking a step, you cannot read these books without starting to study. Journey of miles starts with one step. First step of the child is difficult. In course of time, she runs marathons. Do you understand? If you start, nothing is difficult. You only need determination."

Hesitatingly, Simran said, "*Didi*, can I also study?"

"Of course, you can. I will bring books and shall teach you for two hours every evening. If you work hard, you can pass your X class exam in about three-four years. Dream big but remember, you can realise them only through effort and not through wishes."

Simran was very intelligent. She started studying seriously. Her memory was very sharp, and she picked up things very quickly. With her hard work and the motivation of Dolly she began to show remarkable progress in studies, much to the surprise of everyone.

With Simran's safe future, Rani was now apprehensive of

the reaction of her mother. She was well aware that her mother was extremely revengeful and would leave no stone unturned to make her life miserable. She anticipated serious problems but was courageous enough to fight for a noble cause.

As expected, Rani faced the ire of her mother. No sooner had she stepped into her home, when Kamla dashed to her room. She was highly infuriated and her broad eyes were blazing fire of anger. She pounced upon her like a hungry wolf and wanted to know where she had gone. Maintaining her calm, Rani told her that she had gone for some important work. Unable to know Simran's whereabouts, a red-faced Kamla yelled and started abusing her. Rani did not retaliate. Exhausted, Kamla sat on the bed. Rani brought a glass of water. There was slight swing in her mood. Adopting a soft and reconciliatory tone, she said, "Simran was a neglected child, and had miserable childhood. I wanted rest of her life to be happy and prosperous. Tell me what was wrong in that? You have ruined all plans."

"I am in the proximity of reality and know all your plans. Let me say it straight. You and your so-called cousin wanted to prepare some blue films through Simran. I remember sometime back, you had referred to a person, who had amassed lot of wealth through such nefarious activities of flesh trade. Both of you were now in search of some innocent girl. Suman could not satisfy your greed and your covetous eyes fell on poor Simran. If your motive had been pure, you would have certainly discussed everything with me. Do not try to hide your intentions and befool me."

An arrogant Kamla could not digest these shameful remarks, and flew into rage again. Looking with disdain and raising her eyebrows in anger, she retorted with a violent outburst of threat, "Remember, you will have to pay a very heavy price."

"I do not worry so long as my conscience is clear. For God's sake, have fear at least at this age. Your feet are in the grave, and you are treading such an immoral and disgraceful path. Have some mercy on the innocent child. Let me tell you. Do not play with her life. I can adopt the role of Durga. She is my child, and a furious tigress can attack anyone to save her cubs."

"Are you threatening me?"

With great confidence but all humility, she replied, "No. I am very politely requesting you to stay away from her life."

Thoroughly annoyed and with an extremely frowning face, Kamla left. Rani kept on thinking about the future course of her mother. She was certain of some drastic reaction. Her main weakness was that she was not in a position to afford rent for some other accommodation. Financial stress had forced her to stay in one room of her father's hut. If she could afford, she would have taken a little better accommodation and would have been saved from the pain of separation from Simran. She had to suffer the curse of poverty all her life. With meagre earning of about five thousand a month, she was hardly able to afford two bare meals for the family of five, two young children of her jobless widower younger brother also took their meals with her. She was so magnanimous that she never displayed a frown on her face for this additional load. She always used to say, name of the eater is written on every grain, we are just the means. With all these problems, she was leading a contented life, and never adopted immoral means like her mother and sister.

The impending danger was looming large, and Rani always feared some problem simmering beneath. Every day was passing with increasing mental tension. For saving the life and honour of Simran, her own life was drowned in the sea of distress, and a mountain of trouble fell on her.

□

4

Rani was mighty relieved by placing Simran in the safe and sound hands of Puris. With her ingenuity and farsightedness, she tried to explore love and a secure future for Simran, who was now gravely concerned about the safety of her *maa* due to the despicable plans of Kamla. To all this, was the added pain of separation being equally suffered by both. To minimise that intense pain, Simran daily talked to Rani through the phone of Pooja or Dolly, who were generously allowing her to talk to her heart's desire. Rani also impatiently waited for her call, and was immensely satisfied that she was happy and had started her studies also.

"*Maa*, I am always worried. Your mom is a great trouble rouser. Is she creating some problem because of me?"

"Simmi dear, firstly, don't worry about me. My deeds are pure, and God is always on the side of good people. I am bold enough to handle all types of people. Adversity has made me tough to face problems courageously. Secondly, for God's sake, do not blame yourself. Do not carry any guilt feeling in your mind. You will never be responsible for anything that may happen to me. We all carry the burden of our own fortune."

"*Maa*, if I had not been there, you would not have suffered. Sometimes, I wish if God wanted one life, He could have taken my life instead of that of my mother. All would have been spared of the pain of sufferings. My mother might have been dejected for sometime, but slowly everything would have been forgotten, and normalcy would have returned with the birth of another child. Life of my father would have been full of love and peace. Just to save me, God created problems for so many, with my life also being equally miserable."

"Do not blame God. Destiny does not barter lives. All this was preordained and things don't happen as per our choice. Everything is written and no amount of tears can wash even a single word. We can't fight destiny and have simply to bear with bowed head and folded hands. Problems will always be there; courage lies in facing them. Always pray to God to give you strength to bear the unbearable. Never dwell on worry, for it is not the solution to a problem. It is a virus that impacts the mind, and is more painful than the problem itself. I don't want you to blame yourself for anything, if your deeds are pure."

Kamla was not the stuff to sit idle and began to harbour resentment against Rani. Hungry for revenge, she wanted to settle score and her evil mind finally weaved a wicked plan against her. On Simran's insistence, Rani told her all the details.

"Simran, I will not hide anything from you. My mother hurled all types of vulgar abuses after my arrival here. Having exhausted her scathing verbal threats, she resorted to evil plans to evict me from the one room that I was occupying, but I refused to be cowed down. You will be shocked and dismayed to hear the plan of the wicked lady, if I may call her so." Waiting for a while, she continued, "One evening, she came to me and told me that there was no gas in the cylinder and that her electric heater was also out of order. She wanted to cook some *dal* on my heater and told me that she would put illegal wires on the supply line from the roof, and no one will observe it at night. You know about this illegal practice of power theft from dangerously dangling wires, very common in these slums, which I have never done. Foolishly, I did not object. After about half-an-hour, someone knocked at the door. On opening, I saw a policeman with another person."

"You have taken illegal connection from on the street wire?"

"I was shocked. I told them that I had not done anything and the *dal* belonged to someone else. They were not satisfied with my explanation and told me that the *kanta* and the heater were sufficient proofs of my theft of government resources. The man wrote something and asked me to sign. I could not read and signed. After about a week, a person from the electricity department came and wanted me to sign a notice for illegal use of electricity. It was a breakdown moment, but I stayed calm in those trying circumstances. I called my neighbour. He told the man that the notice was in the name of Ram Saran, and not in my name. He told me not to sign and asked him to hand over the notice to the concerned person. The man asked me address of Ram Saran, my husband. I did not know that. However, I gave him his phone number and he left."

"*Maa*, what is the position now? Did you not tell your mom about the notice?"

"Look at the behaviour of the vamp. She had seen the man, but did not come out of her room. Later developments confirmed that all this had been conceived by her to evict me from the room, and take revenge of my taking you away from her. She came after the man's departure, and pretended ignorance of the whole incident. Relations were on the verge of collapse, and the home could have turned into a battlefield, but I maintained my calm. After two days, the police constable came and threatened that I would be arrested after warrants from the court. I was shaken. I disposed him off by the language that the police understand, and became a regular source for his gratification."

"*Maa*, why did you not consult someone in the society in which you are working?"

"Simmi, I applaud your brainwave. You have become

very intelligent. It is good for your future. I think you should become an advocate."

"*Maa*, don't pamper me. I am too small for that big profession. I want to remain grounded, and cannot aspire to dream that big. Actually, I have been discussing with Dolly *didi*. She suggested this to me."

"I am grateful to her. You can't forecast destiny, but I can predict that a glorious future awaits you. Anyway, I did not want the situation to spiral out of control and talked to an advocate in the society. He told me that since the meter was not in my name, the department could not issue the notice to me. He also told me that a case of harassment will be filed next day against the department. He was kind enough not to charge any fee and charged only court expenditure, which I could pay in two-three monthly instalments. He also told me that Assembly Elections were round the corner, and as a vote catching device from the slum dwellers, government will certainly drop all such cases. He told me to politely show to the policeman copy of the case filed in the court, and offer him only a glass of water. It was a testing time, but I survived the heavy blow."

"*Maa*, this was wonderful. I appreciate the kind gesture of the benevolent advocate. All this is because of your good nature, and the habit of maintaining cordial relations with all."

"My dear child, I always pray that you embrace all noble human values. It is the tongue that creates both friends and foes. I could not study in a formal school, but learnt free from the school of life. This school has no building and is open all the twenty-four hours. We have not to carry the heavy load of books. This school indirectly taught me the values of hard work, courage, love, humility and decent behaviour. I want you to learn from this school, besides the formal school. Remember, education is the most precious treasure, which can never be stolen, and can be acquired everywhere and from everyone at all the times."

"*Maa*, I have already started studying. Dolly *didi* has bought books for me and devotes two hours every day for teaching me. She is a source of great inspiration, and always tells me to dream big and let sky be the limit. After the household work, I go to the KG school and study with small children."

"This is very nice of Dolly. Uncle and aunty are really noble people. You must serve them wholeheartedly."

"*Maa*, I forgot. Did you talk to Kamla about the latest developments?"

"This is very interesting and revealed her true nature, and the purpose of her wicked plan. After coming from the advocate, I posed to be sad and dejected. I went to her and started shedding cold tears. Instead of consoling me, she told me that the police will force me to accept the court summons, as I was still legally Ram Saran's wife. She threatened that non-compliance could put me in jail. I requested her to help me."

"The only solution is that you go to your husband, or shift and start living somewhere else. I will tell the police that I have no idea about your present address. This will save you from any legal action. If you need, I will try to arrange some advance for you. As mother, that is the best that I can do. I have always been concerned about your welfare and that of your son. Imagine his fate, if you are put behind bars. He will be rotting on the road and who knows, may become a criminal. Act fast. Rest is your decision."

"Simmi, all her promises for help were just a lip service. To punish me for my noble deed, she wanted to throw me on the road to beg or to suffer in the house of my treacherous husband. I did not want to be offensive. There is a saying in rural culture. 'Why give poison, if you can kill with jaggery.'" In course of time, the case died its own death and Rani was luckily saved from the crime, that she had never committed.

Pooja was astonished to know the working of the mind of crafty Kamla. She said, "Simran, at times, we suffer even for nobler deeds but remember, in the long run, truth always triumphs. God never punishes you for the sin not committed by you."

"Aunty, *maa* had been so kind to me in life, and I became a source of trouble to her."

"Simran, I reciprocate what Rani told you. You should never blame yourself and never wallow in self-guilt. This leads to depression and lowers self-esteem. Blame yourself only if you wilfully commit some sin. We choose our action, not its outcome, and cannot be blamed for the unforeseen or unforeseeable repercussions of our acts. Sinners suffer, not the virtuous. Your aim in life should be to spread love and happiness all around. This will give you inner satisfaction."

After sometime, Pooja switched over to another topic and asked, "Simran, we are absolutely unaware of what happened to you after Daljeet took you back to Delhi from here. He never maintained any contact in spite of our request."

Simran became tense and joy withered from her face. With some difficulty, she resumed, "Aunty, the most tragic and humiliating period of my life started with my departure from here."

"But Daljeet took you from here to arrange your marriage."

"Aunty, on the night of my arrival at Delhi, when papa and his two friends, Deepak and Sandeep, were enjoying their drinks, I gathered from their discussion that papa had met them in jail, while they were serving three-year sentence for car theft. After his release, papa came to Deepak, who offered him shelter and also lured him in his criminal activities, which he and his friend had continued after their release. Papa did not appreciate, that company of our friends determines the quality of our life. I hated his activities, and thought I will soon convince him to leave the path of crime. I did not realise that one crime generates another, and the cycle never ends. Behaviour of both his friends was normal with me, and I had some consolation that I was of some relief to my father in his loneliness. Perhaps, to strengthen his business relations, papa wanted me to marry his partner-in-crime and opened the topic next day."

"Simran, you are growing now and I have brought you here to arrange your marriage with Deepak."

"But papa, he is not a good man. He is a shady character, and I hate his activities."

Daljeet became aggressive. "But he will soon desert the path of crime and start his own workshop. He is a rich man and will look after you very well. Your future will be safe in his hands."

"Papa, man can change but not his nature. I will prefer a poor noble person to a rich criminal. *Dadi* used to narrate the story of Guru Nanak Devji, who squeezed milk from the coarse bread of an honest poor and blood out of the buttered bread of a dishonest rich. I will prefer not to marry, rather than marry a criminal."

Daljeet was furious and warned, "Remember, I am your father. My decision is final, and I will not change it."

"Uncle, I did not like the threatening tone of my father and decided to leave the topic at that hot moment. At night, when all three were heavily drunk, I heard their discussion."

"Daljeet, did you talk to Simran about our marriage?" asked Deepak.

"Yes, I did. She is adamant. Her response was still cold, but I will convince her soon. From my side, the relation is confirmed. She is your wife. She is your property."

"Don't worry. I will persuade her and am sure, she will

agree. I think by the time you and Sandeep come back from Guwahati, she would have willingly agreed," said the confident Deepak.

"Uncle, I came to know that they had changed the course of their business. They were not stealing cars now, but buying the stolen ones and selling them in North-east, which was a haven for such illegal activities. For this, they had established an office at Guwahati, that was to be managed by papa. These cars were also dismantled within few hours, and the scrap and parts were sold in a market at Meerut, a place about 75 kilometres from Delhi. This job was assigned to Sandeep. Deepak was in charge of the main activities of purchase at Delhi."

"Simran, you should have forced Daljeet to leave the path of crime immediately."

"Uncle, occasionally I did talk to him, but the issue was always sidetracked by him. I could not persuade him to follow the path of nobility in those few days, as he soon left for Guwahati. He also tried to satisfy me by saying that there was no crime in their purchasing the stolen cars."

"What happened after he left for Guwahati?" asked Pooja.

"Papa left Delhi, leaving me at the mercy of the beast. Deepak started bringing costly fashionable dresses and precious gifts, which I invariably refused. I vehemently told him that I was not interested in marriage. I could see the controlled aggression on his face, but did not suspect anything at that stage. His behaviour was outwardly normal, but he would keep hovering around me with smile and lust in his eyes."

Simran suddenly became quiet. Her voice was completely choked. She turned aside to hide the tears suspended on the fringes of her eyes. An anxious Pooja looked at her and said, "Simmi dear, you can hide your wound and tears from everyone, but not from your mother. Tell me what happened then?"

"Three days after papa's departure, Deepak came fully drunk. Normally very talkative, he was absolutely quiet. I did not realise the lull before the storm. He came to my bedroom, tied my hands, gagged me, and sexually abused me. It was a brutally chilling moment. I cried, implored to be left alone, but all my entreaties and wailings fell on deaf ears. I struggled hard to save my honour, but could not match the might of the burly drunk criminal. There was none to hear my piercing shrieks. Tears and solitude were my only companions. I was absolutely devastated. My whole world crashed, and there was a cloud of darkness before my eyes. My chastity and honour were utterly disgraced and I lost everything of my life. Besides the body, my soul was also completely defaced. All brilliant hues of my life faded in those tragic moments and I became a heap of foul and rotten social garbage. My state at that stage can only be imagined and cannot be described in words. He threatened to kill me and my father, if I revealed anything to him. Courage deserted me. I did not want to lose my father, irrespective of his past and present behaviour. Profusely bleeding, I became unconscious."

"Why did you not tell your father?"

"Aunty, I had no phone and did not know papa's phone number. Deepak was a very shrewd man with a seasoned criminal mind and had taken all precautions. He was always around me like a shadow and started guarding me day and night. If at all he had to go, he locked me in the bathroom, whose only window was nailed with a wooden plank. He continued his nefarious acts for over three months, and I became a perpetual victim of his physical lust. I was crying all the time and begged with folded hands to spare me. Even God had closed his eyes and plugged his ears. Destiny completely deserted me."

Expressing his anguish, Ramesh furiously asked, "Did

Daljeet not enquire about you all those days?"

"That is the tragedy of my life. Papa was least concerned about my welfare or safety. For him, I was already dead and now he was satisfied, having handed over my corpse to Deepak. He was perhaps convinced by him that all was well at Delhi, and that I had accepted the marriage proposal. Even if I had contacted him, he would have refused to buy my argument, since he was entirely under the spell of Deepak and depended on him for his living. His concern was his future, not my present."

Simran's throat was suddenly choked. She began to weep. It appeared she wanted to say something, but was hesitating. "Aunty, my plight is inexplicable in words. I was breathing but not living. There was none to apply the healing balm. Pain was the only remedy of my pain. I had no choice but to conceal my wounds and suffer my ordeal alone. I cannot tell you what did he do to me? I wish to cut my tongue before telling you the truth. I wish I had died. I cannot tell you. I can't tell you anymore." Crying and sobbing violently, she suddenly left the place, dashed to the other bedroom and bolted it from inside.

Both Ramesh and Pooja were astonished, though Pooja was less surprised. "What has happened to her?" asked Ramesh.

"I know what happened after this."

"How do you know? Did she tell you earlier?"

"She never told me anything. Being a woman, I can understand the succession of further events from her words, violent cries and sudden departure." Moistening her lips, Pooja continued, "The poisonous truth is that she became pregnant." Ramesh was simply shocked, and was dumb in astonishment. How could Pooja say that? Waiting for a few moments, he said, "I can't believe but if it is true, how could the young innocent girl bear that exceptionally agonising physical and mental pain? She must have been completely shattered. Please ask her to open the door. I am afraid she might do something."

"Let her weep her heart out. She needs some space and time. She will not do anything. If she wanted, she would have done long back. She is only afraid that we may not throw her out"

After waiting for some time and having felt that Simran must have lightened the burden of her heart, Pooja gave a light tap on the door. "Simran, my child, you need not tell us anything. I will not ask you. I am not only your mother but also you friend and well-wisher. I will support you under all conditions and circumstances. Please open the door."

Simran quietly opened the bolt, and seeing Pooja right in front, hugged her tightly. The cries became more violent. Pooja took her to the bedroom. Simran buried her head in her lap. Pooja kissed it, wiped her tears, gave her some water and tried to change the course of discussion.

"Simmi my child, your uncle has been asking me for a cup of tea. You have banned my entry to the kitchen. May I request you for help?"

Little reluctantly, Simran got up, wiped her face with her *dupatta* and went straight to the kitchen. Pooja also quietly followed her. Inside the kitchen she said, "Your uncle is also feeling little hungry. Can you make some delicious onion and potato *pakauras* for him?"

Pooja was very intelligent and fully understood the feelings of the innocent adolescent girl, who was bereft of any support from anyone, and had undergone such a harrowing trauma in her life. To give her some breathing time to regain normalcy, it was essential to change the track of her thoughts. Kitchen was just an excuse. Even after enjoying tea and snacks, she did not continue the previous topic. She started talking about the school, problems of children, her studies and arrangements for the next batch of girls in the flat. At times, both Pooja and Ramesh were cracking light jokes to alienate her fear of throwing her out, and in restoring her confidence in the continuation of her stay with them. Further discussion was postponed for some other opportune time.

After lunch and some rest, Pooja tried to resume the discussion, as she wanted the young girl to let off her mental burden. She knew that in agony, everyone needs some shoulder to put his head on to lighten the heart. She was the best source of consolation for the gravely saddened girl.

"Simran, it is not that I want to hurt you, but as mother, I want to know all that happened to my dear daughter. This will help me to chart the future course of action. Please tell me, did Daljeet know about your trauma?"

"No. I never told him."

Looking inquisitively at Simran, she decided to shoot a straight question and softly said, "Who took you to the hospital for abortion?"

Simran was stunned at the query of her aunt. She had no courage to look into her eyes. Putting her arms around her neck and clinging to her, she hesitatingly muttered, "Deepak."

"Did Daljeet again force you to marry Deepak?"

Still sobbing, and intermittently gaining some breath, she replied, "Yes. He asked me as soon as he came from Guwahati. He was under the false impression that I had already consented to marriage, and was happily living with Deepak. On my persistent refusal, he beat me hard that night, when he was totally drunk. Blood started oozing out of my mouth. Thunder of the slaps still echoes in my ears. My heart-wrenching cries and sobs miserably failed to soften his heart. Bolted in a room, he left me alone. I was heart-broken and completely crushed like a dry leaf."

"I could never imagine that Daljeet could be that cruel."

With pain reflected in her eyes, and grave mental conflict visible on the face, Simran continued, "It was *Amavasya,* full dark night which is a symbol of sin, evil and treachery. The night truly brought complete darkness in my life, with another harrowing tragedy. Next morning, when I got up, I was in some unfamiliar surroundings. I was dizzy and my head was spinning. I found myself locked in a room. It was sparsely furnished, dimly lit and had no window. I was terrified and feared that I had been kidnapped and confined to that room."

"What a tragedy?" Ramesh shouted. "Your misfortunes seem to have no end."

"Uncle, an abandoned and lonely young girl discarded by her father, is a soft and vulnerable target for man's lust and fodder for his sexual hunger. Such people view a woman only through libidinous lens. After about two hours, the door opened. I saw Deepak standing in front of me. He tried to console me by saying that my father wanted to kill me, and for my safety, he brought me to that place. I knew the place was safe not for me, but for his immoral deeds."

Simran was feeling little exhausted. Gaining some breath, she continued hesitatingly, "Sexual harassment continued for two days. On the second night, Sandeep finished his turn and went to the bathroom. My courage collapsed, but soon I gained some strength. I peeped outside the room. Deepak was fully intoxicated and lying motionless on the chair. He was snoring and was fast asleep. This was a golden opportunity never offered to me by him. That pivotal moment was the most opportune time to run away. Initially hesitant and indecisive, I chose to take a chance. Though completely drained and exhausted, I did not lose my presence of mind and trusted my gut and instinct. God gave me courage and strength. To avoid even the slightest noise, I moved on soft tiptoes and slipped quietly with a pair of *chappals* in my hand. Something flashed across my mind. I turned back and picked up a fifty rupee note lying on the bed. In breathless awe, I ran out and headed straight to the nearest bus stop to catch the first available bus for any destination. Fortune favoured me and a bus came immediately. It was for Old Delhi railway station. It appeared that my destiny had begun to turn in my favour."

Simran had courageously narrated all details of her sad story. With tears in her eyes, she said, "Thus ended the disgusting tale of my distressed life. After this, the rest is known to you. Uncle, I feel your coming and my visit to the *Gurudwara* were the turning points in my life. Course of my stars has changed, and I now hope that the tragic period of my life has finally ended under your care."

"Simran, cycle of opposites revolves in every life. Pleasure is followed by pain and pain by pleasure. Accept this fundamental universal truth. I pity your lot, but appreciate your courage and determination. Courage lies in facing adversities and conquering fear. The timid never rise, the bold never fall. The abode of God changed your destiny, and I am sure, your life is now destined for a happy and bright future. God has saved you for some dignified and noble deed," predicted Pooja.

Placing his hand on her head, the determined Ramesh said, "Grieve not my child. Wipe your tears. They only weaken will-power and self-confidence. They are symbol of timidity, and not solution to a problem. Let eyes reflect joy and not shed tears. You have unlimited creative potential and your noble qualities of head and heart are your greatest assets. Unlock the dormant energy trapped in the inner recesses of your heart. Give a new shape to your thoughts, and transform your dreams into reality. Look at sunshine ahead and not the shadow behind. Shed negativity and do not carry its baggage on your back, as miserable memories poison the resolve." Waiting for a while, he said, "Conserve the dormant volcano of your anger to explode later. Keep the fire of revenge smouldering and crush the devils under your foot at the most opportune time. This is for what you have survived."

Simran's resolve was further strengthened. She began to visualise the end of her days of distress. Suddenly, she became little sad and said, "Unfortunately, life is not as colourful as dreams. I always dreamt that my morrow would be better than today but destiny decided it otherwise."

Pooja held her hand and said, "Simran, never blame your destiny. It is a product of time and effort. As a child, you had no power to change your circumstances, and were completely helpless. It is now in your hands, and you are its architect. You can always colour your dreams with brilliant hues by your effort. Remember, wind and destiny can change direction any moment." Waiting to see the reaction, she resumed, "Problems and challenges are a part of every life. Face them. They get diluted with determination. When one door closes, God opens another, but we keep on gazing at the closed one. You are now in safe and protective hands. Dark spell of your life is over. Enjoy the bright specks of your life and explore joy even in small things and in trivial moments."

For some time, there was complete silence. Pooja switched over to another subject and asked, "What happened to Suman? Did her life go smooth?"

"Aunty, one who spreads thorns for others, should not hope to tread on flowers. Initially, both mother and daughter stuck to Vikas like a leach, but the virus of greed soon began to ruin them. Devoid of any source of income and with demands not diminishing, Kamla was frustrated. Her relations with Suman hit a rough patch and turned sour. To further cement his illicit relations, Vikas now offered to marry Suman but she was still adamant and refused. This escalated further tension, and bitterness eroded relations."

"I had anticipated this development. Horse always runs

to the grass and for the sake of money, insatiable Kamla must have forced Suman to accept the offer of Vikas."

"Aunty, your guess is absolutely right. Ambitions cloud logic and Kamla wanted to accept the proposal of Vikas, mainly due to his wealth. Reasons for declining the offer of Vikas were better known to Suman. By nature, she was not keen to remain tied to one man. Whatever the reasons, Suman was firm on her decision, and flatly rejected the offer. This irritated Vikas. He tightened the strings of his purse and declined to meet her liberal financial demands. He had also exhausted his quota of physical lust with Suman, and wanted to explore some fresh and young partner."

Waiting for a moment, she said, "Aunty, another serious development took place during this period. Suman became pregnant."

"Then she should have aborted the child or married Vikas."

"Wealth of Vikas, persuasion of her mother and advancing age had by now mellowed down Suman's stubbornness against marriage. She now wanted to settle down in life and finally decided to accept the offer of marriage. Vikas was hypocrite and a very shrewd man. Inwardly, he never wanted to marry Suman for the fear of the society, and marriage was only a convenient ploy to continue the immoral relations. Revealing his real intentions, he changed his stand and offered to continue the relations without marriage, which Suman now declined. To persuade her, he began to liberally meet her financial demands. Time passed in this tug of war, and it now became too late to abort the child. The fragile relations snapped under the stress of mistrust and she suffered his betrayal. Stubborn as she was, Suman could not share a frosty relation, and shifted to Delhi, much against the wishes of her mother. She thought that Vikas would follow her, but he did not. Toxic relations based on selfishness and sham love, completely crumbled. Such relations eventually meet with a sordid end, and lovers once now became mortal adversaries. Simmering tension also widened the gulf between the two ambitious and greedy ladies."

"Did Suman not go back to Dehradun?"

"In her inflated ego Suman thought that Vikas would apologise and marry her. Her vanity and false faith in her vanishing charm betrayed her."

"This is where the sanctity of marriage plays its role. In her mistaken pride, Suman thought that she would never grow old or would never be deserted by anyone. But man is a very greedy animal and once satisfied, would stalk another prey. She and her mother both failed to anticipate the behaviour of Vikas. In him, they met their own match and had to pay back in the same coin. They failed to realise that one can befool a person all the time, but not all the people all the times. The clever advocate used Suman to his heart's desire and with the withering of her charm, dumped her in the dustbin like a squeezed lemon with an additional life-long load. In the horse-race of life, one moment you are on the head and another on the hoof."

"Aunty, whatever may have been the weaknesses of my father, I still feel that he would have been sincere to her if she had married him."

"I also have absolutely the same feeling. Unbridled greed is the genesis of most human problems. It gives birth to hatred, jealousy and selfishness, greatest stumbling blocks in progress. Materialistic propensities and insatiable avarice of Suman prompted by her mother, ruined lives of both, and those of you and your father. If she had settled for a happy family life and accepted you also as her own daughter, all would have been spared of the life-long pain suffered due to her ambition-driven greed. Remember Simran, not only friends, foes also teach us. Sometimes, a fool is a better teacher than the wise. He unwittingly teaches us something invaluable. Suman and Kamla teach us the painful result of blind faith, broken relations and deceptive confidence in live-in relations. Mistakes are opportunities to learn, but both were blind. If you continue doing the same thing and expect a different result, it is mental bankruptcy. Both mother and daughter fall in this category. But all this was destined. No amount of tears could change the course of destiny."

"Though late, Suman became wiser with the passage of time and after the desertion of Vikas. She now realised that Vikas was not a good man at heart, and had got my father imprisoned in a fictitious case only for his sexual lust. There was a paradigm shift in her attitude towards my father. She began to pay frequent visits to jail and convinced him of her love and sincerity. Pregnancy was a new development that completely blocked her future prospects of some further live-in relation. Realising that all her viable options had been exhausted, she now decided to exploit the innocence of my father and seek shelter under his love and care. She knew that my father, a victim of emotions, was prone to follow his heart and would easily fall in her trap. Trust deficit started vanishing and love of my father brought her closer to him. It may be surprising but papa was still faithful to her and was prepared to accept her in spite of all her failings. She attributed all this to destiny and convinced him that Vikas poisoned their relations. Whatever the reason, her tears and pleadings played upon the weakness of my father, and he promised to marry her after his release. Flaws were amicably ironed out and the derailed lives finally got back on tracks."

Ramesh had been listening patiently. Suddenly, he got little furious and said, "Daljeet was certainly not a man of strong will and was too weak to take decisions in matters of love and marriage. Perhaps, he began to feel that jail sentence had tarnished his image, and to settle down, he could not find any better option than Suman. Clever Suman again played with his emotions, and he ungrudgingly gave her a fresh lease of life. Any other man in his place would have thought ten times before accepting a woman of Suman's character, who had deserted him just for the lure of a few more chips. He did not even care that she was carrying the baby of someone, who had deprived him of his love, and was responsible for ruining ten prime years of his life, by falsely implicating him in a fictitious case."

"Uncle, I also feel that papa is emotionally a very weak person and can be easily swayed to either side. Still, I will be happy if he can explore love and settle down in his life. He has suffered enough pain."

"Simran, tell me frankly, what will be your attitude towards Daljeet, if he desires to marry Suman after his release?" questioned Pooja.

"Aunty, my fundamental thinking is, garbage cannot be cleaned by garbage; darkness cannot be dispelled by darkness. Just as you cannot enjoy fragrance of a jasmine flower in a room filled with filth, you can't have peace in a mind full of hatred. I cannot carry this heavy load of hatred throughout my life and want to unburden myself of this unbearable insidious baggage. It is an impediment to mental peace and stillness of mind. Papa has hated me and has caused me immense pain, but I do not harbour any ill-feeling against him. A troubled conscience never lives in peace, and I will be the last person to nurse any feeling of revenge against him. The pain caused to me is now obscured by the mist of time. Unless, I forget the past, I will be perpetuating unhappiness not only for him, but also for me. He is my father, my own blood. He has suffered due to his own mistakes, and I don't want him to suffer because of me. Moreover, I had promised *dadi* to look after him, and I will always abide by that solemn promise. Forgetfulness is the key to reduce pain and to happily move on in life."

"Simran, I wonder, even at this young age, you have become wiser than sages, who meditate for years to gain that depth of wisdom. Humility is a great human virtue, but rare at such a tender age. It shows absence of ego and any feeling of retaliation in you. I agree that fire of hatred can only be doused by the nectar of love, but there is another side of his character also. By forcing you to marry Deepak, he is completely responsible for all that happened to you that could have been avoided, if he had been careful and sensible." Pooja wanted to further probe her reaction towards Daljeet.

"Aunty, blind faith in the goodness of everyone was papa's basic weakness. He easily fell into the trap of Suman and Vikas, and suffered. His trust in Deepak left me in the clutches of the devil, that ruined my life. I do feel that as a wise man, he should have been more careful. He was certainly casual about my life and future, but perhaps his intentions were not so bad. He did not love me but was not so mean to sell me. I do not wholly absolve him of the blame, but I hold Deepak responsible for all that happened."

Intervening, Ramesh said, "I have my reservations on the issue, but appreciate your magnanimity and decision of forgiveness for the future happiness of all. Hatred is already in abundance in the world. Let us put it in the hearth and let love abound all around."

Simran wanted to change the course of discussion to avoid any further damage to the character of her father. "Aunty, the magical spell of both Rani *maa* and you, has dramatically changed the philosophy of my life. One gave me life and the other two things, peace and happiness. The medium has been the same, love and nothing but unconditional love. I want to repay to all what I got from you. If I perpetuate hatred, I will be setting a chain reaction that will never end. I want to break that chain here and now."

"Simran, let me ask you a more serious question," asked

Ramesh. "What will be your reaction towards Suman, if Daljeet marries her? You must be frank and truthful in your reply."

"Uncle, by nature, I don't believe in telling lies. If she hates me or is still indifferent, I will maintain normal relations. If she is normal, I will love her. If she loves me, I will love and respect her. I will be always a step ahead of her. At least, I will not hate her. Hating her will again cause pain to my father, which is the last thing that I will do in life." Waiting and reflecting for a moment, she resumed, "Uncle, I understand there is phenomenal change in Suman's behaviour and her whole outlook on life has dramatically changed mainly due to papa's love. I will forgive her for all her wrongs done to me not because she deserves forgiveness, but because I desire peace in my life and in the life of my father. Not only her, I will forgive all those who sinned against me, though forgetting them may be little harder. It is said, one who forgives, benefits more than one whom he forgives."

"And to her child?"

"Love. Only love, and nothing but love. I will shower all my care and affection on her or him. Child is not the cause of harm or pain to anyone. I became a victim of that reaction and suffered. I do not want another Simran to suffer like me."

Speechless at her wit and wisdom, Ramesh decided to know her opinion about an embarrassing issue. "Let me know your reaction towards the two rogues who ruined your virginity."

Simran did not take even a fraction of a second. "Revenge through legal course. Punishment will be my aim in life not only for them, but for all those beasts that ruin the lives of innocent girls."

"You seem to be ruthlessly determined to take revenge. Let it never fade away. But remember, when you quench your hostility in revenge, you also create a cycle of retribution. I am not discouraging you, but your adversary may try to dent your dignity in the court, and you may have to face extremely shameful situation."

"Uncle, a drenched man does not fear rain. I am not scared of outrageous remarks. They will further strengthen my resolve. I have shaken off the shackles of shame. Why should I be ashamed? He should be disgraced, isolated and shunned by the society for his morally dubious act. He should hide his face for ruining the chastity of a pious girl. Social thinking has to change. Tolerating oppression encourages the oppressor to repeat and facing oppression, forces the oppressor to retreat. He has soiled my body but not my spirit. My determination to fight shall never be dented."

Continuing after gaining some breath, she resumed, "Uncle, there is a sudden surge in rape cases. I want to liberate the hapless and helpless victims from social isolation and emotional oppression. They must discover and reinvent their lost strength and courage to face the society. Throughout my life, I will continue to fight for such victims and for more stringent rape laws. I want to replace ridicule with respect and not sympathy. I do not want a victim to dwell on her setbacks. I want the people to view things through the eyes of the victim, and realise her pain and plight. Even if alone in life, I will stand by my social struggle. Struggle is the other name of life."

"I salute your resolve for women empowerment. Now just tell me will you spare Vikas for all that he did to your father?"

"Uncle, I have seriously thought of that. Legally, I will not be in a position to prove his role in papa's conviction. However, I will certainly seek justice for Suman's child. Different folks need different strokes. With him, I will try veiled threats to get financial compensation for Suman and her child. In all probability, my persuasion will succeed but if not, then I will take recourse to legal action."

Fully endorsing her decisions, Ramesh said, "Simran, we are glad that your thoughts are so clear, mature and firm.

I appreciate your positive thinking about your father and Suman. Negative thoughts aggravate pain of our wounds. Some nurse wounds the whole life and not only suffer themselves, but also cause sufferings to others. For rape and causing emotional hurt to women, you must devote your life to fight for them. Remember, one who bears injustice is a greater sinner than one who inflicts it. A campaign against stigma attached to the rape victims will be a milestone towards their social restoration."

Pooja was completely astonished at the determination of Simran, and was silently appreciating her wisdom. She said, "Simran, foundation of your bright future is being laid in your present resolve. I want you to leave your gloomy and depressing past behind and let it not come in the way of your future. Live life with head held high and gracefully value everything that life gives. Be a source of strength to others and happily share their sufferings. I am sure, we have further fortified the noble ethical and human values, that were imbibed by you through your grandmother, and nurtured by Rani."

After a short pause and with little seriousness, she continued, "One doesn't know about life but I will say a few things. Be like a flower placed at the feet of God for worship, in the bun of a bride for decoration or as a token of reverence for the dead. It continues to give its fragrance, irrespective of its role, and even if it withers or is trampled under the feet of the meek and the mighty. Also, never tolerate injustice as it is a sign of cowardice. Remember, woman may appear deceptively fragile and vulnerable, but she has the strength of Durga and Kali."

"Aunty, you are my greatest source of strength and came in my life at its most crucial phase to dispel the cobwebs of my mind. I will always remember your sane advice. Your divine fragrance and inspiration are venerable." With a sense of determination, she said, "I will never forget the pain of the past wounds and the trauma that I have endured. More than the wound, hurts the pain of one who inflicts it. I will fight my case in the court and be a model for those who may be too timid to come forward. I will live my life with pride and encourage others to live with dignity. I could have joined any other profession but want to pursue law only for this mission of my life. I have no lust for money and shall give free service to all poor and destitute girls and children. My core life-mission is to spearhead a campaign to prepare them physically, mentally and emotionally to face the world. The challenges are extremely pressing but I will live for them. They only fly who think they can." Reflecting for a moment, she continued, "Aunty, to pursue my life-mission, I will start an NGO and its name will be '*Pooja Rani Nari Shakti Trust*'".

"Simran, I am proud of your resolve. To be a part of your path-breaking movement, we will also contribute our physical, mental and financial resources for the Trust." With little seriousness, Pooja resumed, "But I must warn you. On your path, you will encounter innumerable obstacles. Do not collide with them but pass them, as water passes by the side of boulders and merrily carries on its journey towards its destination. For success, you need relentless dedication. Even ordinary men with extraordinary dedication can work wonders. Start the journey; destination awaits you."

Simran warmly hugged Pooja and said, "Aunty, I am really indebted to you for all your advice and encouragement. You are my greatest strength in life."

"Simran, since we are talking of your future, I want to warn you against the negative impact of possessiveness that might have inadvertently entered your psyche. Right from your childhood, you have lived in a small world of personal relations, protected mainly by your grandmother or by Rani. You were deprived of love and company of siblings and other children and with us also, you were surrounded by only two personal relations. From a very small world of protected relations, you will now be entering the wider world of contacts. There will be challenges at every stage and you will have to trace your steps with utmost caution. Simran, extreme hatred and absence of love create the negative emotion of possessiveness and make one more introverted, or result in withdrawal symptoms. Fortunately, you are quite extrovert and broad-minded, otherwise you would have not revealed all details of your life and future plans to us so vividly. There are no signs of such negative emotions in you, but warning is essential."

Ramesh and Simran were intently listening to Pooja. She continued, "You will be entering a different phase of life, where Rani, Pooja and Ramesh may not be available. You will have to weigh everything on the scale of your own knowledge and wisdom. In the new critical phase of your life, you will create different types of relations than what you have enjoyed or suffered so far. There will be relations with a variety of friends and after marriage, with your husband, in-laws and children. While creating these new relations, Simran, you must maintain the old ones but never remain tied to them. Do not be possessive of any relation. Remember, possessiveness is different from love. Love liberates relations, possessiveness strangulates them. Love is caring, sharing and trusting. Love is giving and not demanding. In love, you have to give breathing space to your loved ones. Selfishness in love leads to possessiveness, and slowly but surely, even best of the relations gets crucified, though you have no intention to do that."

"Aunty, these highly inspiring words are perhaps the most valuable advice that a mother can give to her daughter for her happy and prosperous future life. Even with enough space in *maa's* love and required freedom in your intense love, some negative forces could have certainly ruined my life but I assure you of my positive thinking."

Pooja's eyes suddenly became teary. She took a deep breath and said, "An inner urge impelled me to say all this. In future, you will have to weigh all pros and cons in a situation and come to a positive decision. Whenever in doubt, follow the call of your conscience. To discriminate between right and wrong, and ability to take the right decision are most vital in life. A moment makes a mistake and whole life suffers. I want you to gloss over my words. Your happiness means a lot to me. I have never wished so much for anyone in my life."

Simran hugged her tightly. Tears rolled down her cheeks. She was emotionally so charged that she could not say a word. To lighten the seriousness of the mood, Ramesh said, "Pooja, keep some words of advice for her children also."

All were little relaxed after such a serious discussion, when the door bell rang. Simran got up to open the door. There was a young man with some stuff.

"Simran, open the door and take the material. I will bring the money", said Ramesh. Excitement erupted in the mind of Simran. The box appeared to have cake and some other eatables. Both Pooja and Simran were astonished.

"Uncle, what is all this?"

"A pleasant surprise. We will celebrate your admission in the Five Year Integrated Law Course."

Surprised, Simran hugged Ramesh and said, "Uncle, I don't know what to say?"

"Then you need not say now. Better say when you know it." The witty remark evoked burst of laughter and merriment.

□

5

In the college, Simran was mostly busy with her studies. She remained very reserved and hardly communicated with other students. Her favourite place was library, though most others enjoyed canteen and sitting in gardens. Men and women had friends of their own liking and were generally very free with each other. Simran was perhaps the only woman who never interacted liberally with any other man or even with a woman student. The only classmate with whom she sometimes used to discuss about studies in the library was Gaurav Saxena. He was a handsome, smart young man with elegant social and personal habits. Both were toppers in the class but maintained a healthy competition and were never victims of any mutual jealousy. In fact, each was happier in the better merit position of the other. They did not know much about each other except that Gaurav was from Delhi and had come to Jaipur for studies, and Simran was from Punjab who had also come to Jaipur for studies, and was living with her uncle.

From his very first chance meeting with Simran, warm and friendly Gaurav had been seduced by her physical charm and irresistibly captivating and adorable smile. He always admired her unassuming character and pragmatic silence. Her graceful dresses were often complimented by him, but Simran normally responded only with a soft smile. Though time brought them emotionally closer to each other, their friendship never went beyond socially permissible limits.

Debates and discussions on topics concerning legal issues, visits to courts, preparation of fake cases, and arguments in legal cases were the projects in the last year of studies, and participation in them was a part of the curriculum. In one such project of debate, Simran and Gaurav were pitched against each other and the topic was "*Spurt in Rape Crimes and Quantum of Punishment in Rape Cases*". Both had prepared themselves well for a hot debate, and other classmates were keen to listen to them as they expected it to be dignified, content-oriented and of high intellectual calibre.

Initiating the debate, Gaurav Saxena said, "Seventy years of independence have witnessed a spurt in rape cases. Though there is exponential rise in other cognisable crimes also, increase in rape cases is highly alarming. National Crime Records Bureau has revealed horrifying increase in rape by whopping 870%, child rape by 336%, abduction of women by 380% and kidnapping by 750%. Estimates suggest that a woman is raped in India every 20 minutes. Worldwide figures are equally disturbing. As per UN data, one in three women has reportedly experienced physical or sexual violence, mostly by an intimate partner. Most developed countries like America, Canada, UK, France, Germany and Sweden are the most immersed ones in this crime. India is known as one of the world's most unsafe countries for women and it is essential to treat the safety of women on top priority. It is an irony of fate that though we worship Shakti, Durga, Kali, Lakshmi and Saraswati, all female forms of divinity, yet we do not respect women. Our ancient philosophy also believes "*Yatra naryasya pujyante, ramante tatra devta*", meaning where women are worshipped, gods reside there."

Dressed in simple matching *salwar-kameez* with hair tucked in a low loose bun, Simran was looking glamorous and was at her magnetic best. She noticed the admiring glances of Gaurav and responded with a faint smile. Reacting to the introductory remarks of Gaurav, she said, "Rape is one of the most heinous forms of assault afflicted on a human by another. I fully endorse the view that there is exponential rise in rape crime cases in India. Take any newspaper. There will be at least one case of rape of a woman, a teenage girl or even a child. Adolescent boys are also getting more into the act. This reported increase may be due to awareness among women and role of media. Rape is a complex crime to analyse, but it is believed that about 70% cases, particularly from rural areas, go unreported. This is mainly due to retaliation, humiliation, social stigma and fear of being disowned by families. Several disturbing cases of alleged harassment at workplace have also been aired recently, involving men in position of power making advances on vulnerable young women. Acid attacks are other vicious, potentially life-threatening crimes, but I am restricting my discussion to only rape victims, as that is the subject of debate. Woman in Indian culture was always held in high esteem, but molestation, rape and gang-rape tarnished our image in course of time. Besides our epics, it is also said in *Gurubani*, "*So kyun manda aakhiye, jitt jamme rajaan*", meaning why debase one, who gives birth to kings. Woman is in distress today. There is none to listen to her raining woes, leave aside protecting her. The situation is extremely pathetic and needs to be checked and remedied."

Continuing on molestation of women, Gaurav said, "Besides disrespect to women, provocative, disrespectful, vulgar, puerile and insulting statements, and irresponsible comments on rape crimes by our leaders are most disgusting and shocking. In male chauvinism, our elected representatives misuse the right to freedom of speech and expression. Instead of shaming the crime, some justify rape by describing it as a social crime that can be "right sometimes, wrong sometimes."

Some defend the rapists by saying that "Boys will be boys." Some say, "Men are men and will do such things." In one case, a politician stated, *"Itne bade sheher mein chhota hadsa ho jaata hai".* Another equally insensitive politician said, *"Yeh to sab karte hain."* For a candidate for assembly elections, who was in jail on rape charges, a former Home Minister of a State remarked, "At least he could have raped after the election." One woman politician stated that girls should not be so 'adventurous' to move on the road at night. It is not only the politicians who make such undignified off-the-cuff remarks, even one defence lawyer shamefully commented in his interview in a documentary, "If you keep sweets on the street, then dogs will come and eat them." Such is the thinking of our legislators and educated class of the society. They believe that women are of lesser value and that, daughters, wives and sisters should be locked at home in order to "protect" them. Surprisingly, mobile phones have been the focus of patriarchal ire before also by *Khap panchayats*. Some blame "influence of western culture" and "vulgar dressing" for rise in rape crimes."

Supporting the views of Gaurav, Simran added, "Such disgraceful remarks of politicians and legal luminaries dilute the gravity of the crime. They view a woman as an object for sex and exploitation. It shows a dangerous dive in their maturity level and is not indicative of a seasoned democracy. They suffer from verbal diarrhoea and seldom take responsibility for their irresponsible and undignified remarks. Their cryptic, outrageous, insensitive and chest-thumping statements are an insult to the dignity of women. They are made in an effort to gain cheap popularity. They only encourage the rapist and dilute the gravity of the crime. They provide cover to heinous crimes and still get away by making bizarrely and shameful sexist remarks. Such powerful people lose ability to see things from victim's perspective. Besides, rape originates in the mind, and is never a product of the victim, their choices, clothing or neighbourhood. Instead of women, men should be blamed for all kinds of sinful thoughts, that cross their minds when they see a woman. There must also be a Line of Speech Control. Violation should be a punishable offence and should not be permitted. Freedom of Speech of one should not disgrace the dignity of the other. Legislators who disgrace women deserve to be censured by the Parliament and State Assemblies. Yardstick for commoners and politicians should not be different, when it comes to punishing people who insult women through their thoughtless utterances. Such remarks send a wrong signal to the molesters, and police also begin to share similar attitude. Let us defeat such politicians at the ballot box, to teach them a lesson for being insensitive to woman, the goddess of human creation."

Continuing her argument Simran said, "Why blame the politicians and advocates, even judges sometimes hold different views. In a 1982 judgement, judge Bertrand of Ipswich Crown Court let off a car driver of sexually assaulting a woman, who had taken lift from him on a lonely street in the dead of night, with a fine of 2,000 pounds. The narrow minded ground was that the woman was also guilty of "contributory negligence" for request for lift at that time of night. Again, in June 2007, another British judge, Julian Hall of Oxford County Court, awarded a lenient nine-month prison to a rapist. The reason given was that the ten-year old victim "liked to dress provocatively" and looked as if she was sixteen. Not to talk of re-victimising a rape victim by clever advocates to save their clients, even a US judge asked a rape victim, "Did you close your legs?" In India, the SC acquitted two policemen of rape charges in 1978. Reasons, the sixteen-year old girl did not raise any alarm, while being sexually assaulted inside the police station and that the behaviour of the girl suggested that she was habituated to sexual intercourse. However, the SC has changed its approach in rape cases since then. It rightly observed in one of the cases in 1991, that a woman is "equally entitled to protection of law. Therefore, merely because she is of easy virtue, her evidence cannot be thrown out."

The moderator of the debate competition intervened and said, "Both the debaters should now confine themselves to the question of quantum of punishment for the rapists."

Without waiting, Simran immediately took the first turn. "Let us look at the problem of punishment from the victim's point of view. A rape victim has to suffer emotional pain and social abuse. She has to carry the baggage of shame throughout her life. The oppressor leaves, but the pain caused by him continues for ever. The emotional residue of rape pain stays in the psyche of the unfortunate victim, and manifests in the negative emotion of low self-esteem. Fence sitters can hardly grasp the trauma of pain of a rape victim. Thrown into dark deep pit of infamy, it becomes impossible to regain the lost prestige. Rape-crime takes minutes, justice takes years, but the trauma and stigma that the rape victim suffers from, survives for a lifetime. Stained in shame, the rape victim is ostracised by people. She normally drops out of educational institution and at times, has to change residence also. Society tries to shun the victims and their families. People constantly stalk her and she fears of being killed. She becomes an easy prey making her rehabilitation almost impossible. She is humiliated again and again in the court. All her wails and pleas fall on deaf ears in the stifled closet of patriarchy. Why do we adopt dual standard for the rapist and the victim? The police question the survivor more than the rapist. Its attitude is usually anti-survivor from the moment she sets foot inside a police station. Police also sometimes waste more time in deciding jurisdiction. Precious time is wasted in debating non-human issues, without caring to look to the immediate needs of the helpless victim in peril. She struggles to survive on the road, while the onlookers are busy taking photographs. There is none to even cover the nudity of the poor victim. On the other hand, the rapist coolly puts on his dress, raises his collar in pride as if he has won an Olympic Gold and merrily walks away. Unmindful of his crime, the unbridled bull fiercely runs amok on the road for another vulnerable catch. He behaves in the society and in the court as a hero. The whole society has been polluted by such brutal beasts.

The punishment for the rapist must send a clear message to the society. It must be strong enough to check him and others from committing more such heinous crimes. It must be at least life imprisonment, and I mean life, and not less than that. Murder after rape is being followed more these days to destroy evidence. In case of death of the victim or some permanent life injury, it should be nothing short of death sentence. Desperate diseases need desperate measures. The deterrent must be stringent enough to make others shiver from even thinking of committing such a crime. Besides, a minor above 16 years of age should also be treated as an adult, if he is an equal contributing partner in the act of rape.

A subject related to the quantum of punishment is the rate of conviction. Out of 86% charge sheets filed, conviction rate is 32%, which is abysmally low. Our legal system is also skewed and marginalised against the deprived. Poor rape victims are unable to seek justice for want of proper legal advice and free legal aid. This also encourages the affluent to exploit loopholes and escape the clutches of law."

Loud claps were indicative of staunch approval of audience. Murmurs slowly died down and Gaurav took his turn. "I appreciate the emotions of my fellow debater. It is not that I, as a man, feel less about the plight of the rape victim. But here we have to consider the punishment from legal point and not emotional. Views on awarding death sentence in general have differed at all times. Whereas some advocate death penalty, others do not support it and suggest life sentence. Law Commission headed by Justice Ajit Prakash Shah, has recommended abolishing capital punishment, except in terrorist cases. Some believe that death penalty is an inhuman punishment in a civilised world, especially in a democratic country. History proves that there is no relationship whatsoever between the presence and absence of death penalty with respect to the rate of crime. We must delve deep on the issue of capital punishment and should not be carried away by our sentiments. Punishment should be proportionate to the crime committed, and here death penalty is disproportionate to crime. Law is said to be a double-edged weapon. While it protects the rights of a person, it can also be used to throttle the liberty of the opponent. These days, false and fictitious cases of sexual abuse are common weapons for revenge, extraction of money, and for similar other reasons of exploitation. The law has to guard the innocent and victims of consensual sex. I firmly believe that death penalty is not a more effective deterrent than alternative sanction of long-term imprisonment. Keeping a person alive in solitary confinement is certainly a greater punishment than death. In capital punishment, a person loses his life in seconds; in life sentence, he 'dies' with every breath.

Chemical or surgical castration can also be explored after release. This is followed in some states in the US and in some European countries. Let the culprit realise throughout his life that moment commits crime but whole life suffers. I endorse the view of life sentence, which should not be restricted to only 14 years, but should be more and even for the whole life. For rape crimes, tough action against the rapists, including minors above 16, is needed. Psycho-babble or socio-babble from our politicians, *netas* or religious leaders is just an eyewash. It is also important to refrain from one-size-fits-all approach to gender crimes. I support that punishment should be an exemplary deterrent to future rapists.

To this, I would like to add formation of fast-track courts for rape cases. The hearing should be on day-to-day basis with no adjournments. Protection of witnesses is of paramount importance. Mindset of the police needs tremendous change. Urgent reforms are needed for the victims to have unflinching trust in police and legal systems."

The moderator again intervened and wanted to conclude the debate, giving two minutes to each debater to suggest measures for checking rape-crime cases. Gaurav Saxena took the first turn. "My primary stress would be on inculcation of moral and social values. Human irrationality and faulty passion needs to be checked, and foundation for this must be laid in childhood. Home is the cradle of all virtues, and all values are imbibed here. Children that grow in homes where women are considered inferior and are not respected, are more likely to indulge in sexual violence. Next to home is our education system. It has to channelise and change the perverse mindset of the youth. It has failed to impart the values of equality, resulting in gender sensitisation and disrespect for women. Strengthening the value system should be part of our school curriculum. Another neglected area is rapid urbanisation. In urban areas, criminal behaviour has direct correlation with building environment. Crime germinates in unhealthy social and physical environment. Population in modern cities is from different walks of life having no affinity with one another and this has further eroded the value system. With rapid urbanisation, country's towns will populate to dangerously high levels, which will reach 50% in another two decades. The current 30% of slum dwellers will become double. Average family and private space has shrunk, and this has driven crimes, including rape crimes to high levels. Police force has not increased in proportion to these changes. Better street lighting, public transportation, more surveillance cameras and widening network of shared facilities are essential to minimise incidents of sex abuse.

Besides failure of our education system, gender discrimination is strongly embedded in our social class for centuries. Female infanticide has been common due to poverty, dowry system and lack of other support systems. Their sense of inferiority encourages rape and sexual abuse. Female infanticide and sex determination are also due to this discrimination. Normal infant sex ratio is 93.5 girls to 100 boys, which becomes 92 by the age of 6. In some states, the plight of girls is shocking. In the state of Haryana, overall child sex ratio is just 76 girls against 100 boys. Many of the girls are being killed in the womb. The situation is fast improving due to government schemes like *Beti Bachao Beti Padhao*, but a lot still needs to be done. In theory, citizens have been given equal rights in India, but, in practice, society disempowers women in matters of marriage, divorce and inheritance. Gender inequality and other stereotypes have resulted in socio-cultural collapse. For India to be a global power, we must pass and implement laws that respect and empower women." With this, Gaurav resumed his seat.

Taking her turn, Simran said, "Crime thrives in situations of anonymity and impersonality, where there is desperate search for a community. Lonely and emotionally deprived social isolates are possible sources for the rapid growth of such crimes. Family and society provide education, and lay foundation for culture and morality, which builds up slowly through the environment in which the child develops. Children living in brutalised areas grow up to become amoral machines of violence and death-defying instruments of regimes. Community and family ties have weakened, and are crashing and crumbling. Social relationships have thinned, which have adversely affected respect for women. Family values that promote and nurture solidarity and love within the family, have been eroded by urbanisation. This is the price of modernity, its ruthless urban-industrial vision, and version of hard-nosed individualism. Indian society is patriarchal, where women are treated as second-grade citizens. Fundamental rights like right to freedom and equality are severely compromised for women. This devaluation of women must cease.

The nature of rape is deeply rooted in man. Increasing violence against women and children needs to be confronted and curtailed by government action, and strict enforcement of laws. These crimes also do not happen without the active connivance or abject disregard of some basic norms by the police and the judiciary. Police stations are conspicuous by the absence of women officers. The victim is uncomfortable, narrating her ordeal to a male officer. The result is writing incorrect words in victim's statement, which dilutes the case. The investigative agencies are also bitten by the male chauvinism bug. Appointing more police officers, prosecutors and judges, and improving their training, skill and resources will certainly minimise rape cases. Women cops in plain clothes should be posted in sensitive areas and vulnerable localities, to be a deterrent to criminals. Special cell may be created to monitor cases of rape-crime and sexual abuse against women. Police and judicial reforms should be on top priority, if we are to lay claims to being a civilised society. Zero tolerance approach to rape crimes will eventually result in drop in crimes. Unfortunately, we lack social and political will to root out crimes against women.

Our blood boils when we hear about a ghastly rape incident. We hold candle light marches, flock to the streets and stage *dharnas*, but soon become victims of memory loss. Slowly, we forget everything and wait for another distressing day to repeat our anguish. The process goes on. There is certainly awakening, and appreciable change is visible, but crucial change is coming in micro steps. The system needs to change much more and much faster to check socio-cultural degeneration. A society that does not equally respect men and women can never progress. A one-winged sparrow can never fly. We need a social revolution, a crusade for women empowerment in general and rehabilitation of rape victims with dignity in particular. We dream emergence of an India that is more humane, progressive, self-confident and one envisaged by the founding fathers of our republic. Only a nation that respects and empowers its women, can become a global power. I am confident, that dawn is not very far off. With this pious hope, I conclude my presentation."

The debate was often disrupted by thunderous applause and thumping of desks by the spectators for both the speakers. "Shame", "Shame" was also heard from some corners on the remarks of the politicians for rape victims. Besides language and facts, presentation, diction and proper aggression were the significant aspects of presentation and had an electrifying impact on the listeners. There was a panel of five judges and to avoid any criticism of bias, three were men with two women. At the end, the Chairman, a woman, praised it as one of the most fruitful debates witnessed and judged. She particularly admired the spirit of both the debaters, saying that debates these days on TV and other places are more of shouts and fights with none even listening to the other, not to talk of respecting the views of the opponent. Non-issues are raised by debaters to sidetrack the main topic for want of adequate preparation, proper knowledge and arguments. Soul-stirring description of the plight of a rape victim by Simran Kaur was particularly praised, and she was declared the winner.

The hall thundered with claps, warm rounds of applause and standing ovation. Listeners congratulated both. Gaurav got up from his seat and was the first to warmly compliment his fellow debater. With a genuine smile and spirit of appreciation, he said, "Congratulations, Simranji. You certainly deserved to win. It is as if you had felt the pangs of sufferings of a rape victim and painted them in your remarkable words, that came straight from the depth of your heart. Congratulations once again." Simran stood speechless. She had great respect for her classmate and his benevolent gesture. His heartfelt appreciation further raised his prestige in her heart. With a faint smile, she could simply murmur, "Thank you very much." Responding to the congratulations of others, she folded her hands and soon left home with Ramesh and Pooja, who were also present in the hall. They were immensely delighted at her achievement and Pooja hugged her warmly. "Simran, we are so proud of you. There was a high quality of maturity in your words and narration. Time has made you wiser at this young age. Stars might have been unfavourable in the past, but I can predict today that you are destiny's child to lead a crusade for women empowerment. Just as foundation of the present was laid in the past, foundation of future is being laid in the present. My prayers and wishes will always be with you."

Ramesh was equally delighted and said, "Simran, there have been dark spots in your life but you never got blinded by them. Pain and grief have given you mental strength and fortified your determination. It is now time to face the world at large."

With the end of exams, academic career of Simran also came to an end. Ramesh and Pooja now decided to talk to her about her marriage. "Pooja, it is time for Simran to settle down and establish her family life. It will be better if you open the topic and try to convince her for an early marriage. Let us complete our duty as her guardians and well-wishers. Also, try to get her views about Gaurav. In my opinion, he will be a very suitable match for her."

"You have taken words out of my mouth. I had also the same idea in my mind. Both of us have seen Gaurav from close quarters. He is sober and mature, and also belongs to a respectable family. He seems to be the only person in the college, with whom Simran is emotionally close and comfortable. I have observed that she also has a soft corner for him, and I am sure, she will be very happy with him. Sometimes, I have an unfounded fear that having had devastating experiences with men, she might even decline to talk about marriage. Marriages are arranged in heaven, but I will try to convince her."

The same evening, after dinner, Pooja came to the bedroom of Simran and started the topic. "Simran, your exams are over, and you must be mentally quite relaxed. I was also free and thought of talking to you about something personal."

Simran was surprised. Making her aunt more comfortable, she said, "Aunty, why should you be so formal with your daughter? Please tell me if anything is bothering you."

"Simran, if not earlier, a mother starts thinking of the marriage of her daughter as soon as she completes her education. I also want you to get married and settle down in life, so that I can also enjoy the love of your children, before I close my eyes." Pooja said without mincing words.

Taken by complete surprise, Simran looked at her aunt and groped for a suitable reply. She was least prepared for this unexpected topic. After waiting for a few minutes she gained some composure and said, "Aunty, I can understand your keen concern for me as a mother. Every mother wants her daughter to be married and happily settled. But I feel it is too early for me to even think of it. Humbly, and with all due respects to you, I will say that mentally, I am not prepared for marriage and have never given even the slightest thought to this subject."

"You might have not, but it is the ripe time to decide."

"Aunty, I want to be very frank with you, but please do not take my frankness as a sign of disrespect. I do not want to marry in life."

Pooja had already anticipated that negative reply. Maintaining a sweet smile on her face, she said, "I appreciate your frankness. I am happy that you have opened your heart. I can understand something, but want to have your reasons for not marrying in life."

"Aunty, nobody knows my past better than you. Tragically brutalised by men, even thought of an association with man hurts me, and shakes my conscience. Though outwardly I maintain good relations with all, the very sight of man makes me shiver. If someone else had asked me for marriage, I would have straightaway refused to even talk."

Pooja maintained her admirable calm and did not show any annoyance on her face. "Simran, I can understand the pain of your past. You are justified in saying anything against man. Is it that good men have never come in your life? In this world, there are all types of people. On the spectrum of life, we have men and women, who are good and bad, wicked and virtuous, and devils and saints. You cannot generalise."

"You are absolutely right, aunty. You and uncle have strengthened my faith in marriage and family relations. If I had not come across Ramesh uncle, I would have hated all men in the world. But the general picture of man in my life has been of a devil and not a saint."

"Simran, you don't stop walking on the road just for the fear of a stumble or an accident. You need care and not scare to trace your course in life. While plucking a rose, you have to be watchful, and not fear the prick of the thorn. I will say one more thing. Though one has to be one's own support in life, you always need family, friends, husband or society to stand by your side in crisis. You need the support of a pot to boil water; fire and water alone are not enough. Same is the case with life. With all humility as a mother, I will say that we stood by you in the most delicate period of your life. Imagine what would have happened in the absence of any strong support system? Today we are here, tomorrow we may not be. We want to create some support for you before we depart."

With moist eyes, Simran said, "Aunty, please don't talk of leaving me. I cannot live without you. I will always need your love and care."

"That is exactly the point that you have to bear in mind. Death is inevitable. Sooner or later, we have to leave this world, and with this will wither the support. It may be a harsh reality, but we have to gracefully accept it. Besides, we may decide to go to America to live with our children. Our greatest wish is to leave our treasure in safer hands."

"For that aunty, marriage is not essential."

"May not be essential, but is desirable. Marriage is an important social bond and the most secure social support system. You may not realise it today, but you will understand the wisdom of my words when I will not be there, and it will be too late to understand."

Simran had no answer to her aunt's very strong arguments on marriage. Thinking her deeply pondering, and feeling that her words were having some desirable impact on her, Pooja put her arms around her neck and continued, "Simran, there is no hurry, but it should not be too late. You can carefully ponder over the issue and once convinced, we can discuss again."

"Aunty, my case is different from others. Even if I give it a serious thought, no one will accept me after knowing my past."

"Simran, I do understand your concern. You are scared because of your past. Your fear is justified. But once you are serious about marriage, we can find a suitable person. I will say that you must tell all details in case of a viable proposal. The world is not short of nobler persons. Why should you be blamed? Think in a broader perspective. You are a victim, not a culprit. You have not committed any crime. Never carry that guilt feeling in your mind. You are as pure as Ganges."

"Aunty, you are thinking with the heart of a mother. All persons will not have that perception."

"You are right. But all do not crave for lust. Most want love and trust, the very foundations of a solid married life. Moreover, I am not talking of all persons. I will be interested only in one. I know at least one, who understands you."

Simran was amazed at the strange revelation of her aunt's mind. Her heart suddenly began to throb. She was intelligent enough to guess, but still wanted to know the man in her aunt's mind. With a little optimistic smile on her face, she said, "Aunty, it seems you have already decided everything for me. Let me know the person in your mind."

"You know him. I am talking about Gaurav. He is very calm, quiet and sober. He can be your suitable life partner. Your cracking chemistry is palpable, and both I and your uncle have often observed and felt your emotional closeness. Extend your hand; he is longing to hold it."

Simran was taken aback at the sudden and straight proposal of her aunt. The offer was to her heart's desire, but she never thought that Pooja aunty was so fascinated by Gaurav. She said, "Aunty, you are saying as if you have peeped deep into his heart. Our assumptions are sometimes deceptive. I know Gaurav is a good human being. He is a thorough gentleman, and has all the good qualities of head and heart. But I have never seen him from that angle. Moreover, how good he will be after knowing the details of my life?"

"Purity of gold can only be tested by putting it in fire. Reveal everything to him, as suppression of facts raises probability of their reappearance. Let us test him. If not satisfied, we will be the last to suggest his name. There is nothing wrong in trying. You can't be sure unless you try."

"Aunty, Gaurav is certainly a broad-minded person with modern ideas, but his parents may be reluctant due to social prejudices. Even if they agree under his pressure, they may backtrack later. Lies they may tolerate, but truth they may hate. A girl from a well-off family with tainted background may be acceptable, but not a middle-class girl with noble values. Besides, love is like a flower. It gives fragrance for some time, but withers soon. Gaurav's love may cool under social pressure. Pain of heartbreak later will be distressing."

Holding Pooja's hand affectionately, she resumed, "Aunty, I will prefer not to marry, than to suffer pain of broken relations and shed tears the whole life. Hurt sentiments matter more than hurt bodies. Relations are like bangles; they mingle and jingle, but cause pain when broken. And if there are children, the pain will be unbearable. I will not rush for marriage till I am fully convinced that love is true and lasting. Besides, marriages are falling apart on trivial issues, and divorces are becoming very common these days. Incidents of strained family relations and abusive marriages are on the rise. Also, I do not want my most cherished dream of women empowerment to be drowned in the sea of marriage."

"Simran, I appreciate your very intelligent analysis of the institution of marriage. Rise in incidents of divorce is because of ego, and lack of adjustment. When relations break, normally both have to share the blame. Differences of opinion are certainly there, but what is needed is harmony of hearts. Both partners need love, empathy and support of each other. It is a common saying that prosperity comes to homes where love resides." After waiting for a few moments to let her words sink deep in the mind of Simran, she resumed, "So far as your dream is concerned, if your partner also supports your views, even a daunting task becomes easier. It all depends on the stand of your companion. But do not trust a partner, who suffers from commitment phobia."

"Aunty, life is so unpredictable; it is like a drop of water on a lotus leaf."

"Of course, you can't predict future but can certainly create it. You are a bold girl, but fear seems to be troubling you. You are laying more stress on the negative aspects of marriage. Think of the positive values of this sacred institution."

"Aunty, I am downright confused."

"Don't worry. Confusion is the genesis of decision. Wisdom will dawn, once the cobweb of confusion is removed. Sit back, introspect, and your wavering confidence will bounce back. When in doubt, follow the inner voice. My advice is, think, reflect, and decide. Once decided; implement."

Simran was completely speechless. Pooja also thought she had given enough food for thought to Simran. She wanted her to digest the same and come to some decision. It was better to wait and watch for her reaction, rather than press further. Looking at the clock, she said, "Oh! It is past midnight. You must go to sleep now. Before leaving, I will say that we could have discussed your past with Gaurav, but it is better if you meet him tomorrow and reveal all details to him. Let life swing either way, rather than remain in a state of uncertainty." Saying this she got up, went near the table, picked up the trophy, wiped it with her *dupatta*, kissed it and reverently placed it again on the table. She looked at Simran with eyes brimming with optimism and left the room.

Simran was surprised to watch all this. She wondered if her real mother had been as loving as Pooja aunty, who was a symbol of grace and humility. Ramesh uncle sometimes got little aggressive. At that poignant moment, she would keep quiet and move away from the stimulus. She would open her heart at the most appropriate time in words least hurting to anyone. She was an embodiment of courage, calm and care.

Simran tried her best to sleep, but deeply drowned in the turbulent sea of faith and fear of marriage, she tossed from side to side. Her aunt's proposal both pleased and disturbed her. She had a brief wink of sound sleep at the crack of dawn.

Dynamics of love cannot be understood and explained easily. Emotions erupt simultaneously in loving hearts, irrespective of time and distance. Simran's enigmatic charm and mental alertness had slowly made way deep into Gaurav's heart also, and created an emotional turmoil. Yearning to probe into her mind and know about her personal life, he stayed at Jaipur after the exams. He rang her up next morning and requested for meeting in a garden. Equally anxious Simran gladly responded.

Simran was completely confused about the subject of discussion, but Gaurav was mentally relaxed. He wanted to know more about Simran in the hope of emotionally coming closer to her. On meeting her, he came straight to the subject. "Simran, I think recent past has brought us closer, though we do not know much about each other. I want to remain your good and intimate friend. Before I ask you anything, let me tell you about my family. My father, Rajeshwar Saxena, is Assistant General Manager in State Bank of India, and is posted at Delhi. My mother, Lalita, is a housewife. We are a small family and enjoy very cordial mutual relations. We have a three-bedroom flat in a society, and my education has been in Delhi. You can ask me anything more about my life. I do not know much about you, except that you are from Punjab and live with your uncle and aunt. May I request you to tell me something more about your life?"

With an indifferent attitude, she replied, "What is there in my life? It was normal like that of any other girl."

Gaurav was taken aback at the unexpected tone of her reply, but retained his calm. Body language, facial expression and aggressive tone indicated that Simran was trying to hide something vital. Patience and perseverance were the only remedies to get the truth out.

Simran did not raise her eyes and maintained stony silence. Gaurav tried to touch her emotional chord and said, "Simranji, eyes never tell lies. Your lowering the eyes shows that you are hiding something. I have an intuition that you have no blood relation with uncle and aunt. How did you come here to live with them?"

Before coming for the meeting, Simran had made all mental preparations to reveal her past to Gaurav. Suddenly, courage failed and head got blocked. She was in the grip of some queer feeling of nervousness. Unable to decide anything, she replied rather rudely, "Have you called me to know all these things?"

Gaurav was not the man to accept defeat. He realised that Simran's indifference was an indirect indication of love, otherwise she would have not come for the meeting. Stirring her emotional chord, he said, "Simranji, I think time has brought us to a little higher level of friendship. I want to come little closer to you in life, and feel a right to know more about you."

Simran had similar feelings in her heart, but suddenly became apprehensive of opening up. She did not want to be offensive, and replied most politely, "Gauravji, it is true that I have no relation with uncle and aunt. I lost my mother on the day of my birth, and they have brought me up as their own child."

Gaurav was getting optimistic, and in an effort to dig some more facts, he asked her about her father. Simran was not prepared for such an embarrassing question. Revealing details of her father would open a Pandora's box, and the beans of her past would be disgracefully spilled. She heaved a sigh and in frantic desperation replied, "He left me under the care of uncle and aunt."

"Simran, truth can't be wrapped in layers. You can delay it but not demolish it. Perhaps you are not treating me as a trustworthy friend, and I know for sure, that in the grip of some stress you are hiding a lot from me. Remember, holding facts creates suffocation; getting out opens solutions."

Simran raised her eyes and lowered them again. She decided to maintain her usual calm. Gaurav hesitatingly placed his hand on Simran's hand and said, "Simranji, I cannot open my heart, but can say that you can confide in me. Telling me little more will further cement our relations. I know you also feel the same in your heart, but are struggling to open up. I want to be your partner on life's pathway."

Warmth of Gaurav's hand aroused her emotions. There was a conscious coupling of the two loving souls. Simran's heart began to throb violently. She also wanted to come emotionally closer to him, but her faith in the sincerity of man had been smashed by the past experience. She was still not prepared to open the past of her life. Courage deserted her and fear sealed her lips. Though earlier prepared to reveal everything, she was awfully confused. In the state of uncertainty to say or not to say, she preferred solace in silence. Fortunately, nature came to her rescue. Thick dark rain clouds indicated onslaught of heavy downpour. It suddenly started raining. Both were getting drenched to the bone. Holding her *dupatta* fluttering in strong breeze, she suddenly got up, left without uttering a word, slowly struggling her way towards the gate through the muddy rain water. Gaurav kept on looking at her steps moving away from him in the fond hope that she would turn back and look at him. She did not. He was heartbroken but he knew that he had created deep ripples of love in her heart. He was sure that next meeting would bring them closer as life companions.

Back home, Simran simply told Pooja that she could not talk to Gaurav about her past. At night, she cried and wept to lighten her heart. Ashamed of her timidity and stubborn attitude, she was cursing herself. Gaurav never lost his patience, and had been so calm and composed, while she was so rude. Her heart wanted to come closer to Gaurav, but head held her back. Drowned in these thoughts, she kept on rolling in bed. Night of intense emotional turmoil and unrest passed with great difficulty. In the wee hours, she took a vital decision of her life. She would meet Gaurav and tell him all details of her past, and then leave the rest to fate. This would also decide the ambitious proposal of her aunt. Pigeons perched on the sunshades had started cooing, giving an indication that it was time to be up. Crimson light of the dawn began to peep through the slits of the curtains. A new day of her life had dawned. She rang up Gaurav and conveyed her intention of meeting him in the same park.

Gaurav reached the park before time. As soon as she arrived, Gaurav could see an adorably different Simran. She was more smartly dressed, had confidence in her gait, radiance in her eyes and courage on her face. With a sense of determination, she started the discussion.

"Gauravji, I have been very upset by my yesterday's indifferent behaviour. I have inexhaustible faith in you, but I want you to keep to yourself all that I am going to tell. You may break the friendship after that, but promise that you will not reveal anything to anyone without my permission."

The very introduction further aroused Gaurav's excitement. Holding her hand warmly, he said, "Simran dear, I swear in the name of God, that I will never ever betray your trust."

There was profound awakening of love that forbade Simran to escape the grasp. Eyes communicated the invisible emotions. Her heart also began to throb with excitement. Taking a deep breath, she said, "Gauravji, my life has been full of unbelievable tragedies. I have suffered the worst that a woman can suffer in life. As I told you, my mother died at my birth and my father discarded me. Destiny played hide and seek with me and..."

Simran narrated all details of her life, without hiding even an iota of truth. She did not waver or falter at any point. Her whole narration completely shocked Gaurav. Her frankness, courage and determination about her mission further cemented his love and respect for her. At the end, she said, "Gauravji, life became a burden and I struggled to carry the weight of my dead body on my broken shoulders. With time, I regained strength to bear the trauma of my life and determination to fight. Please do not betray the trust reposed in you, otherwise my life would be totally shattered. I will lose complete faith in man, and will have no option but to seek peace in solitude."

Emotions sealed the lips of Gaurav. His tongue was tied, and he had no strength to utter even a word. He softly placed his both hands on the hands of Simran and said. "Simmi dear, I could never imagine that one could suffer so much in childhood and bear so much pain in adolescence. Your frankness has further raised your respect in my eyes and trust in my heart. I request you not to be chained to the baggage of gone days. It hinders joy and adds to pain." He did not bottle up his feelings, assuming that Simran will understand. Gripping her hand more firmly, he said without hesitation, "So long as I am alive, I will never betray your trust. I love you and want to be your life partner."

Simran was simply mesmerised to hear such sweet and loving words from Gaurav. She was instinctively drawn towards him. Unsaid emotions of deep love were passionately churning her heart. Shyness faded. Sucked in the whirlwind of intense love, she came closer to him. She also clasped his hand tightly, and cradled her head on his shoulder. Both began to share a warm equation. The decision had been taken and conveyed. Words failed; emotions mirrored their feelings. Lips remained sealed; eyes conveyed the thoughts. Such was the state of the two loving hearts that were beating fast, Simran's being little faster. Few moments spontaneously decided the whole future course of life without any discussion. Intermittently, both looked into the eyes of each other. Gaurav was drowned in the depth of the large crystal eyes of Simran that were sparkling with love. She further tightened the grip of her hand and could only say, "I also..." She could not utter the two other words that Gaurav was longing to hear, but her expressive eyes and language of silence had conveyed everything. It was getting dark. People had already left. Birds were returning to their nests to join their mates. Gaurav hugged her warmly. Simran responded with equal warmth. Their relations had moved to a higher pedestal. The two remained there for some more time to fully enjoy the solemn moments.

Breaking silence, Simran said, "Gauravji, it is easy to fall in love, but difficult to stay in it. You are sympathetic at this moment. With the passage of time, emotions will wither and when logic returns, your views may change."

"Simranji, only time can prove my love and trust. I swear I will prefer to remain alone, rather than hold another hand. I will never ever betray you. You are my life. You are my present; you are my future."

Revealing her life-mission, Simran told Gaurav that she wanted to fight for empowerment of women and work for the destitute children. She was prepared to sacrifice everything, even her marriage, but could not relinquish her mission.

With a steely resolve in his voice, Gaurav replied, "I will not be a hindrance in your mission. On the other hand I will compliment your resolve and share your vision in life. From today, don't say *'I will fight'*; say *'We will fight'*. For every mission, replace *'I'* with *'We'*. You are not alone now. I am your life-partner in pleasure and pain."

"I have now more faith in you than in myself. But there are factors in life beyond our control, that may not favour your decision. I want you to tell all details of my life to uncle and aunt. You are their only child and must respect their decision."

"I am sure they will support me, but if by any chance, they decline, I can tell you I will never marry in life. I will spend my life in serving them, but my heart will always long for your love, wherever I may be. I will still remain your partner in the pursuit of your sacred social mission."

"Please don't take such vital decisions in emotional haste. Think over all aspects of life coolly and calmly. I certainly do not want you to go against their wishes. You are their hope. Take care of them even at the cost of our love. One can have everything in life, but not mother and father. It will be extremely distressing for me, and I will always blame myself for their pain and sufferings. With all sincerity, I say that you must respect their decision, even if it is against marriage. Do not force your decision on them." Looking deep into his eyes, she resumed, "If they are not in favour of our marriage, marry the girl of their choice. Tell me the truth beforehand. Do not keep me in the dark. Hiding truth would be unbearably painful, and my love and trust would crumble to pieces. Betrayal of trust will completely shatter me. Please, never ever hurt my faith in you."

"Simran dear, I promise I will never betray your trust and shall never conceal the truth from you. Give me some time to discuss with them. It will be foolish to madly rush into the arena. Right thing at right time and right place bears fruit. Even right thing at wrong time or wrong place can result in failure. The best would have been to discuss with them, and place the proposal after their meeting you, and knowing you more closely. That would be possible only if you move to Delhi or at least pay more frequent visits to Delhi."

"Moving to Delhi will depend on uncle and aunt. I cannot sacrifice their comforts for me. Marriage is too small a sacrifice for all that they have done. I can forgo everything in life, but would not cause a scratch to them. Of course, the idea of frequent visits can be explored."

"In life, time is destined for everything. When not able to decide, leave things to time to chart the best course for our lives. You may have to bear some patience."

The same night, Simran revealed all details of her discussion with Gaurav to her aunt. She was thrilled to know such a sudden action on her suggestion. She asked, "What was his reaction?"

"It was very positive. He himself offered the proposal for marriage after listening to all details of my past and future life mission. He is prepared to accept me with my past."

"That is highly gratifying. Your uncle will be mighty pleased to know. This is his greatest wish in life."

"Aunty, let him first discuss and reveal all details to his parents. He is confident of their approval, but I have some lingering fear and inner apprehensions. Orthodox social beliefs may not accept a girl with tainted past. I categorically told him to take a decision with their concurrence and approval. He also suggested that I should pay more frequent visits to Delhi for his parents to know me more intimately and closely."

"I think that is a laudable suggestion. Let us wait for the decision of his parents, and then we will go to them and put the formal proposal."

Time often dilutes such emotional decisions taken in desperate haste, but here relations further blossomed and gained strength. Gaurav deliberately extended his stay at Jaipur to enjoy the company of his heart-throb. Both were now free to remain together for almost the whole day. He became a more frequent visitor to Puris, who were getting further enthralled by his qualities of head and heart. They were optimistic that the two will happily enjoy matrimonial bliss in the near future. They silently prayed for the fulfilment of their most cherished dream of happily settled Simran.

□

6

On the chess board of time, events were moving fast and silently changing course in unpredictable directions. Gaurav moved to Delhi to join his parents, and Simran got involved in the service of her uncle and aunt. Mutual promises of eternal love had emotionally brought the two loving hearts closer to each other, and separation after a long and close association was unbearably painful. It was difficult to fathom the depth of their grief, as pangs of pain of separation can only be realised by the sufferers. Strange is the nature of time. In joy, hours fleet in moments, while in distress moments take hours. Days became long and nights still longer, and passed in rewinding past-loving memories. Simran would often look in vacant spaces, and wonder when the harrowing time of separation will come to an end. Human mind is a source of infinite burning desires, but her only aspiration was to have wings to fly and be with her beau. Emotional quotient of pain of separation was equally high in Gaurav, and he desired to have his dream-girl in his arms.

Earlier, Gaurav had suggested to Simran to move to Delhi, for his parents to know her more intimately. Asking uncle and aunt to shift there, would have been too selfish. She was prepared to sacrifice all her desires, but not cause any discomfort or pain to them. For emotive satisfaction of the two lovebirds, the only solution at present was long telephone calls.

Strange is the course of stars. They play their game

unmindful of gain or loss to anyone. Earlier, Simran lost her mother for her to suffer, and Daljeet to move away from her. Now Pooja was being sacrificed for Ramesh to suffer and Simran to move closer to Gaurav.

As a part of her daily routine, Simran used to be first to get up and prepare tea for all. About two months after her exams, she got up one day and woke up her aunt, who was late in rising.

"Aunty, you are little late today. Normally, you are up before everyone. Are you all right?"

"I don't know but I am feeling very weak. Night was very restless, and I could not sleep properly. There seems to be something horribly wrong with me."

Simran touched her forehead and said, "There is no fever. Take tea and you will be all right."

After preparing tea, she tried to wake up Pooja. "Aunty, your tea is ready. Please get up."

There was no response. Simran told her uncle that aunty was not feeling well. He also called her, but there was no reply. He touched her. She did not move. He shook her. She just slumped on one side. She was lifeless. He cried but Pooja had already left this mortal world, leaving all in tears. In a span of only a few minutes, lives of many were miserably shattered. Simran called the doctor who declared her dead. A massive silent cardiac arrest had taken her life. Dolly and Rohit came from America. Before leaving, Dolly suggested to her father to dispose of all his assets in India and move to America. Rohit also endorsed the views of his sister. "Papa, staying here alone would not be a good option. Pain of loneliness will be unbearable. Staying with children and grandchildren will be more enjoyable. I will arrange your visa and then permanent citizenship."

"Rohit, I have decided to sell the school, as it will be

difficult for me to manage it. At present, I am not in a stable frame of mind. Give me some time to decide."

Both Dolly and Rohit left. They again requested their father to decide as early as possible. For the present, they were satisfied with his stay at Jaipur, as Simran was there to look after him.

After a few days, Ramesh opened the topic with Simran. "Simmi, both Dolly and Rohit insisted that I should settle in America. I have been seriously pondering over the issue, but have not been able to decide anything."

"Uncle, loneliness is perhaps the biggest problem after the loss of life partner. Old memories will always haunt you particularly, when aunty loved you so intensely. The loss is devastating, but one has to grapple with it."

Ramesh was inconsolable in grief. With tears in his eyes, he said, "Loneliness in old age is a great curse. I could never imagine this tragedy to happen. It is as if she will come out of the room and say, 'Why are you late? Get ready, we have to go to the school'. She was so caring, so loving."

"Uncle, your life is shattered and so is mine. I have lost my second mother, under whose love and care I had grown. I can imagine what would be your state, when you had spent your whole life with her."

"I am completely ruined. In tears or smiles life will pass but I will not be able to bear her separation. She loved me so much. I had not lived without her even for a day. I want to sit in a corner and cry."

"Uncle, I still remember that momentous day, when I came here, and she instinctively hugged me without a moment's hesitation. She did not care for the ridicule of the society and loved me like her own child. Sometimes, I wonder what would have been my fate if she had not accepted me. Suicide would have been the only option. I am alive today, only because of her. She gave me second birth. She was so careful that within days of my arrival, she told me that uncle sometimes loses his temper, but his anger vanishes as fast as it appears. She advised me not to take anything to heart, and to come to her in case of any problem." Waiting for a while she continued, "But uncle, we have to bear the unbearable. She cannot come back. Only her memories will remain. It is very easy for me to say, but you have to accept the loss with courage. You have to decide your future now."

"I am in a fix. Sometimes, I feel that I should go to children. But there also I will be a prisoner of loneliness. With all working and children going to school, I will be alone almost the whole day. Children will hardly have any time to even talk to me. If I stay here, I will be a burden on you."

"Uncle, please don't say this. When I came here, was I a burden on you? You treated me as your daughter. You are my father. A father cannot be a burden on children. Please never say this again. It hurts me. It will be my pleasure and duty to serve you." Simran clung to Ramesh like a child, and began to cry.

Consoling her, Ramesh said, "I am sorry. I did not mean to hurt you. You are my child, and a source of pleasure and pride. I do not know what to do? Tell me just one; one out of the two options. Should I go or should I stay? In the state of uncertainty, your decision will be final"

Without waiting even for a fraction of a second, Simran confidently said, "Uncle, my decision is you stay here."

"You have said what I wanted. I am also inclined to stay here. It is finally decided. I will stay in India. I will also sell both these flats and move to my flat in Delhi. Life will be more comfortable there, and time will easily pass in the company of old friends. Besides, prospects of your legal practice shall also be better there. Both High Court and Supreme Court are there, and you will have better exposure in your career. After marriage also, you would have moved to Delhi. But I will not go from here unless you are willing."

"Uncle, I will reveal a secret to you. Aunty also wanted you to stay here." Surprised, Ramesh looked at her. She continued, "About three months back, one day very early before dawn, aunty knocked at my door. I was studying. She was not feeling sleepy, and wanted to gossip with me. Casually turning over the pages of a book, she started talking about you."

"You know Simmi, your uncle is so careless. He does not pay attention to his medicines, food or clothes. He has to be reminded like a child. When he had to go to the office, I had to check his purse, handkerchief, car keys and other things. He would just pick up the purse and go, without caring whether money was there or not. I always used to put money in it." Suddenly, she stopped, took a deep breath and resumed, "For sometime past, a strange dream is haunting me. In full bridal dress and make-up, I am leaving in a train and you are all wishing me a happy journey."

"I looked at her, hugged her and said, 'Aunty, such dreams are just nightmares.'"

"Simmi dear, dreams may not be true but end is a certainty. Death is an inevitable reality. You will be soon settled. What will happen to your uncle? Even after your marriage, I want you to stay with him or take him along with you. Rohit and Dolly are very affectionate and will certainly take care of him, but I want you to look after him. You know all his needs. Please do not leave him alone. He will not survive."

Narrating this, Simran's throat was choked. She could not speak. Gaining some strength, she said, "Uncle, there were tears in my eyes. I placed my head in her lap and began to cry. Affectionately, she started stroking my hair. It was at that moment, that you entered. Do you remember the day?"

"Yes, I do remember. I also remember my asking that Pooja must be complaining against me."

"When she replied that there are many secrets between mother and daughter, and you asked why were my eyes wet and appeared as if I was weeping." A little reflection and she continued, "I remember how intelligently, she diverted the topic by saying that I was worried about the welfare of my father."

Heaving a sigh, Ramesh said, "Simran, she was so caring. She never wanted me to get worried about anything. She would bear all pain, and never let her worry trouble me. There are numerous incidents that show her magnanimity."

"Uncle, it was as if she was making a frightening prophecy. It appears she was anticipating some tragedy to happen." Ramesh also shared with Simran that Pooja wished to play with her children. Simran was simply dumbfounded. This showed that Pooja loved her like her daughter.

"Simran, she was very far-sighted. Considering all aspects, she inwardly wanted me to stay here. Let me tell you frankly. I had also been thinking of the same."

"Uncle, my biggest worry is your loneliness. It is a great curse, and its pain is distressing. I am too young to say but sooner or later, this situation comes in the life of everyone. It is very difficult to imagine how fragile life can be without your loved one, unless one actually passes through that state. A life has left, but her love will haunt you every moment. You will always be gripped with a state of helplessness. Sleep deprivation may predominate." Waiting for a moment, she resumed, "Uncle, normalcy in life may be difficult, but to reduce the pain of separation there is one more thing in my mind. I have been hesitating to say."

Simran suggested to Ramesh that Rani *maa* may stay in the servant room of the flat at Delhi. She would look after his food, medicines and other necessities that would relieve Simran of his loneliness, during her absence in the court.

Ramesh was mighty pleased, lovingly looked into her eyes, warmly held her hand and said, "Simmi, my child, how intelligent and caring you are? It is one of the most sensible suggestions. I could have never thought of this. Moreover, her son and daughter-in-law have virtually thrown her out, and she is staying with Suman." Waiting for a few moments, he said, "But she will not live as a maid. She will live as a part of the family. She may look after the kitchen, but a maid will be engaged for cleanliness."

"Uncle, you are so considerate. This will not dent her dignity and our relations. I also suggest that you adopt a pet, if you like. Dog is the most faithful companion of man. You can keep yourself busy by playing with him, and in looking after his feed. He will be like your child. In his company you will forget your loneliness. You can take him for a walk every morning. Your blood pressure will improve and knee pain will be reduced. This will widen your social circle and children will throng to you to pat your pet. Besides this, you can spend your time in listening to music of your choice, which is the best remedy to ward off loneliness. You can play cards and other games with your old friends in the society. You may invite them for lunch, as there will be no problem of cooking. Time that stagnates in solitude, fleets with friends. It may be very difficult to forget your love, but all these measures will minimise the pain of the unbearable loss."

Ramesh was surprised at the far-sightedness of Simran. Affectionately looking at her, he said, "Simran, Dolly and Rohit may feel bad, but I have finally decided to stay here in India. I can occasionally go to them and enjoy the love of children and grandchildren,"

Simran hugged him warmly, and with tearful eyes could

only murmur, "Uncle, I am grateful to you for that trust and confidence in me."

Simran's result was declared. She expected to be among the top rankers and was fifth in the University. Gaurav was third. She was not jealous of that and was happier at his position than at her merit. Finally, Ramesh Puri shifted to Delhi in his flat along with Simran.

After shifting to Delhi, Simran's first desire was to pay a surprise visit to her father. Rani had already told her that Daljeet had married Suman and was living happily with her and Aarushi, her daughter. Daljeet was immensely delighted to see his grown-up daughter. He was speechless and kept on looking at her. Finally, he gained composure and said, "Simran, my child, how are you? Rani had told me that you have also shifted to Delhi, but I had no courage to meet you. I was so ashamed of my past that I could not dare face you."

"Papa, I have always loved you and had been longing to meet you all. I hope you have not forgotten your daughter. I had been regularly enquiring about your welfare through Rani *maa*. I have not come here to discuss the past. It is over and recalling it will only cause pain. Life has taken a full circle. Today, I have come here to meet you all."

"Simmi, my child, I know I have wronged you, but at heart I always loved you. I sincerely apologise with folded hands for all that I have done to you. I am ashamed of my conduct as father. Please forgive me for my sins." Daljeet folded his hands and continued, "Let me open my heart. Death of your mother completely shattered my life, as I intensely loved her. Without her, life became meaningless. I was moving like a lunatic. I began to hate everything in life, including you and my mother. Let me confess. The root cause of my many problems has been my impulsive nature to take decisions without forethought. I became a slave of my emotions and was easily swayed by others. Blind trust in others ruined my life and caused sufferings to you and others."

Holding Daljeet's hands, Simran said, "Papa, all that happened was our destiny. Let us bury the past and move with the present."

Turning to Suman, Daljeet continued, "Simran, today I want to say everything to lighten my heart. Suman came in my life and I began to love her. I wanted to marry her, but Vikas dropped from nowhere, and ruined her life and ten precious years of my life also. Embers of love cannot be extinguished, and she regularly met me in jail. Unfortunately, she was helpless and could not do anything. Motherhood brought a radical change in her whole outlook, and she appreciated the meaning and value of love, after the birth of her daughter. A tired soul, she has very wisely decided to settle down in life. We are now a happy family."

"Papa, this is the best decision of your life. Remembrance of past pollutes the present, and its forgetfulness is the key to happiness. Forgive everyone and start life without past prejudices. A good painting can only be made on a clean canvas. My earnest request to you with folded hands is to wholeheartedly accept the child. Neglecting her would be disastrous for both of you, and also for the innocent child. She is almost as old now, as I was when I came here. Look at her innocent face and captivating smile. She is so cute and beautiful. I do not want another Simran to be born. Destiny was kind to me and I survived due to the care and protection of Rani *maa*. Another Simran may not be fortunate enough to get a Rani. This is the only thing that I want for Aarushi."

"Simran, I repent for the sins committed against you and do not want to commit more. With no fault of theirs, children suffer due to the mistakes of their parents. She is *my* child; she is *our* child. She is the sweetest creation of God and cannot be blamed for the slip of someone."

"Papa, though late, decision of both for marriage and settling down in life is laudable." Looking at Suman, she said, "I will also love and respect her as my mother and the child as my sister."

Suman got up, came close to Simran and said with folded hands and eyes full of tears, "Simran, I have no words to beg forgiveness, but please forgive me though I do not deserve it. My sins are unpardonable, but you are such a large-hearted girl and will certainly forgive me. In youth, I was blinded by lust and greed. I realise all my mistakes now, when I am also a mother. I have no words of apology. I am your culprit and ready for any punishment." With hands still folded, she bowed down before Simran. Unstoppable stream of tears of repentance was struggling to wash the stains of her guilt.

Holding her hands and kissing them, Simran said, "Mother need not apologise to her daughter. Bestow your love on all of us. My only wish in life is happiness of all of you. Our days of misery are over and a bright dawn awaits us now. Let us welcome it."

Simran was mighty pleased at the astronomical change in the behaviour of the once haughty and proud Suman. She was now so calm, composed and sober. One could never believe that she was the same Suman. Simran took Aarushi in her lap, pleasantly complimented her nice dress and kissed her affectionately. The little baby was comfortably sitting in her lap, as if she had known her for years. Simran took a five-hundred rupee note from her purse and gave it to her. With a streak of smile on her comely lips, she instantly handed it over to her mother. All were astonished at her gesture. "Aarushi, remember me. I am your elder sister, your *didi*. I am sorry I could not come earlier to meet you. Now we will often meet. Next time, I will bring some more presents for you. Give me a sweet kiss." Overwhelmed with joy, Aarushi immediately planted a sweet kiss on Simran's cheek and all had a loud and hearty laugh.

Simran asked Daljeet about his job. He told her that he was working in a factory, but was now planning to start a small car service station at his land in the village with residence at the back of the same. His problem was of loan that Simran promised to arrange.

Turning to Rani, Simran said, "*Maa*, I have not talked to you. I have some other plan for you. Next time when I come in a few days, you please pack up your things and get ready. I want you to live with me. I will discuss details with you."

Back home, Simran got mentally occupied with the process of filing the case of her rape and kidnapping. Before taking this vital step, she decided to first discuss with Ramesh uncle.

"Uncle, you remember my decision to fight two cases after completing law? Time has now come to take up the first. But before taking a final decision, I want to have your views. You are aware of the bone-chilling tragedy that engulfed my life, before you brought me to Jaipur. I cannot get rid of the pain and trauma that I suffered in those days. Distressing memory of the worst tragedy of my life terribly haunts me. It is as fresh in my mind as on the day it happened. I lost the peace of my life. Now I want to file the case and seek justice."

"I appreciate your undeterred resolve, but it is an issue that must be considered carefully before you take up the final step. Reversal may not be possible. Once decided, you will have to take it to its logical conclusion. Let me know your vital reasons for going ahead with the case."

"Uncle, there are two reasons. Before I state the first, let me make it clear. Love, humility and nobility are the essence of my life. Pain caused by others results in vengeance, and cycle of hatred and revenge continues to fester in our mind. It is a poison that you drink expecting the other to die. It gives further sufferings and causes irreparable damage to our psyche. To put a stop to pollutants of hatred, remedy is to forgive and forget. Revenge and hatred are not a part of my personality, and I firmly believe in forgiving and moving ahead. With this as the core of my conviction, the first reason for filing the case is that I want the culprits to be punished not as a part of any revenge, but as a lesson for all rapists, who ruin lives of innocent girls. I want to be a model for other such women, who suffer in their lives, but have no money or courage to pursue the case in the courts. Secondly, I want to start an NGO for the empowerment of such pathetic women and destitute children. I want to enkindle their self-confidence, grit and determination. Power resides in the mind, and once the spark for justice is ignited in the mind of the victim, destination is never far off."

Waiting for the reaction of Ramesh, she resumed, "Uncle, they reach destination who explore it, and not those, who just sit and ask its way. Some walk on other's footsteps; some create their own. I want to create my own and be an inspiration and beacon of light to others. I want to create social ripples, that in course of time may become mighty waves and turn into a tsunami of public outrage. The tirade of peoples' movement, thus launched, will become an irreversible momentum. There may be fierce resistance, but I will fight to light up the dark and deprived lives, and set rolling wheels of social change towards a new horizon of women empowerment."

"Both the reasons are convincing and highly commendable. The danger is damage to your prestige. You may have to face uncomfortable situation in the court. The case will immediately catch the attention of media and may affect your future, particularly marriage and legal practice."

"Uncle, in war one should not think of loss but of gain. To achieve something, some sacrifice has to be made and greater the achievement, greater the sacrifice. My prestige is too small a price for my cherished social mission. I feel my dignity and status will multiply manifold. If I am sincere in my work, there will be no damage to my legal practice. On the other hand, it will prosper manifold. So far as marriage is concerned, I have already revealed all details of my past and my mission to Gaurav, and am awaiting the decision of his parents. If he loves me despite my past and cares for my ideals, he will certainly agree. If he declines or his parents have any reservation, and there is no other person ready to accept me with my past, I will prefer to remain unmarried. Marriage is too trivial a desire in comparison to my noble mission. Whatever the consequences, I want to resolutely fight."

"And the dread of failure?"

With all the courage at her command, Simran promptly replied, "Uncle, I do not fear failure. Determination not only dilutes fear, but can even defeat destiny. Fear is only an imaginative fright, and I have learnt to conquer it. My effort will not fall by the wayside. Even if I fail, I will continue with renewed effort. Courage is not in avoiding a fall, but in getting up after every fall. Failure in fact, strengthens determination and teaches more than success. Success is also built on failures, and when failure stares in the eyes, success is only a step ahead. Besides, there is ample evidence to nail the culprits. I am certainly conscious of the pitfalls, but chances of failure are very grim, if not nil."

"Simran, you must carefully think and decide, as even best of the plans crack under uncertainties and feeble execution. A game can overturn any moment. You are not a winner till you win." Waiting for a while, he resumed, "I still feel that you may fight for the empowerment of women, but should forget your case and move ahead in your life."

"Uncle, I remember, Pooja aunt's words. 'God has saved

you for some dignified and noble deed' and 'you are destiny's child to lead a crusade for women empowerment'. The most befitting tribute to her life and memory would be to respect her prophetic words. I have carefully considered all aspects, and want to fight my case to set a personal example for the future victims. My decision is steady like a rock."

"I appreciate your self-belief and indomitable spirit. I know you will have no peace in life unless you file the case. I fully endorse your conscious decision and will always be morally at your back. I feel Pooja would have also complimented your resolve. However, I want you to discuss with Gaurav before you take a final decision. His consent is a must. You should not go against his decision, particularly when he is keen to marry you. Also, who will fight the case? Will you fight it yourself?"

"Some time back, I had discussed my life mission with Gaurav, and he whole-heartedly supported my decision. Idea of requesting Gaurav to take up the case has been spinning in my mind. I can fight it myself, but I have decided in favour of Gaurav. If he is reluctant or refuses, then I will fight it myself."

"Simran, I am confident of his sincerity, and hope he will have no inhibition. Besides, this will also be an acid test of his sincerity for your future relations."

Deeply engrossed in some serious thought, Ramesh resumed after some time. "Simran, I am glad your vision is crystal clear, thoughts full of wisdom and determination rock firm. I am often surprised. With a practically ruined childhood, how did you adopt all these noble human values?"

"Uncle, living happily even in a state of abject adversity was taught to me by Rani *maa*. She was poor and virtually uneducated, but faced the problems of life courageously. My life was a barren desert, and she was an oasis. While my formative years of childhood were shaped under her care, in adolescence, I was bestowed by love, humility and sacrifice of

Pooja aunty. Herself well-educated, she inspired me to work hard and study. She was a woman of determination and a pillar of strength for me. She pulled me out of the ashes of despair, taught me to live life with dignity and head held high."

With moist eyes and holding the hand of Ramesh, she resumed, "Uncle, she was the epitome of divinity, and her compassion was through words and deeds. Seeds of nobility in my life were sown by her. She taught me to retain serenity in crisis and in frustrating times. She believed, every crisis could be turned into an opportunity. Crisis, she said, is a double-edged sword. Its pain is like contraction of labour; too much to bear, but easily forgotten with the joy of new birth. These two ladies are the solid foundations on which my life has been laid and built. One gave me walk; the other wings. Hatred of my father indirectly taught me to love others. From you, I learnt courage, clarity of thought, to be meticulous in life and live like a family."

Deeply drowned in the judicious analysis of the contribution of all to her life, Ramesh waited for a while and then asked, "Coming to your vital issue, how do you want to proceed?"

"Subject to your approval, I have thought of preparing a brief of the case, call Gaurav next Sunday for lunch, invite his suggestions and request him to take up the case."

Next Sunday, after lunch, Simran placed the brief before Gaurav. "Gaurav, you know my most cherished aim of life. Time has now come to execute my first decision of filing the rape and kidnapping case. I have prepared the brief for your perusal and suggestions. Please go through it so that final decision may be taken."

Gaurav was aware of all details and it did not take him much time to go through the brief. He asked, "Have you thought of engaging some competent and experienced advocate?"

"Competency and experience have their own place, but most important quality of an advocate is sincerity of purpose. There is only one who qualifies on that test. He is Mr. Gaurav Saxena. This is my decision and has uncle's approval also".

Surprised, Gaurav looked at Simran. "I am grateful to you for reposing so deep confidence in me. God willing, together we shall win."

Turning to Ramesh, Gaurav asked, "Uncle, I want to have your opinion on one point that has come to my mind. Should the case be filed now or after marriage?"

Simran immediately intruded, before her uncle could say anything. "Sorry for the interruption. It must be filed now and certainly before marriage."

Ramesh was amazed at the firm assertion of Simran. Gaurav was equally surprised at her sudden and forthright reply. Apologetically, she clarified, "Gaurav, you might have been offended by my unexpected interruption. I have very solid reason for that. I request you to show the brief to your parents. Let them know everything, before they take a decision on marriage. I certainly do not want them to succumb to your pressure. After they have read, you clarify everything to them and leave the decision to their wisdom. Gaurav, I do not want to hide anything. They are my parents, and parents must know everything about their children. Lasting relations are based on trust, and not on deceit. Revealing details after marriage, will be cheating."

Supporting Simran, Ramesh said, "Gaurav, you should not mind the decision of Simran. There is sincerity in her thought. Trust is first priority in any relation. If your parents come to know of any fact later on, they will lose their faith in all of us. I think you must show them the brief, and then explain all details of Simran's past without hiding anything. I visualise an auspicious beginning of your lives on the horizon."

"Uncle, hindsight also convinces me to do as suggested by you and Simran. There is certainly wisdom in her thought, and I appreciate it. Anyway, I do not refute your suggestion, am prepared to take up the case and shall discuss all details with mom and dad."

"Gaurav, there is one last thing that I have been waiting to say all these days. I will say in straight and clear words. My wife would have also joined me in this request." Charged with heavy emotions, Ramesh said, "Trust is the foundation of all relations. If love is lost, relations are lost but if trust is lost, life is lost. I do not doubt your sincerity but temptations and allurements or any social pressure can always cause problems in life. Relations must be strong enough to stand rock firm against any pressure of society or these forces of greed. Simran can bear everything but not betrayal of trust. Tell her if you or your parents change the decision. Truth will be acceptable; hiding will be devastating. I do not want my daughter to suffer any mistrust."

Waiting for a while and after clearing his throat, he resumed, "Marriage decision taken under emotional haste or under any pressure is always short-lived, painful and generally ends in disaster. Regret in the decision will be suicidal for both, and my child will not be able to bear it. As a loving and obedient son, go after the decision of your parents. Simran is your love; they are your responsibility. If they do not approve, tell us the truth. Concealing will be deceiving, revealing will be sincerity."

"Uncle, I will never hide the truth. Greed of gold or any other temptation has no place in my life. Love and sincerity are my primary concerns. Simran is my life, and she will always be safe in my hands. You will have no regrets in life. We need your blessings."

"They will be always with you. Decision of your parents is the concern."

"Uncle, I could have married without informing them, but that would be cheating. I want to be faithful to them as to all of you. Their concurrence and blessings are a must. Both are broad-minded and have always been very supportive. My dad may have slight hesitation in the beginning, but my mother will easily convince him. By God's grace, the final outcome shall be positive."

"Gaurav, I appreciate your incredible optimism, but must say one thing very clearly. Take the decision of marriage only and only if both your parents fully and whole-heartedly agree. Even if one has some inhibition or hesitation, respect their decision. Simran would be happier alone, rather than suffer in distressed relations. I live for her happiness, and would never see her suffer more in life. I repeat, tell the truth, and do not hide anything."

"Uncle, I swear I will never hide anything from you or from Simran." Waiting for a few moments, he asked "Simran you have been quiet. Have you to say anything?"

"Uncle has said everything."

The most significant moment in the life of Gaurav had arrived. Though sure of the approval of his parents, there was some odd fear lurking in the recesses of his heart. His father was more money-minded, and would certainly oppose in the hope of marrying him in a rich family. He might deny the proposal on account of the tarnished past of Simran. He might try to postpone it, on one pretext or the other, and may even hide the truth from him. In the grip of curious mixture of hope and despair, and with prayer on his lips, he handed over the brief to his father. "Dad, this is the first case that I have decided to take up. I request you to go through it, and also discuss it with mama. I shall disclose more details after dinner."

Being a holiday, Rajeshwar Saxena did not take much time to go through the brief. More he read, more was the shock. He was simply stunned, and his heart sank to know the real life of Simran. The facts were unbelievable and to grasp them, he read it several times. He explained all details to his wife, who was virtually in tears. They could not wait till dinner, and decided to immediately discuss further with their son. Holding the brief in his hand, Rajeshwar said, "This is utterly shocking. Simran is such a nice girl full of all the nobler qualities. In this short period, she had come so close to us."

Reciprocating the feelings of her husband, Lalita said, "This is absolutely unbelievable. How much the poor girl had to suffer in life? How did she pass her days under such emotional stress and social stigma? She had endeared such a loving place in our hearts. I was totally mesmerised by her physical charms and qualities of head and heart. She is so affectionate, caring and respectful to us."

"Mama, the whole story is full of nothing but tragedy. This brief does not contain even half of her life story."

Gaurav did not want to miss the opportunity and explained all details of Simran's life right from childhood to the present day. Both were gravely sad, but Lalita was repeatedly wiping her tears. Being a woman, she could more severely feel the pain suffered by the young and adolescent girl at the hands of destiny and the cruel society. She repeatedly appreciated her determination to silently bear the trauma, and fight all odds of life. Gaurav did not say anything at this stage about his intention of marrying her. He wisely decided to resume after dinner, when the emotions would have cooled down.

After dinner, Gaurav decided to open the topic of his love for Simran, and his intention to be her life partner. Instead of coming straight to his objective, he decided to introduce the subject in a different way. "Dad, since you have read and understood all details of the life of Simran, I want to have your opinion on two vital aspects. First is, should she file the case?"

Gaurav's father immediately replied, "Opinions may differ, but my firm view is that she should desist from filing the case. This will absolutely dent her professional career and ruin her future matrimonial prospects. She will be simply lowering her prestige in the society."

Lalita seemed to be seriously pondering over the whole issue. "My view is diametrically opposite. I am of the firm opinion that she must file the case and fight it in the court. It will not dent her career. On the other hand, it will prove her to be a bold and courageous advocate. More cases will come to her. Her action will teach a lesson to the rapists, and be an inspiration for other girls. I am all praise for her decision and appreciate her resolve. Today, we need such daring and brave women, who can take up the cause of the poor and down-trodden. If left unpunished, the unbridled wild horses will run amok, and lives of many more innocent girls will be ruined. Since she has personally gone through the trauma, she will be able to fight the case with more sincerity and determination. So far as marriage prospects are concerned, I also feel that it may be adversely affected. Even though outlook of society is changing, we are still chained to orthodox and rigid customs. We may be liberal to give opinion to others, but are not flexible to accept them ourselves. People still look at such victims with myopic vision. Her courage for fighting the case will be widely appreciated, but for marriage, she may have problems."

"Dad, look at the problem from broader social perspective. We should fight for women empowerment. They must get justice, otherwise the rapists will get encouragement. She wants to launch a crusade and be a motivation to the distressed. I also support mama, and feel that this would raise her dignity and respect as an advocate."

"May be, but I feel the greatest damage will be to marriage prospects. She may gain some praise as an advocate, but her personal life will be completely ruined. She may file the case only if she is prepared to sacrifice her marriage."

Gaurav thought time was ripe to throw the gauntlet in the ring. "Dad, if you have to decide marrying your son to such a girl?'

Shocked and bewildered, Rajeshwar immediately reacted to the most unexpected question. "I will never agree."

"Any specific reason for your disagreement?"

"Gaurav, emotions block logic. They distort and impair critical thinking. Today, we may be sympathetic to her but once sympathy diminishes, result will be nothing but regret. In decisions of marriage, we must go by logic and follow the established social norms. Age-old wisdom cannot be put on the back seat. Society is a collective movement of people. We are its part, and cannot survive in isolation. News associated with social stigma and character of a girl travel like wild fire, and become fodder for public gossip."

"What is your reaction to my question, mama?" asked Gaurav.

"It is a sensitive issue. I am downright confused. Without being offensive, I will say that though concerns of your dad are legitimate, Simran is certainly not to be blamed and cannot be held responsible for the act of the rapists and for the crime committed by someone else. Her personal character is certainly pure and blotless. One should appreciate her courage and determination to fight. What if this happens after marriage? What if she had hidden the facts? Truth must be appreciated and rewarded, rather than smothered. Most such girls never come out with truth even when probed. Besides, she is so charming, and her qualities of head and heart are so rare in a modern girl. She may take care of us in old age and the marriage may be happy and prosperous. So far as society is concerned, it is like a bottomless pit, has no stable norms and can consume anything. I would, however, leave the decision of marriage to Gaurav."

Gaurav was immensely delighted at the positive response and support of his mother. Pushing his point more aggressively, he said, "It is certainly a complex social issue but times are changing fast. To continue with decaying social customs is mental slavery; to support desirable social customs is mental freedom. Let us not view the problem from narrower social parameters. There is now realignment of the orthodox social compulsions, and we must shake off the shackles of redundant social orthodoxy. So far as the view of the people is concerned, it all depends on the perception of the beholder. Problem is not in the view, but in the viewpoint. Some look at the glass as half empty and others as half full. There may be criticism from some quarters, but in broader perspective, you will earn the admiration and appreciation of the society."

Waiting for the reaction of his father, Gaurav continued, "Dad, if you care for the society and go after the people, you can never have peace. You must consider the character of the girl. She did not hide anything. She has been so respectful and affectionate to those who loved her in life. For them, she is now prepared to sacrifice everything. It is difficult to find such girls. She knows how to maintain relations, and will certainly be a source of harmony and happiness in our family. Relations easily break today due to ego and undue demands of a partner. See your own family. More than half homes are suffering with distressed relations. Some are fighting divorce cases in the courts. Love, peace and harmony should get precedence over narrow social outlook."

"Your arguments are highly laudable. I agree to what you say. She is immensely graceful with all adorable human qualities. One cannot find even one negative aspect in her personality. She is a self-made woman, full of determination with empathy, humility and nobility. But besides rape, pregnancy and abortion, we must also keep in mind that her father has been involved in a drug peddling case, and married a woman of loose character. I am certainly against the decision of marriage."

"Dad, with all humility and due respect, I am inclined to say that your views are self-contradictory, and arguments self-destructive. On one hand, you appreciate her noble qualities and on the other, you discard her for marriage. I think what is more significant in matrimonial relations is adjustment, love, care and respect for elders. Simran is an amalgamation of all these and many more noble qualities. The irony of our thought is that we perpetuate criminality and crucify innocence. A father is prepared to marry his daughter to a rapist, who is a slur on womanhood, but is reluctant to marry his son to an innocent rape victim, who is not responsible for the crime. This is double standard of our thought, and is biased towards male dominance. If every father starts thinking from that angle, half the girls may remain unmarried. Without being offensive to anyone, let us place our own daughter or sister in her place, and then give our judgement. Winds of change are there regarding stigma surrounding the rape victims, and we must change our complexion. By denying rehabilitation, we repeatedly bleed the victim and continue bleeding her for whole life. Instead of applying the healing balm, we continue to deepen the wounds and trauma of pain. Society should warmly embrace such victims, rather than treat them as culprits and discard them as waste paper. We must weigh things from the point of view of the innocent victim, and not worry about what people say. Happiness of the couple and the family should be the primary concern, and not the society. Dad, the problem is not that society is strong; the problem is that we are timid. Qualities should be the determinants of marriage and not the incidence of rape. Simran is grace and beauty personified."

Waiting for a while, he continued, "So far as the case against her father is concerned, it was concocted by an evil-minded advocate, who wanted to deprive him of his love. Marrying a woman of so-called loose character is an act of sincerity in love. He remained faithful and did not betray the woman, whom he loved. We must not view things with biased notions."

Contemplating critically over the convincing arguments of his son, Rajeshwar said, "I certainly appreciate her adorable qualities. I also agree that this tragedy can happen after marriage, but you can't knowingly swallow a fly. One must choose a companion with great care. It is a lifetime decision. Emotions should not drive our actions. Decisions taken in the flow of heat are generally painful."

"Dad, I have deeply pondered over all aspects of the issue for about a year. My decision has not been taken under any emotional haste. Simran is a pure soul. It is difficult to find girls of her calibre and quality. You are not aware of relations these days between boys and girls before marriage. Most have illicit relations and even maintain them after marriage. They believe in hiding their illegitimate relations, and are quite clever to cheat their partners. They hide not only their relations, but even pregnancy and abortion. Here in this case, Simran has not cheated anyone. Suppose she had decided not to file the case, no one would have known her past. Even her father was not aware of the developments. The issue could have been easily buried deep for the whole life. Lie could have easily survived by strangulating the truth. Would that have been better or is revealing the facts better? If you start punishing honesty, truth, sincerity, purity and innocence, nobility would be crucified and only crime will prosper."

Rajeshwar seriously pondered over the thorny issue. He

was a very shrewd man, and knew that he would not be able to win over his intelligent son. To buy some time, he said, "Let me discuss the issue from all angles with Lalita and will give you our final decision tomorrow. However, I morally support Simran to fight the case and pray for her success."

"Dad, your decision is highly gratifying. Tomorrow can't be envisaged today and future is always unpredictable, but I can assure you both that you will never regret your considered decision in favour of marriage", said Gaurav with utmost humility and confidence.

Lalita looked at her husband and preferred to remain silent. At night, Rajeshwar opened the topic with her. "Lalita, I am certainly not in favour of Gaurav's marriage with Simran."

"But if Gaurav does not agree?"

"Gaurav is too timid to oppose my decision. Moreover, I will create such a situation that greed for gold will blind his vision, and he will himself reject Simran. I cannot afford to eat a rotten egg with eyes open. I will certainly ensure that Gaurav does not marry her."

Waiting for a moment, Lalita shocked her husband. "And what is the guarantee that the other girl will be pure?"

Stunned, he fumbled and replied, "One is a certainty; other will be a chance, may be one in million. If the other is also not good, then it is Gaurav's destiny. But Simran is certainly rejected. I have a plan by which, as the saying goes, the snake will be killed and the stick will also not break. I did not tell you, but I have been in touch with Rakhi for about a month. Since I had looked after her so well as brother, she wanted to do something for Gaurav. She wants him to come to America. Due to the failing health of her husband, she wants Gaurav to manage her business of petrol pump and grocery shop."

Lalita was furious with her husband for hiding all these facts from her. Rajeshwar had not revealed even a hint of his plan, as his wife could never hide a secret for a long time. He tried to mellow down her anger and said, "Anyway, now behave normally with Gaurav. Let him not have any suspicion of our plan. Meanwhile, Rakhi will also choose a suitable girl for Gaurav from a well-off Indian family and he will have a bright future. Once emotions cool down, allurement of the green pastures will shake off the ghost of Simran from his head. Considering all aspects, I am certainly not inclined to his marriage with Simran."

"But this is deceit."

"Life is a game and in a game, there is nothing like deceit. There is only a plan; a move."

Lalita had no courage to oppose the decision of her dominant husband. Rajeshwar resumed, "Tomorrow morning, you tell Gaurav that we agree to his proposal. I will inform Ramesh Puri accordingly, and that marriage will be solemnised after the case. This way, we will gain some time. I know how to arrange his departure. Keep everything to yourself and leave the rest to me. Just wait and watch."

Next day early morning, managing some fake smile on her face, Lalita informed her son about their approval of his marriage with Simran. Mad with joy, Gaurav touched the feet of his parents and dashed to the flat of Simran with a box of sweets. On seeing her, he tightly hugged her, lifted her in his arms and shouted, "Darling, my parents have approved our marriage." There was a wave of rejoicings all around, as the most cherished dream of Ramesh and Rani had been fulfilled. Meanwhile Rajeshwar rang up Ramesh, conveyed their decision of Gaurav's marriage with Simran, and that the marriage would be solemnised after the case.

Lalita outwardly displayed normal behaviour, but was gravely distressed at heart. Rajeshwar had always kept her under his thumb, and she had been too timid in life to oppose her stubborn husband. Selfishness blinded her vision also. Mesmerised by the plan of her husband, she also began to dream a glorious future for her son. However, she had all the sympathy for Simran, who was being deceptively sacrificed at the altar of Saxena's wily ruse. Gaurav was, of course, unaware of the plan of dumping his soul-mate and crushing her under the feet of treachery. In his sincerity, he continued his normal relations with Simran.

□

7

Rape, abortion and kidnapping were the three vital aspects of the case contemplated by Simran. Gathering evidence and seeking support of witnesses on all the three, that had happened about six years back, had to be handled deftly. Both Gaurav and Simran were still raw in their profession and feared to face more experienced and astute opponents. Many such genuine cases fall flat for want of evidence, betrayal of witnesses and uncomfortable questions to the victim. Though courts are careful not to permit questions damaging the dignity of the victim, yet clever advocates find ways to save their criminal clients and make victims uncomfortable, fragile and helpless. Both carefully considered the case from all angles, as they were determined to nail the culprits, and set an example for future rapists. In war, forewarned, is forearmed and so they decided not to reveal all facts, evidence and witnesses immediately. They wanted to keep their cards close to their chest, and shoot the proper arrow at the appropriate time, without giving even breathing time to defence.

First step in the process of filing the case was to file a police complaint. While discussing the details, Gaurav suddenly became serious and asked, "Simran, I have been hesitating, but want to ask you something if you don't mind. Had Daljeet uncle played any negative role in this whole episode?"

"Gaurav, it is good you asked me this question. At heart, papa was a thorough gentleman and was not responsible for any of these criminal acts. He has certainly not played any negative role in rape and kidnapping. His only fault was his emotional weakness, blind faith in Deepak and considering my marriage with him without careful thought. Deepak also convinced him that he would leave the unholy path of crime, and would soon establish a car repair workshop. Due to his weak willpower he easily fell into his trap. His intention was not bad, but execution casual. He was certainly careless about my future, but had no direct or indirect role to play in the criminal acts of the rapists. If he had any hand, I would have certainly told you and would have not spared him."

"I asked you this question fearing that he may not get implicated later on, which would be the last thing that we would like to have." Waiting for a few moments, he resumed, "To tame the lions in their own den, we need present address of Deepak and his friend. For this, you contact uncle and try to find from him address of the accused."

Next day, Simran went to her father to reveal vital facts of the tragedy of her life and then request him to get the latest address of Deepak and Sandeep. On reaching, Aarushi immediately ran towards the outstretched arms of Simran, and clung to her legs. Simran had brought a nice dress and gave the same to her. This time, she had brought presents for Rani, Suman and her father also. After exchanging some family matters, Simran asked her father, "Papa, I have come for another purpose, besides the reason of meeting you all. Let us go to the other room."

Simran briefly revealed facts of her tragic past after Daljeet had brought her to Delhi from Jaipur. "This is the brief story, though details are very tragic and too painful for a father to hear and bear. I have decided to file a rape and kidnapping case against both, and want to know their present address."

Daljeet was completely shocked. Ground slipped from

below his feet. He was extremely furious, as was visible from his reactions. "Simran, I never imagined all this, though I knew their nefarious deeds. Whatever have been my failures, I could have never tolerated such immoral activities against my daughter. I know, and I confess that I neglected you, but my sincere intention was your settlement. Now I feel that I have been responsible for all your miseries in life. My head is hung in shame. How could I do all this to you? I curse myself. God will never forgive me." Daljeet buried his head in his hands and began to weep. Wiping his tears, Simran said, "Papa, do not feel guilty. Let us not lament and grieve. All this was a part of my destiny. Now our good days have come. Please tell me first, do you know their address?"

Gaining little composure, he replied, "I knew Deepak's earlier address and also his address in Narela. I can easily trace his present residence, if he has changed. Tomorrow, I will let you know the exact address of both."

"But you will have to be extremely careful. They should not suspect your real motive. Pay a casual visit to him, and try to find out the whereabouts of his friend. If he asks you about me, just say that you failed to trace me after my escape from the flat, but perhaps I had gone back to the village to my maternal uncle. Everything is to be kept as top secret till the case has proceeded little farther in the court. Slight suspicion, and they will run away, destroy evidence, threaten witnesses and success of the case may be ruined." Considering the gravity of the problem, Daljeet promised to be careful. Simran also told him not to disclose anything to Suman or Rani.

As decided earlier, Rani also came with Simran to stay in the flat of Ramesh Puri. She occupied the so-called servant's room. Kind-hearted as she was, she began to look after the kitchen and all the personal needs of Ramesh as a part of the family. Life also began to run smoothly for Gaurav and Simran.

Both shared a chamber with an associate, and started their practice. Both were intelligent, hard-working and devoted to their profession. They expected their practice to pick-up slowly. At this stage, they wanted to fully concentrate on their own case.

Next morning, Daljeet went to the village of Deepak and came to know about his residence from one of his friends. He was staying in the same flat, where they had been staying earlier. Fortunately, Deepak was present there and was completely astonished to see Daljeet.

"Daljeet, how are you here? It is a pleasant surprise. I thought you had forgotten us. What are you doing these days?"

"I am absolutely jobless. I could not marry my earlier partner, as she also deserted me, and is now living with some other person and is the mother of a child. In fact, I have come to you with great hope. Please help me. I am at your service."

Deepak told him that he and Sandeep were now in the business of sale-purchase of stolen cars. He welcomed Daljeet to join their business. While discussing the past events, Deepak asked, "Daljeet, could you locate Simran after her escape from the flat? Where is she? Is she married?"

With a defiant gesture, Daljeet retorted, "As I told you then also, I hated her right from her birth. It is good that she herself vanished from my sight. I did not try to locate her but a relative told me that she had gone to the village and is living with her maternal uncle. I have no idea of her marriage. For me, she is dead."

All this completely dispelled any suspicion from the mind of Deepak, and he was fully convinced of the sincerity of his new partner-in-crime. Fortunately, Sandeep also came. All shared some beer and shook hands for the revival of their friendship. Daljeet promised to shift next day.

Having achieved his desired goal without creating any

suspicion, Daljeet returned home and immediately conveyed to Simran the residential address of both.

The complaint had to be first filed in the police station at Rohini, in whose jurisdiction the kidnapping and rape incidents had taken place. The application simply stated that Deepak Dabas and Sandeep Yadav had raped Simran Kaur in their flat at Rohini, and then kidnapped her and raped her in their house in Narela, from where she managed her escape. The present address of the rapists and that of house in Narela were revealed with year, dates and time of various acts. The idea was to swoop down unaware upon the victims and get them arrested. Since both were advocates, police was also careful in dealing with the case, lest they get trapped in any legal lapse, favour or delay. The fact of abortion was deliberately hidden at this stage to avoid erasing of vital evidence, destruction of hospital record and intimidation of the doctor as witness.

Next day, Simran went to the police station as complainant and Gaurav accompanied her as her advocate. Placing the complaint before the SHO, Simran said, "Sir, I want to file a complaint of rape and kidnapping against two persons, Deepak Dabas and Sandeep Yadav. Here is my application."

"Who is the victim?"

"I am the victim and the complainant."

The SHO looked at Simran and was spell-bound at her confidence and boldness. Introducing him as advocate of the complainant, Gaurav said. "Our request is that police may immediately take action and arrest the culprits, as one of them is certainly in his flat, address of which is given in the application. Since the case is about six years old, the accused may run away, and try to destroy the evidence or intimidate the vital witnesses. Laxity of action will certainly help the accused to escape from the clutches of law."

Since both the complainant and her advocate were

practicing lawyers, the SHO could not afford to delay for the fear of any implication of police in helping the accused. Moreover, he had been told that both had criminal background, and had served imprisonment term of about three years each. The SHO warmly complimented the courage and determination of Simran, and promised all possible police help. The police immediately swung into action, and fortunately, both Deepak and Sandeep, who were waiting for Daljeet, were arrested. Being experienced in the field of crime, Deepak denied all charges and immediately contacted his advocate, who came to the police station for their bail. He was told that this being a rape case, bail application may be moved in the court next day, when they would be produced.

Next day was the first day of appearance. It is customary in some homes to give yogurt and sugar to the person going for an exam, an interview or for any other auspicious purpose. When Simran was about to leave for the court, Rani brought the same for her. Simran reverently touched her feet and got her blessings. She was only told that Simran was appearing for her first case, in the court. Ramesh Puri had arrived from America for the case and also to solemnise Simran's marriage after the case. Simran touched his feet and got his blessings also. With eyes full of optimism, Simran left for the flat of Gaurav, who had to accompany her to the court.

As the court resumed work, police produced both Deepak and Sandeep before the magistrate, and their advocate moved the bail application.

"Your honour, though my clients had been earlier convicted in a case of car theft, they are now leading a very honourable life. They have a clean record for the last about six years and deserve to be granted bail."

Gaurav stood up and said, "Your honour, prosecution vehemently objects to the grant of bail to both the accused.

Firstly, it is a rape case that happened about six years back, and both being persons of shady past will certainly try to destroy the evidence and intimidate the witnesses. Secondly, the contention of defence that both are not involved in any case now is not borne out by facts. Both are history-sheeters and have been sentenced for short periods later on also. They are still continuing with their illegal activities and have been recently charged for the sale of scrap of stolen cars in Meerut, and the case is under police investigation. Honourable court is requested not to be misled by their cloak of innocence. Prosecution strongly opposes grant of bail to both the rapists due to their criminal background, and the strong possibility of their adversely influencing the course of justice."

The judge adjusted his glasses and said, "Bail application of Deepak Dabas and Sandeep Yadav is rejected. The case shall be taken on day-to-day basis and both may be produced tomorrow."

Simran looked at Gaurav with a sense of great satisfaction. They had won the first battle of the long drawn war. She also decided to go to Suman and disclosed all facts to her. Back home, she revealed all details to Rani also to avoid being blamed for concealing the vital information of her life tragedy. She clung to Rani like a child and said, "*Maa*, I sincerely apologise for having hidden all these facts from you. I did not want to hurt you. Please pardon me."

Rani was absolutely devastated to hear all the heart-wrenching details of Simran's ordeal. Her face went pale as the narration progressed. Tears rolled down; voice was choked. She said, "This is really shocking that you had to bear all this physical and mental pain and I could not do anything. I think Daljeet is responsible for all this."

"I do not blame papa, as he had no knowledge of all that happened with me. He had brought me from Jaipur with the idea of marrying me to Deepak, who took advantage of his emotional weakness. His intentions were not bad, but his blind faith in his friends ruined my life." Waiting for a few moments, she continued, "But *maa*, let us forget all this. I have now filed a rape case against the culprits, and they are in lock-up. The case will start from tomorrow." Rani wanted to attend the court daily to follow the proceedings. She prayed that both the scoundrels may be hanged for their outrageous and shameful act.

This being the first important case of his life, Gaurav decided to do some shadow practice in the evening to regain the required confidence. It was also a testing time for Simran, as she was on the verge of the fulfilment of the most cherished dream of her life. Howsoever courageous a person may be, anxiety, fear, and restlessness do disturb his mental state at such a critical moment. Her determination and patience were being put on the anvil. It was time to summon all her courage and resolve. As a keen observer, Ramesh saw nervousness on her face and said, "Simran, you appear to be little tense. Worry and discomfort are normal. Be relaxed. Concentrate on your action and do not worry about the result. If mind is fixated only on result, performance is hampered. Lord Krishna said in the Gita, 'Action thy duty, reward is not thy concern.'"

Regaining her courage, she replied, "Uncle, this little nervousness will disappear in thin air as soon as I am in the court. Like Arjun in Mahabharta, I will then concentrate only on the eye of the fish to shoot my arrow. I am confident that with your blessings and your presence in the court, I will have no worry or fear. Though there are others, you have always been my greatest source of inspiration and strength."

"That should be the spirit. Maintain that in life. Now pray to God. When chips are down in trying time, solace is in prayer. More things are wrought by prayer, than the world dreams of." With all those words of encouragement, night was still restless.

The regular case started. Due to media hype, the court room was flooded with visitors keen to follow the proceedings of one of the rare cases of an advocate. There were no signs of nervousness on the faces of both Gaurav and Simran. They were smiling and looking right into the eyes of the spectators, including media persons. As soon as the judge resumed the chair, Gaurav stood up and with all the confidence at his command, started proceedings with the order of the court.

"Your honour, before I start, I want to make one request to the honourable court. Honourable Supreme Court and honourable high courts have ordered in their judgements that in rape cases, care should be taken that honour and dignity of the victim is maintained. It is against this background, that I wish to pray to the honourable court that my client is a respectable citizen of the society with absolutely unblemished record, and is pursuing a dignified profession. We have stated all facts of the case to the honourable court, but do not want everything to be revealed to defence, due to secrecy of evidence and protection of witnesses. Prosecution will disclose every fact in stages, and defence will have full opportunity to argue the case."

"I object your honour. It is the right of defence to have a copy of the complete complaint for the justice to be fair."

"Objection overruled. Revealing all facts immediately to defence will certainly jeopardise the course of justice in such a sensitive case. Defence will have full opportunity as and when facts are revealed by prosecution." Looking at Gaurav, the judge said, "You may proceed now." Gaurav thanked the court and desired to start with the examination of Deepak Dabas.

Deepak Dabas was summoned to the witness box. After the customary oath and a few introductory questions of name and address, Gaurav adjusted his gown and said, "Mr. Deepak Dabas, what is your profession?"

"We live in a joint family and have about five acres of agricultural land. I am a farmer."

"Mr. Dabas, you live a very decent life style and have a BMW also. Is the income from that small piece of land sufficient for you and your joint family?"

"Actually, I earn from sale-purchase of cars also."

On further questioning, Deepak revealed that his office was in a rented flat in Rohini, where he and his business partner, Sandeep Yadav, had been living for about six years. He also agreed to produce bank statements and balance sheets of his business.

On further questioning, Deepak informed the court that he knew Daljeet Singh, whom he had met in Dehradun jail, when he was serving his term of imprisonment. He also informed that while in jail, he casually told him that if he ever needed, he could come and stay with him. After the completion of his sentence, Daljeet stayed with him at Delhi, and joined his business.

"Do you know any girl by the name Simran Kaur?"

"Yes. She was the daughter of Daljeet Singh."

"Did she also stay there with her father and you?"

"Yes. Daljeet Singh brought her as he wanted to find a suitable match for her marriage. He also said that if the marriage was delayed, he would send her to the village."

On further examination, Deepak informed the court that Simran Kaur was then about nineteen or twenty years old. In the beginning she behaved like a normal girl but soon became very reserved since her father did not behave well with her. He often used to scold her on the issue of marriage.

"Did Daljeet Singh put her marriage proposal to you also?"

"He was very keen that she should marry me."

"What was your reaction to the proposal?"

"I told him that I had no objection, if his daughter agreed."

During his interrogation, Deepak revealed that to expand his business, he opened an office at Guwahati also, that was looked after by Daljeet Singh, while he managed the main business at Delhi and Sandeep shuttled between Delhi and Guwahati. He also informed the court that Daljeet Singh left Simran Kaur at Delhi with him, so that she could understand him better and then agree to marriage. She stayed alone with him for about three months.

"You also sometimes hurled crude and insensitive barbs and deliberately rubbed your shoulder against her body."

"Never. I always respected her. However, I often used to persuade her to marry me as per the desire of her father."

At this stage, Gaurav wanted to mentally break Deepak with a fusillade of relentless questions. With a defiant look, he said, "Mr. Deepak Dabas, let us discuss some details of that period of three months when Simran Kaur stayed alone with you. Before answering, remember, truth can be delayed but not destroyed. It may be concealed by even hundred lies, but finally, it triumphs." Gaurav came closer to the witness box, looked straight into his eyes and very politely said, "When did you first rape Simran Kaur?"

Deepak suddenly flew into rage and shouted, "What are you saying? Why should I rape her? I am a man of noble character and have always respected women. There has been no case of my molesting any lady in my life. This is not correct. This is a lie; a blatant lie."

"Mr. Dabas, I just asked you one simple question and you became so emotional. You are clutching the arm of the witness box. Your body language and aggressive tone speak volumes about the inner turmoil of your mind. You have been absolutely normal so far. Why should you be so agitated? Let me tell you. This is a clear indication of wilful subversion of facts."

The defence counsel was completely stunned, as he was not aware of any such fact. Deepak had never even hinted at his illicit relations with Simran. Observing drops of perspiration on the face of his client, and fearing that he may get aggressive, the defence counsel immediately got up and said, "Your honour, I strongly object to those slanderous remarks of prosecution. My client is a gentleman, and is just being provoked to lose his cool. He is not in proper frame of mind and needs some rest. I request that further proceedings may be deferred till tomorrow."

The judge looked at Gaurav, who immediately responded, "Your honour, prosecution also feels that Mr. Dabas needs some rest. We have no objection to the postponement of further interrogation till tomorrow." The court was adjourned.

All through Simran sat patiently by the side of Gaurav, concentrating on the course of the proceedings. She had prepared flash cards to ensure that no point or sequence of proceedings was missed. She looked at Gaurav with a sense of complete satisfaction at the development of the case. In fact, they had decided to provoke Deepak to lose his temper and play upon his emotions. Today, the intention was to take the interrogation only up the to rape incident. If defence had not requested for postponement, prosecution would have. Request from defence gave Gaurav a chance to earn the goodwill of the judge, defence, and the accused. It was pre-planned to take up abortion proceedings next day. Copies of the relevant documents had already been procured, and the doctor had confirmed her evidence. In the evening, both went to the doctor, requested her once again to be present in the court next day with original hospital record.

At the end, Ramesh congratulated Gaurav and said, "Gaurav, I appreciate your confidence and determination with which you dealt with the proceedings. There was maturity in your thoughts and actions. Even very experienced advocates could have not done better."

"Uncle, it is all due to the blessings of the elders. How could I falter with innocence of Simran in my heart and her determination in my head? It is as if all had happened with me personally. I was feeling the pain that Simran had suffered from this ordeal. Her agony gave me the required mental strength. The credit for all that I have done, goes to her. I was simply the mouthpiece of her words."

Appreciating his magnanimity, Simran said, "Uncle, this is his character, his generosity. For his achievements, he always gives credit to others."

"This is the sign of a virtuous human being. I will always pray for peace and happiness for both of you." All reached home, had a well-deserved cup of tea and got involved in the preparations for the next day.

Next day, Gaurav continued with the interrogation of Deepak Dabas. Armed with a battery of questions, he came closer to him and placing his hand on the arm of the witness box, he said, "Mr. Dabas, I hope you had the desired rest last night."

Giving a quizzical look, Deepak kept quiet with clear signs of nervousness on his face. This was the right time to pile up staggering pressure on him. "Mr. Deepak Dabas, yesterday I asked you if you had ever raped Miss Simran Kaur during the three months that she stayed in your flat without her father, when you got agitated. You were nervous and suddenly exploded. Relax, today I will not ask you about that."

As an intelligent advocate, Gaurav knew that Deepak must have mentally prepared himself for further questions on rape. He completely evaded that topic to avoid playing on his strength. He systematically confronted him with a series of most unexpected and embarrassing questions to floor him in the mind game. With a little fake smile on his face, Gaurav asked if he had ever taken Simran Kaur to a doctor. Deepak replied that he had taken her once to a doctor, when she had fever and bad cold. He pretended that he did not remember the name of the doctor.

Gaurav retorted sternly, "Mr. Dabas, this is mysterious obfuscation of facts and a shameful pack of lies. The sinner never remembers; the sufferer never forgets. You are very conveniently forgetting every fact. Let me say, you are a consummate liar. Your denial is a ruthless suppression of facts and you are manufacturing lies. I say it with certainty that you remember everything, but are lying and deliberately trying to mislead the court. Remember, truth can't be imprisoned. It breaks all barriers and pops up with greater force. I will remind you, and your edifice of lies will crumble to pieces." Gaurav was getting progressively offensive. Dropping a bombshell at that defining moment and pushing him to the brink, he said, "You took Miss Simran Kaur to a hospital and not for fever or bad cold, but for her abortion."

The silence and stillness of the court was suddenly disrupted. There was chaos and commotion all around, and a mixture of anxiety, excitement and loud murmurs among the audience. The judge had to call the court to order. Deepak was utterly shocked and gravely agonised at the belligerent charge of Gaurav, as he did not anticipate the direction of the incoming storm. He was shattered and so was the defence counsel, as Deepak had never even hinted at any fact about rape, abortion or kidnapping. He had only told him that the whole case of molestation had been cooked-up by Daljeet Singh to extort money from him. The situation was downright hopeless, and Deepak was now completely at the receiving end. Displaying his anguish and frustration, he got violent and shouted, "Your accusation is outrageous. You are again levelling false charges against me. I had never had any sexual relations with her, as I told you earlier. The question of abortion does not arise. It is only exploitation of an innocent person."

"Mr. Dabas, you are displaying nervousness as before. I will remove all your doubts. Get ready for the proof."

Springing an unexpected surprise, he took out a paper from his file and handed it over to the court.

"Your honour, this is a copy of the application for abortion, signed by both Mr. Deepak Dabas and Miss Simran Kaur, where Mr. Dabas has stated that Simran Kaur is his wife and is an adult. The original is with the doctor."

This took wind out of the sail of Deepak. Fretting and fuming, he was thrown out of gear, and stood stunned. The least expected revelation shocked everyone in the court, including Simran's family members. They looked at each other, and shook their heads in utter disbelief. There were whispers all around, and the judge ordered silence.

"Your honour, the doctor of the concerned hospital is present in the court with original record. Permission may be granted for her evidence."

The doctor was ordered to come to the witness box. She informed the court that her name was Dr. Pratibha Gupta, and she was working in City Hospital.

"Dr. Gupta, do you maintain some record, when husband and wife come to your hospital for an abortion request?"

"Yes. They have to sign an application when they come for abortion request, and we also enter the relevant details in a register."

Placing copy of Simran's abortion application before the doctor, Gaurav said, "This is a copy of the abortion application of your hospital. Is the original with you?"

It was a nail-biting moment for Simran. She was sitting with folded hands praying to God. Fate of the whole case hung on doctor's evidence. The doctor took out the original application from her records, and handed over the same to the court. Simran was mighty relieved.

"Deepak Dabas, did you sign this application?" asked the judge.

With words not matching the language of his eyes, he faltered and said, "I have never signed any such paper. I totally deny the charge being levelled against me."

"Dr. Gupta, you had mentioned that you enter relevant details in a register also. Is the register with you now?"

The doctor handed over the register to Gaurav, who presented the same to the court. After going through the details of the record, the judge ordered, "Prosecution may continue."

"Your honour, to a discerning observer, the application and entries in the register are ample testimony to the proof of abortion." Turning to the doctor, he resumed, "Dr. Gupta, do you recognise the husband and wife, who came to you?"

"Normally, it is difficult to recognise and remember all our patients, but I remember Simran Kaur due to a remarkable discussion still etched deep in my mind."

"Can you please enlighten the honourable court about the details of the same?" asked Gaurav.

"Your honour, when both Deepak Dabas and Simran Kaur came to me, I found that Simran Kaur was absolutely quiet and did not answer even simple personal questions that I asked her. She appeared to be mortally afraid of something. Thinking that she might be scared of the pain of operation, I tried to console her on the operation table. 'Simran, don't be afraid of the operation. It is very simple and you being a young and healthy girl, will be able to bear it without any problem.'

Without moving even her eyelid, she lay down quietly. After the operation, when she got up, I asked her, 'Was there any pain?'

I vividly remember her reply. With a divine spark in her eyes, she thundered with great confidence, 'I am not afraid of the pain of your knife and scissors. They are so gentle. I wish some doctor to cut to pieces the beast, who caused this cruelty, mental agony and social stigma.' I was astonished to hear her sweet but fiery voice for the first time. Adjusting her dress, she said with unwavering determination, 'Destiny has always been very cruel to me, but the kind hand of God saved me just at the moment when all appeared lost. If God is kind again, as in the past, I will meet you. Please remember my name. I am Simran Kaur Gill.' Saying this, she opened the door and made a hasty exit without even looking at her husband. I was stunned at her wisdom and confidence. My eyes remained wide open staring at the door for a long time."

Murmurs of those present in the court disturbed the proceedings. With resumption of silence, the doctor said, "At times, her words of deep philosophy haunted me, and her face often flashed before my eyes. I still remember the whole incident, as if, it had happened just yesterday. In retrospect, I now understand the cruelty of man that she was referring to. I am sure, she will now realise that the doctor for cutting to pieces that beast who caused cruelty, mental agony and social stigma to her is here in the court, and has the instrument that is mightier than the sharpest sword."

All through, Deepak stood motionless with teeth clinching and eyes spewing venom. Even in his wildest dream, he had not expected such a course of the case. He knew that he was running out of luck and was fighting a losing battle. The game was over and his fate was sealed. Inwardly, he was itching to devour the doctor, but was helpless. With hands on his cheeks and elbows resting on the table, the defence counsel just watched the proceedings as a mute spectator, realising his inability to save his client from the clutches of law. With hearts in their mouths, the pulsating moments passed and finally, both Gaurav and Simran heaved a sigh of relief. Silently, they thanked the doctor for her brutal honesty. Though convinced of their success, they were always apprehensive, since justice is slave of evidence, and it is evidence that opens the gates of justice. Truth without evidence is also a lie. One slip and tables could have been turned against them.

The judge was highly impressed and was deeply engrossed in the words of Simran. He quoted them in his judgement. Feeling that it was time to end further proceedings, he said, "The court is adjourned for the day. It will resume tomorrow morning."

Simran kept on sitting for some time, to let the feeling of immense satisfaction sink deep. Gaurav jolted her shoulder to wake her up from the deep dream. Both were immensely satisfied. Confirmation of abortion was a proof sufficient for rape also, though only the statement of the victim was enough to nail the culprits.

Next day the plan was to take up the kidnapping case. This was another thorny matter, for which there was no direct or even indirect proof. CCTV footages, if any, at the society gate had been deleted by this time. No such cameras were there near the place, where Simran had been taken. But truth always triumphs. By sheer coincidence, a lady came to Gaurav as he was coming out of the court with Simran.

"I was present in the court since morning and keenly watched the developments of the case. Your systematic proceedings and strong arguments were highly commendable. I am sure the culprit will be suitably punished."

"Thank you very much. But sorry, I cannot place you."

"We have never met earlier. I am Poonam Thakur, Principal of a Government Girls Senior Secondary School. I have some information, but am not sure if it relates to your case." Gaurav requested her to reveal the same.

Poonam Thakur narrated the incident. Hope swelled in

Gaurav's heart, and he immediately said, "This is exactly what we had been looking for. We had been groping in the dark for some concrete proof. We shall be highly indebted to you, if you could come to the court tomorrow and be a witness in our case?" The lady immediately agreed to give her evidence. Gaurav was now sure that the culprits could not escape the charge of kidnapping.

Next day, as the court resumed, the judge asked the prosecution to continue. Gaurav stood up, came close to Deepak Dabas and said, "Mr. Deepak Dabas, let us start from the night, when Daljeet Singh came back from Guwahati. Can you tell the honourable court what happened on that night?"

"Since Simran Kaur had outright rejected the marriage proposal, Daljeet became violent and in an inebriated state, he repeatedly slapped her. Blood started oozing out of her mouth. She kept on weeping and without eating anything, went to sleep. All of us also slept. Early in the morning, Daljeet got up and wanted his daughter to prepare tea for him. Not finding her, he came running to our room. Both I and Sandeep were sleeping. He woke me up and said that Simran was missing. We wanted to go out to search her but found the door open. She had run away. Daljeet began to cry. I told him that all this was because of him. He had beaten her so violently that she decided to leave the house and might have committed suicide."

"Did Daljeet file a missing complaint with police?"

"He told us that he went to the police station and lodged a missing report. He showed us a copy of the same. I do not know what happened afterwards."

"Is it not a fact that you threatened him that if he reported to police, you would give evidence that he had beaten her, and then he would be arrested? He was terrified and did not pursue the report further."

"It is false. Why should we threaten him? Actually, he was

himself afraid that she may not complain about his brutality, and he may be put in jail again. He told us that he was happy that the burden was off his shoulders. He also told us that he hated her right from her childhood, and wished her to die."

Looking into the eyes of Deepak, Gaurav asked, "Did you and Sandeep drug her and kidnap her in your car on that night?"

"Again false charge is being leveled against us. It is an absolute lie. We were all sleeping and got up in the morning after Daljeet got up. How could we do that?"

"I will tell you. You drugged her, put her in the car, took her to your home in the village and before daybreak, came back to the flat and slept." Deepak lowered his eyes and was dumb. His silence was a clear indication of his guilt.

The defence counsel was enraged. He immediately got up from his seat and said, "Your honour, the case is getting mired in unnecessary controversies, and prosecution is levelling all types of false and fabricated charges against my client."

Gaurav was unfazed by the intervention of defence and said with recharged confidence. "All our charges were false and fabricated when leveled but all proved to be true. We will prove this charge also with eye-popping concrete evidence."

Turning to the judge, Gaurav said, "Your honour, our next witness is a respectable lady, Mrs. Poonam Thakur, Principal, Government Girls' Senior Secondary School, Rohini." On the request of prosecution, the court granted permission for her evidence and she narrated all details of the incident.

"On the night between 25th and 26th May, I, along with my husband, his sister and brother-in-law were coming after attending the engagement ceremony of my husband's nephew. At the tri-junction near the Japanese Park, the traffic light on our side was green, and was red on the other side. As we were crossing, a car suddenly came at dashing speed and the driver just managed to stop the car. The crash was very fortunately averted. My husband shouted, "What are you doing? Can't you see the red light?"

"*Ganju*, we are in a jovial mood otherwise we would have dug your grave right now in the middle of the road," said the man driving the car. The other person on the front seat laughed rudely and yelled, "And named it '*Ganju Chowk*'". With a loud piercing horn, they raced away. As they crossed, I had a fleeting view of a woman lying on the back seat. I told my husband, who wanted to inform the police. Since none of us had noted the number of the car, we dropped the idea."

After waiting for a moment, she resumed, "Your honour, the other day, I saw the photograph of the man arrested by the police, and immediately recognised him. Stringing together the scattered facts and pieces of puzzle, I thought over the incident that we had come across, may be related to this case. I came to the court yesterday, and talked to Mr. Gaurav Saxena and discovered that the incident certainly related to Simran Kaur's rape case. It is because of this reason, that I am here."

The defence counsel immediately got up, clapped, laughed and said, "You honour, the case has become a fairy tale. The prosecution has no witness and suddenly someone drops from heaven, and narrates a fanciful fable. All these are fictitious and concocted stories, with cooked-up witnesses."

"The doctor did not drop from heaven. As a pure slice of luck, Mrs. Thakur herself came, because she is concerned with the honour and dignity of women. Her sudden appearance surprised us also, but these are glorious uncertainties of life. There are brave and courageous people in the world, who fearlessly and voluntarily expose crimes. Perhaps God doesn't want truth to be defeated."

The defence counsel was aggressively intrigued at the detailed narration of the witness, and kept on staring at her in astonishment. He got up and retorted, "What is the evidence with prosecution to prove that the incident happened on the night between 25th and 26th May?"

"Your honour, here is a copy of the application that Daljeet Singh filed with the police regarding his missing daughter. It is dated 26th May, and was filed on the day following Simran's disappearance." Gaurav handed over copy of the application to the court.

After waiting for a while, Gaurav looked at the defence counsel and said, "Defence may cross-examine Mrs. Thakur to confirm the veracity of the facts."

"Madam, I appreciate your flight of fancy in cooking up the story of your seeing the victim in the car. How could you remember all these details after about six years?"

"Let me tell you. My memory is very sharp and photogenic. I remember names of most of the two thousand girls studying in my school. Principal of a girls' school has to be extremely vigilant to be successful. If in doubt, please come to my school and check it."

Simran was all the while sitting and watching with hands folded and prayer in her heart. The nerve-racking moments passed. With God on the side of the victim, defence had no courage to further cross-question the witness. He resumed his seat.

"Your honour, prosecution would like to produce another crucial piece of clinching evidence as proof of the confinement of the victim in the house of Deepak in Narela. This will prove everything beyond a shadow of doubt. It will demolish the edifice of lies, and will be the last nail in the coffin of both the accused." Gaurav took out a bus ticket from his file. Placing it before the court, he said, "Your honour, here is the DTC bus ticket purchased by my client on the night of 27th May, while escaping from the confinement of Deepak Dabas and Sandeep Yadav."

The ticket was presented to the baffled defence for perusal. "It is really surprising that the victim preserved this ticket for about six years. However, defence would like to verify the authenticity of the ticket."

"Your honour, it is just a stroke of good luck that this ticket remained with my client all these years. I will explain this. After her kidnapping by Deepak and Sandeep, she was confined for two days to the house of Deepak Dabas in Narela. Displaying amazing grit, she managed to escape from the place of confinement. She picked up a fifty rupee note lying on the bed. With this, she purchased a bus ticket from Narela to Old Delhi railway station. Since she had no purse or pocket in her shirt, she secured the ticket and the balance in a corner of her *dupatta* for the fear of losing the same. When brought to Jaipur, her benefactor purchased some new dresses, and my client kept her old dress as a token of remembrance of her last dress before escape. While discussing about the proof of kidnapping, she suddenly remembered her dress. It was will of Providence and pure good luck, that she accidentally stumbled upon this vital piece of evidence. Defence may like to verify the authenticity of the ticket as it pleases. The balance money was also recovered from the *dupatta* and is with me." Though not of any legal relevance, Gaurav showed to all, the money held in his hand.

Deepak stood in the witness box like a lifeless mass of flesh. His whole body was benumbed, and he was drained of strength to move any limb. A man who was highly emotional and would flare up and give vent to his anguish on the slightest provocation, was looking pale and dejected. He lived under a false illusion that Simran would never come back in his life to reveal the mystery of rape and kidnapping. Destiny always waits for the opportune time to punish the sinner. Howsoever hard one may try, truth always prevails and divine justice finally nails every sinner.

With complete silence of defence, Gaurav stood up, looked at the judge and resumed, "Your honour, if the defence counsel has finished, I would now like to call Mr. Sandeep Yadav."

Sandeep Yadav came to the witness box. There was very little that the prosecution wanted to ask him, as Deepak Dabas had answered all the queries. Sandeep informed the court that he was a business associate of Deepak Dabas, and had been living with him along with Daljeet Singh and Simran Kaur. Gaurav tried to play on the emotions of the timid Sandeep and asked him if he wanted to go through all the rigour again or wanted to minimise damage to his dignity. Realising that it was impossible to get out of the grip of law, Sandeep completely buckled down under pressure. Impelled by his conscience and apprehensive of profound consequences, he pleaded guilty and said, "I will tell the truth. Forced by Deepak, I raped Simran Kaur twice in the flat and once in his house. I have no role in pregnancy and abortion." He also confirmed that he did not drug Simran Kaur and had no hand in kidnapping her in connivance with Deepak. He did accompany Deepak in his car.

"Thank you, Mr. Sandeep Yadav. I will request the honourable court to consider your acceptance of truth while delivering the judgement."

With the end of the cross-examination by prosecution, the court gave full chance to defence to go through the facts, recall the documents and cross-examine the witnesses. Defence counsel wanted to gain some time to prepare his defence and wanted to cross-examine Daljeet Singh and Simran Kaur. He also requested the court to grant him permission to talk to his clients privately for about an hour.

Both Simran and Gaurav were most satisfied with the successful proceedings in the court. They were sure of the conviction of the rapists. With tears of joy, Simran looked into the glistening eyes of Gaurav and congratulated him. She could not say anything more, and all left the court.

Next day, the court proceedings started with the cross-examination of Daljeet Singh. He informed the court that after the death of his wife, his daughter was mostly looked after by his mother. As soon as he shifted to Delhi he brought her and she lived with him.

"You are deliberately bypassing the facts. The fact is that you never loved your daughter and, in fact, hated her. She was totally under the care of the elder sister of your live-in partner, whom you did not marry, and who never wanted to see Simran's face."

"My daughter was looked after by Rani, the elder sister of Suman, whom I intended to marry. Since Rani had no daughter, she loved her intensely and brought her up."

"Rani might have loved her, but the fact is that you hated her and never cared for her. Even later on also, you left her there when you moved to Dehradun." Daljeet did not say anything and defence resumed, "Coming to another point, "Was it advisable for you to bring your minor teenage daughter in the company of two young men, who had a criminal background?"

Embarrassment was discernible on the face of Daljeet. Picking up little courage, he replied, "Deepak appeared to be a changed person. We thought of starting a car repair workshop. I wanted to settle my daughter in about a year, and found Deepak to be a suitable match for her future prosperous life."

"You brought your daughter back from Jaipur not for her future, but for your future. You had no source of income and decided to sell your daughter to Deepak."

Gaurav immediately got up and retorted, "I object to that offensive and derogatory language."

"Objection sustained." The judge ordered.

"Daljeet Singh, you intended to marry your daughter to Deepak and in lieu of that, you wanted a favour from him to support you financially and give you ₹ 2 lakh for starting your workshop. The correct position is that by your plan you wanted to continue enjoying his financial luxury."

Refusing to be bogged down by the accusation of defence and emphatically rejecting the charge, he replied, "It is absolutely wrong. I never wanted any money from Deepak or from anyone else. I did want to start my business, but not at the cost of dignity and honour of my daughter. I strongly deny that fictitious charge."

"Did Deepak offer you some money?"

"Yes. He offered me ₹ 2 lakh for marriage, but I refused point-blank. I am Simran's father and was not morally so low, as to bargain for her life. Moreover, I had enough money from the sale of my property for establishing a workshop on my ancestral land in Patiala."

"What did you do when Simran vehemently declined the proposal?"

"I did not like her decision. There was heated altercation, and I was furious with her."

"Did you beat her when blood started oozing out of her mouth?"

"I did that but not with the intention of hurting her."

"Next day, when you saw her missing, why did you not pursue her search?"

"Both Deepak and Sandeep threatened me that if I reported to police, they would give evidence against me. I was terrified, for this may again land me in jail. Still, I lodged a complaint with the police, and then left their residence. I started working as a mechanic in a factory and began to live by honest means."

"Why did you not make any serious effort to locate your daughter?"

"I tried my best. One day when I went to Rani, I started

weeping. She consoled me and told me not to worry, as Simran was safe and enjoying her life. She also asked me not to probe further. I trusted her sincerity, and with her assurance, did not pursue the search further."

Daljeet's replies were as per the directions of Simran and Gaurav. Jail term had made him wiser in criminal law and he did not falter even once at any stage.

"Your honour, Daljeet Singh is primarily responsible for the ordeals of Miss Simran Kaur. The truth is that he hated her right from her birth, due to the death of his wife. Unmindful of her care, he did not take her to Dehradun also. He was a mature man, but did not realise the grave consequences of leaving the lamb amidst the wolves. His continuous stay at Guwahati, without caring for the safety of his young daughter is an ample testimony to the fact that he deliberately and willingly offered his daughter to the youthful lust of Deepak. If we look at the genesis of the whole problem, the grave tragedy of Miss Simran Kaur could have been averted if, and only if, Daljeet Singh had not fallen a prey to his ambitions of leading a comfortable life with the resources of Deepak, and had performed his sacred duty as father. In fact, he is the only person entirely responsible for the sufferings of his daughter, and not Deepak or Sandeep. It is a tragedy that selfish parents willingly sacrifice the dignity and honour of their daughters for their own greed and comforts. Daljeet Singh is at the centre of the storm for the woes of his daughter, and should be charged for his casualness and grave negligence of his young daughter. Both my clients, Deepak Dabas and Sandeep Yadav, just became sacrificial lambs. Both should be acquitted."

"Since Daljeet Singh is not named in the complaint, this court can take no cognizance against him", ordered the judge. However, in his final judgement he took a note of the fact that if parents are careful, none can dare cast his malicious eye on the child, and many cases of sexual abuse and even kidnapping can be considerably minimised.

After the cross-examination of Daljeet Singh, the defence cross-examined Simran Kaur. "Miss Simran Kaur, I would refrain from asking you any uncomfortable question considering your unblemished character and present status in the society. However, I would like to know why did you not report the incident of your rape and abduction to the police at that time, and why did you wait for such a long period?"

"Financial resources and lack of support from any quarter were the main reasons for that."

"You could have taken the help of Mr. Puri, with whom you stayed at Jaipur?"

"I was still a minor and survival was my first priority at that time. Puri uncle and Pooja aunty were very supportive, but in the face of a court case, they could have abandoned me and I would have lost my last chance of life. The only option then would have been suicide. I wanted to live. The whole situation must be perceived from the point of view of a minor girl, bereft of all financial and moral support. I also got involved in my studies."

"In your heart, you are aware of the role played by your father in your neglect, and all the resultant tragedies of your life. Why did you not make him a party in the complaint? You are an intelligent advocate and know that he is the chief villain in the tragic drama of your life. Don't you think if he had cared for you and performed his moral duty as a father, your life would have been different?"

"My father had his weak moments in his life. He was extremely frustrated after the death of my mother. At heart, he is a gentle soul and had suffered because of a concocted case conceived by a person, who deprived him of his desire to live a peaceful life with a woman whom he loved. If these developments had not taken place in his life, he would have certainly taken care of me. Blaming him is not justified from any angle."

"You are trying to save him only because he is your father."

"That is your perception."

The edifice of defence woefully crumbled. There was no scope for further examination. Both rape and kidnapping had been established beyond doubt. The proceedings virtually ended. There was a sense of satisfaction and wave of exuberance on all faces on the splendid victory of Gaurav. Simran kept on sitting alone in the courtroom for some time to let the feeling of satisfaction sink deep in her heart. One of her most cherished dreams had been fulfiled. With folded hands, she thanked God in her heart and bowed down before Him.

On the way back home, Simran was rather serious, instead of celebrating the success of the case. Looking at her, Gaurav said, "Simran, why are you in such a pensive mood? It is an occasion to celebrate our victory. I am sure the rogues would go behind bars for at least fifteen years. I will plead maximum punishment under law for rape, abortion and kidnapping. Come on, be cheerful and give me a warm, sweet smile."

"Gaurav, the achievements are certainly worth celebrating. Taking a trip down memory lane, the brutal and harsh reality is that fortune of my roller coaster life has been turning like a wheel. Happiness came in life, but kept on slipping from hands like dry sand giving way to sorrow. In life, I had more thorns and fewer roses. Fortunately, at every step when misfortune stared at me, some angel came from somewhere to my rescue, and held me in his lap without causing even a scratch to my body or soul. Laced with pain of hatred and neglect in childhood, *dadi* saved me from sliding into depression. Life was fading into oblivion, when Rani came as a goddess of love, care and protection to save my life from devastation. Abused by the beasts, I was like a cork floating in the ocean with an unpredictable current, and fate could have drifted me to any destination. I luckily fell in the lap of two noble souls, who could have discarded me and thrown me on the road. They saved my ruined adolescence from further damage, treated me as their own daughter and motivated me to study. Now you have come in my life as my greatest support. You embraced me despite my soiled past, and have promised to be my partner in life. Your determination and courage are responsible for the accomplishment of my most cherished mission of conviction of the rapists. I feel mentally relieved today." She gently placed her hand on his shoulder so as not to disturb him in his driving. With a tinge of lust in her eyes, she said, "I love you and want to give you a warm hug for all the moral and emotional support that you have given to me."

To lighten the tense emotional situation, Gaurav gave a sweet, loving and broad smile, and teasingly remarked, "Darling, let me stop the car and enjoy the warmth of your arms. I do not want to miss this opportunity, for who knows this sudden burst of romantic mood may soon wither."

Reciprocating with a similar smile and eyes radiating love, she replied with equal warmth, "It will not. Look in front, and continue driving."

Gaurav looked at her. Simran blushed and lowered her eyes. Her heart began to churn violently and lips desperately longed for a soft, loving kiss. The breathlessly captivating spectacular sight of the glorious sun meeting the horizon further added to the communion of the two loving hearts. There was none to disturb them in their trance, except the soft whisper of breeze. Soaked in the warmth of love and thoughts of passionate romance, they reached Simran's flat.

"I think I deserve a cup of coffee."

"Please come." Alone in the lift, Gaurav took advantage of

the few precious moments, hugged her tightly and planted a light sweet kiss on her warm comely quivering lips that were also longing for that loving gesture. Deeply drowned in the moment of joy and surprise, she was too shy to return the love immediately, and reserved it for some other appropriate occasion. Eyes brimming with love, both remained silent for some time to enjoy the rare moment of their life. Sweet dreams of a happy married life began to flash before their eyes.

Meanwhile, the defence counsel met both Deepak Dabas and Sandeep Yadav in jail. It was wisely decided that any further pursuance of the case would be utterly futile and the best course was to plead some leniency towards the term of sentence. The court held both guilty of rape and kidnapping of a minor girl. Deepak Dabas was sentenced to fifteen years for rape and ten for kidnapping, with both sentences to run concurrently. A little lenient view was taken in case of Sandeep Yadav, as he was persuaded by Deepak in rape and was a minor contributing partner in kidnapping. He was sentenced to seven years for rape and five for kidnapping. For him also, both the sentences had to run concurrently.

□

8

With the curtain finally drawn on rape and kidnapping judgement, Simran had to concentrate now on the second part of her determined mission to fulfil her solemn promise. The problem of getting justice for Aarushi and Suman began to haunt her day and night. However, they had to go according to the wish of their families, as it had been decided earlier that after the conviction in the rape case, Gaurav and Simran will first get married before proceeding further. The second problem had to be put on back burner, and physical and mental energies had to be transferred towards marriage preparations.

Rajeshwar Saxena had his own plans to postpone the marriage, of which none except his wife was aware of. For rejecting Simran, he had divided his plan into three parts. The first was to postpone marriage for about a month. For this, the plea was lame excuse of inability of his sister to come to India due to the health of her husband, and some business commitments. Ramesh Puri had come to India for the case and for marriage. He could not prolong his stay and suggested solemnising the engagement ceremony before his departure.

"I thought of the same. But I want the ceremony to be performed on a grand scale. After all, this is the first important function in our families. We will perform it a few days before marriage. My sister and her family will also be able to attend, as otherwise she will have to come twice." Rajeshwar cleverly turned down the suggestion of Ramesh again using his sister as the lever.

Poor Ramesh had no choice. He reluctantly agreed, though he did not appreciate the attitude of Gaurav's father. No one, not even Gaurav, suspected anything from the plausible excuse of Rajeshwar's request.

A day before Ramesh Puri's departure, all gathered at his residence to plan for the marriage date and bid farewell to him. After some time, when all were still enjoying, topic of secrets of a happy married life came up for discussion. Rajeshwar Saxena was of the opinion that trust and faith were the basis of any relation, and certainly of a happy married life. He believed that relations should be based on unconditional mutual support and selflessness. None of the partners should conceal anything from the other, as hiding facts destroyed married life. Lalita laid stress on adjustment. "Difference of opinion is becoming more predominant not only in family life, but also in society at large. Boiling point of people has become very low, and respect for other's views is dwindling. In our times, differences were certainly there, but these were amicably resolved. Ego had no place in relations. Today, minor issues lead to clash and become source of unhappiness in relations. The need is for greater tolerance. I feel ability to smooth over differences is key to a long-lasting happy life. However, adjustment is not compromise. Adjustment is a sign of wisdom, while compromise is to secure your interest, without following any principle. Adjustment should not be sacrificed at the altar of basic principles and values of life."

Expressing his opinion, Ramesh said, "I will lay stress on two key points. Firstly, trust is the solid foundation on which all relations are based, and betrayal is the enemy of love. Secondly, though difference of opinion is a part of human nature, at least one partner should maintains calm even if the other is becoming little volatile. I had the privilege of such a spouse. The moment I was angry and my wife felt that things were spinning out of control, she immediately kept mum at least at that hot moment. She invariably moved away from the spot to let the blazing situation cool down. She used to say that we have to put water to douse the fire, rather than fan it. She would express her view most calmly at the appropriate time. I give credit to peace and happiness in my life to this cardinal virtue of my wife."

Daljeet looked at Suman and said, "I feel faith is the base on which happiness of life is laid. If you love someone, be faithful and never desert her. I also feel, trust builds relations and strengthens love. Deceit ruins all relations."

Rani was a mute spectator and maintained stony silence all the time like a monk. She listened intently to the views of more intelligent participants. Suman suddenly shot, "Rani *didi's* marriage experience may be widely different."

"My married life was full of thorny relations, and I learnt everything treading on those thorns. Rural culture is different from urban one. A married rural woman has to bear the brunt of everyone in the family. Her time passes mostly in kitchen, rearing children, serving elders and in other domestic duties. Support from husband and in-laws is normally lacking. Mother-in-law considers the daughter-in-law to be her personal servant. Giving birth to girls is a stigma in rural culture, though I was spared from this accusation. Arguments, anger and minor quarrels are a part of every married life. We have conflict with people whom we love but each life-partner should stand rock-solid in support of the other in case others point a finger. Both must respect each other's priorities. Love deficit ruins married life, and a home, bereft of love is just a house of four walls. Common saying is, do not break the delicate thread of love. You can't join it, and if joined, there is always a knot. Infidelity ruined my married life. Often brutally kicked and slapped, I left the hell in search of peace. If relations begin to give pain, it is better to change course. Instead of having a negative impact, pain of life taught me love, humility, courage and determination."

There was a meditative silence all around. All looked surprisingly at Rani and wondered at her deep philosophy of life. She waited for a few moments to let her views soak deep into the heart of everyone and resumed, "I have one more point to add to this. Keep your childhood alive in you. Children get angry, argue and even temporarily stop talking, but soon forget everything, and start sharing their toys and chocolates. Ego and pride have no place in their lives. Trust, sharing and sacrifice are the basis of their friendship. So should be the married life."

"I appreciate Rani's deep understanding of life. Blessed with divine gift of wisdom, she learnt everything from the open school of life." Waiting for a moment, Ramesh continued, "I think we should compile these resounding experiences into a book, *'Tips for a Happy Married Life'*. Though well-educated and intimately known to each other for years, the discussion will further help both Simran and Gaurav in their married life. You learn from your experience after bearing pain, but learning from other's experience is painless."

With everyone having enjoyed the discussion, Ramesh said, "I think it is time to depart. I will leave tonight and shall be here a week before the decided marriage date. If you need anything from America, please let me know. I also extend my invitation to all to visit America. May God bless you all."

Gaurav and Simran were dejected at the postponement of marriage. They started concentrating on their legal practice. Simran did not want to hang her boots and planned to fight for her second most solemn aim of life. She had taken a vow to teach a lesson to Vikas Pandey, who had ruined the life of her father in a fictitious case, and also deprived him of a possible happy married life. Question of filing a case in the court against Vikas for the concocted case against Daljeet was carefully considered, but finally given up due to lack of any solid evidence.

For seeking justice for Suman and Aarushi, there were two courses open. One was to file a case in the court for sexual relations with Suman, false assurance of marriage and depriving the baby of her legal rights. Pursuing a legal battle at Delhi was not a problem, but this could drag on for years, and was finally dropped. The second was to try for an amicable mutual settlement. In their wisdom, they decided in its favour, as it would certainly save time and energy. Simran had to be very careful as the wily advocate was a difficult nut to crack. She rang up Vikas one day. Keeping her personal and professional identity purposely under wrap, she requested for a meeting to discuss a case. Vikas consented, considering Simran to be a normal client.

On the decided day and time, Simran reached the office of Vikas Pandey in Dehradun. After formal greetings, she said, "I am Simran Kaur and am practicing as an advocate at Karkardooma Court in Delhi. I have come to you for some personal work."

Vikas was simply shocked, as he did not expect that it was an advocate from Delhi, who talked to him the other day. What personal work could she have? "I don't think we have ever met before."

"No, we have never met each other. Let me give my full introduction. I am Simran Kaur, daughter of Daljeet Singh."

The introduction triggered an uneasy calm in the mind of Vikas. He was completely taken aback on hearing the name of Daljeet Singh, and apprehended some serious purpose of her visit. The whole chain of past events flashed before his eyes. Concealing any sign of nervousness, he said, "I am sorry I did not know that. What service can I do for you?"

"I have not come to discuss the past of my father. That tragic period is over and deserves to be forgotten. I will be very frank and say everything in clear words." Dropping a bombshell, she said "I have come to discuss something about Suman and her daughter."

Waiting for the reaction of Vikas, who was speechless, she hit a caustic punch. "You know Suman was your keep, if I may say so, and her daughter, Aarushi, was born out of your relations with her. I have come to seek justice for them, particularly for the innocent child."

Vikas showed some annoyance, and replied sternly with eyes filled with intense hatred and rage. "I don't remember any such relation."

"But I am here to remind you everything", came the prompt reply. "Of course, you have now deserted both but still owe legal and moral responsibility to compensate them for the past relations."

Hissing in lethal anger, the impolite and arrogant advocate lashed out wildly, "I have told you I am not concerned with them at all. She is a bloody bitch, and I don't know whose weight was she carrying?"

Simran became little more firm, and in a threatening tone said, "Your remarks for an honourable lady whose love you enjoyed for years are very derogatory, and unbecoming of a gentleman. Besides, there is a fatal flaw in your argument. You know I am also an advocate, and am aware of law and tests to establish relation between father and child." Waiting for a while to see the reaction, she said, "Remember, both Suman and Aarushi can seek compensation from you in the court."

This further aroused the wrath of Vikas, and in an

outrageously hostile and offensive pitch he shouted "Are you trying to take revenge from me on their behalf?"

"No. I am seeking justice. Do not confuse justice with revenge."

With a devilish smile and extremely aggressive body language, he shouted with all guns blazing, "Are you threatening me?"

"Only the guilty feel threatened, not the innocent."

Vikas was absolutely tongue-tied. He was simply stumped at the blunt reply of Simran. With a defiant look, Simran resumed, "I am not threatening you. I am simply warning you politely, very politely."

Clinching his jaws, Vikas was exasperated. He stood up, suddenly exploded in rage and with disapproving looks replied aggressively, "If I refuse?"

Simran was not the character to be intimidated by such threats. In an assertive tone, she replied, "Then you will be playing with fire and should get ready to fight on multiple fronts for your mulish obstinacy." She knew that she could negotiate only from a position of strength. Staring hard into his eyes, she continued, "Do not underestimate the power of my steely resolve. You cannot rattle it. As a very intelligent and experienced advocate, you know that I have come here with full preparations and will not leave empty handed. If you kick the cordial means, doors of court shall be open for them."

Waiting for the reaction of an agitated Vikas, she tried to mellow him down. "I suggest you carefully ponder over all aspects of the case. You may have to repent later on for your stubbornness and emotional decision, but then golden opportunity of amicable reconciliation would have slipped. In case of legal recourse, you will suffer on two counts. You command good prestige in the society and will not be able to tolerate social stigma and fall from grace. Your honour will be spilled in the court and on the streets of Dehradun and Delhi. Your wife and children will simply hate you and may even desert you. Again, the compensation, which may be little delayed, will be very heavy as compared to what I will suggest. Give it a cool and careful thought."

Engaging witty and more intelligent Simran in any confrontation would have been suicidal for Vikas. He slumped in his chair and virtually lost his steam. He cooled down a bit though anger was still visible on his face. "Let me know your proposal."

"That should be the spirit of a gentleman. Everything can be negotiated at a price. I will ask only that, which will be necessary for the child for her future." Without mincing words, she resumed, "I want you to buy a two-bedroom flat for her in Delhi and deposit ₹ 10 lakh for her education and upbringing. It is the barest minimum. I am not demanding anything for Suman."

Displaying an annoying emotion on his face, he shouted, "Do you think me to be a fool?"

"Certainly not. I know you are a very sensible, intelligent and reasonable person. That is why the demand is so meagre and a peanut for you." Pressing his painful nerve, she continued, "In the court, the demand and compensation will be for both, and may be tenfold, considering your assets." Waiting for the reaction of her assertion, she continued, "Vikasji, rigidity is not desirable. Rigidity today can be stupidity tomorrow. I want you to relax and think coolly. There is no hurry. You can take your time. With time, better sense will prevail. May be you did not expect all this to happen, and are so agitated."

"Let me ask you. How are you concerned with them?"

"They are related to me. Suman is now wife of my father and Aarushi, in relation, naturally becomes my sister. Besides, I am a social activist and fight for the cause of women and poor girls. I run an NGO for the welfare of women."

In a humiliating gesture, he ruthlessly replied, "Don't try to scare me with this background. I care a fig for such wretched organisations, that are formed simply to mint money from business houses and usurp government grants."

"That is your presumption borne out of ignorance and prejudice. You will realise the might of a powerful honest body, once you confront it. In future, you may hear more about *'Pooja Rani Nari Shakti Trust'*. Better remember this name."

Vikas Pandey reflected for a little while. Simran kept on looking at him, knowing full well that her plan was working in the right direction. She was waiting for him to move his piece on the chess board. Suddenly, Vikas threw a surprise. "I suggest a better solution. I am prepared to take the custody of the girl and shall give some compensation to Suman. I am sure you will have no objection."

Simran was not prepared for such an eventuality. Her basic strategy was to play to her strength, and not fall to the strength of Vikas. She knew that Vikas was trying to spin a yarn, and his ruse smacked of some treacherous design. Witty as she was, she wanted to nip the evil in the bud and defeat Vikas by solid reasoning. She immediately shot back. "I am sorry your absurd suggestion is ostensibly meaningless, lacks prudence and sound judgement. Let us consider it from both legal and social angles. Legally, Suman is not your wife and you cannot take the custody of the child. She is now the child of legally wedded Daljeet and Suman. Socially, you will naturally not reveal all facts to your wife and children. Fear of fall of grace will compel you to keep her away from your family. Your suggestion smells of some vicious plan to dump the child in trash. I am not prepared to ruin her childhood and deprive her of the deserved love of parents. I do not accept your proposal from any angle. This is absolutely ruled out. The only solution is what I have told you. I give you one week to ponder over my proposal and give me your final decision."

Vikas was speechless at the soundness of Simran's arguments. He was no match for her intelligence and legal knowledge. He knew that he was badly trapped. Amicably getting out of this unexpected maze was more advisable. When weak, wisdom is in compromise. He virtually decided to surrender. "Can the proposal be diluted?"

Sensing the success of her mission, Simran resumed with confidence, "Once you ponder over the seriousness of the problem, I am sure you will realise that the demand is nothing. It is the barest minimum, and in this meagre compensation, there cannot be any deviation. Not even a paisa. You accept or reject in totality."

On a tight leash, Vikas had no option but to gracefully yield. To save his face, he said, "Give me some time to think and I will come back to you."

"That is a very sensible decision. Think it as a good and noble human cause, and as father of a child. It will be an admirable gesture. Money you can earn, but prestige that you lose will never return. It is said, you don't die with loss of life; you die with loss of character. Your conscience will always prick you for doing injustice to an innocent child, who is a product of your love and has come in this world due no fault of her own. Let her not be a child of sin. Let her not be a slumdog and wallow in its marsh. Don't let this golden opportunity slip out of your hands. I leave the decision to you." After a little pause and seeing an appreciable change on the face of Vikas, she said, "I will wait for your call. Best of luck and God bless you all."

Besides creating a fear of law and social degradation in the mind of Vikas, Simran had also tried to stir his conscience. After the whole discussion and the reaction of Vikas towards the end, she was sure that her mission was almost accomplished. Back home, all details were discussed with Gaurav. The ball was now in the court of Vikas, and there was no option but to wait. Simran did not think it proper to talk to her father or Suman at this stage when the issue was still half-baked.

Vikas was extremely restless at night, and could not have a wink of sleep due to the inner turmoil. The choice was hard but had to be made. Locked in a no-win situation, he knew that in business, you can't get what you desire; you get what you negotiate. Oscillating like a pendulum between rupee and respect, wisdom dawned and he decided to let go the former. Next morning, as both Simran and Gaurav were getting ready to leave for the court, the phone bell rang. It was a call from Vikas. With prayer in her heart and fingers crossed, Simran picked up the call.

"Simranji, I thought over the whole issue carefully from all angles, and particularly, from the point of view of the child. I have decided to go with your plan." Simran folded her hands, and silently thanked God for the accomplishment of her mission.

"That is very nice of you Vikasji. Please tell me how would you like to proceed?"

"Since the issue is settled in principle, delay would be futile. You may look for a two-bedroom flat in a society in Delhi. I am sure you will keep my interest in mind. As soon as you have decided, I will come, sign all papers for the purchase of the flat in my daughter's name and also transfer ₹ 10 lakh as fixed deposit in her name."

"Vikasji, we are professional colleagues. Rest assured, I will certainly keep your interest first and foremost in my mind. Why should I deceive you when my purpose has been amicably achieved? Since you are so magnanimous, and have reposed so much confidence in me, I will value your sincerity and will not dent your trust."

All legal formalities were completed and Vikas prepared all documents to his satisfaction, so that Suman or anyone else may never raise any claim at any later stage. The whole deal remained a secret between Simran and Vikas.

Gaurav complimented Simran on her success. "By God's grace, both your missions have been accomplished. And now, turn of my only and most cherished desire, the marriage."

Simran blushed. Her rosy cheeks were radiating love. Waiting for a while, she said, "God has been so kind. I pray for the day when we will be one body besides one soul." Waiting for a while, she heaved a deep sigh and resumed with some seriousness on her face, "Gaurav, sometimes, my heart sinks due to some unknown fear. Marriage is getting unduly delayed."

Hugging her tightly in his arms and looking lovingly into her eyes, Gaurav said, "Honey, your fear is unfounded. Get rid of it. God will soon fulfil our wish." Both got locked in the dreams of their happy future life.

In the evening, Gaurav and Simran went to Daljeet's house along with Rani. Simran immediately picked up Aarushi in her lap. Merrily flaunting her new dress, she said, "*Didi*, look at my dress. Papa brought it for me."

Planting a sweet kiss on her comely cheeks, Simran said, "You are looking so beautiful in this dress and with your ponytail of long curly tresses." Waiting for a few moments, she sprang a surprise. "Aarushi, you do not know how lucky you are? You are a rich girl today."

Everyone was astonished, including Rani, to whom also the secret had not been revealed. None could have dreamt in their wildest dream, the news that Simran was going to break. "Simran, what has happened? Please tell us," asked the anxious Suman.

"Guess?" I will give you three choices."

Suman, Daljeet and Rani all started thinking, but none could hit the nail. Quizzically looking at each other, Daljeet said, "Simmi, please unveil the puzzle. We concede defeat."

"Papa, I have achieved the second greatest wish of my life. I will not keep you all guessing as your hearts must be beating fast. Vikas Pandey has given a two-bedroom flat and ₹ 10 lakh to Aarushi."

All were surprised and looked at each other. Normally calm and composed, Daljeet could not curb his aggression, suddenly lost his temper and shouted furiously, "I don't want my daughter to live on the bounty of that scoundrel. She is *my* daughter and it is *my* duty to look after her. I do not want to see his face, not to talk of taking even a penny from him."

The whole atmosphere suddenly turned serious. Everyone was shocked at his outburst. Little Aarushi was terrified and clung to her *didi*. Suman was bewildered, but maintained a neutral facial expression and did not say anything.

"Papa, I can understand your sentiments and the hatred that you carry against him for having ruined the best period of your life. But please calm down. I have strong reasons for what I have done."

Supporting Simran, Gaurav said, "Papa, your anger and sharp reaction are justified. He deserves all the curses of heaven for all the sins that he has committed against us. It is a stark reality and naked truth that he criminally concocted a case against you, but it was not possible to do anything now for all the damage done to you. Substantial evidence against him is lacking, and there is no proof of his role in your sentence. An appeal against the judgement could only be made within permissible time limit. He could only be punished for his crime against mama. Here also the only thing would have been financial compensation, nothing else. This would have taken a few years. What Simran has achieved without any legal hassle, must be appreciated. Let me tell you. Long back, she had taken a vow to avenge her rape and kidnapping, and get justice for mama and Aarushi. Please get to the bottom of the problem, and ponder over the issue from this angle."

Rani normally maintained silence in such heated arguments, but she was also strongly convinced of the action of Simran. Supporting her whole-heartedly, she said, "Daljeet, your anger is justified and concern for Aarushi is commendable. Do not be emotionally swayed. Simran's intention is not to humiliate you. What Simran and Gaurav have done was the only punishment that could be awarded to Vikas for the crime committed against us. Do you want him to go absolutely scot free and move in the society with a clean slate?"

Gaurav's convincing explanation and Rani's healing balm softened Daljeet. He became calm and looked at his daughter. "I certainly appreciate Simran's concern for Aarushi, and all that she has done for us. In fact, I shall always be indebted to her. I cannot repay her debt in seven lives. She has given me everything, though I did not deserve anything. For hatred, she gave love not only to me, but also to Suman and Aarushi, with whom she had no relations."

With tears shimmering in her eyes, Simran came closer to her father, hugged him and said, "Papa, please do not say all this. I did nothing. It was my sacred duty as a daughter. My relations with mama and Aarushi may not be of blood, but I love both of them from the core of my heart and shall always love them in life. What was my relation with Rani *maa* and Pooja aunty? They came in my life as angels. I have learnt all this from them. Blood may create relations, but it is the heart that determines and cements them. My intention has never been to disgrace you. That is the last thing I would do to you or to anyone. I wanted to seek justice for the innocent child. I know you will provide her everything in life, but it was essential to make Vikas Pandey realise his sin and pay for that. He will think ten times before repeating it again. I would have done it for any other girl in place of Aarushi. I am determined in life to empower women, inspire them to fight for their cause and help children discarded by parents and society, wherever they may be. I have the strength and determination of Gaurav, who is the backbone of all my efforts and achievements. Please accept our endeavour with love and humility, and not with any sense of shame. I wish I could take revenge for his crime against you. Legally, it was impossible now."

Daljeet could not bear all this. He wiped her tears and said, "Simmi, my child, I am sorry for all that I said in anger. There was nothing against you or Gaurav. You are my greatest support at this age. But for you both, I would have been in dust. I know I could have been easily convicted along with Deepak and Sandeep, but you did not cause even a scratch to me. You covered all my mistakes. I am here with my family only because of your magnanimity. I apologise for my sudden and violent emotional outburst. Please pardon me."

A wave of jubilation returned on all faces. To break the seriousness of the atmosphere, Rani said, "Now forget the past. Everything has been done with pure and noble intentions. Let us enjoy this moment of happiness. I have brought sweets. Suman will prepare some tea. Look, how happy is Aarushi with her chocolates. She will appreciate the benevolence of her *didi* much later in life. Let us celebrate this as day for justice and empowerment of children, particularly the girls."

Bringing a piece of chocolate closer to the mouth of her father, Aarushi said, "Papa, why are you so angry with *didi*? She is never angry with you. She loves me so much. She is so nice." Daljeet kissed her affectionately. She ran to her *didi* and offered her a chocolate. Simran immediately hugged her. "I love you, my Aashu."

With her ponytail bobbing in excitement, she said, "I love you too."

"Who has taught you all this?"

"Mama says this to papa."

Aarushi's innocent remarks sent all into peals of laughter. Embarrassed, Suman felt shy and covered her face with her hands. Teasing Daljeet and infusing some humour, Rani said, "Daljeet, be careful now. Someone spies on your activities."

"Mama says this to me also when I say, 'I love you, mama.'" Aarushi rescued Suman from the embarrassment.

"Who loves you more, mama or papa?" asked Simran.

"Without waiting even for a fraction of a second, Aarushi pointed her finger to Daljeet. Looking at Suman, she resumed, "Of course, mama also loves me. But she is sometimes sad. Papa always tells her to be cheerful. He also brings books and reads good stories to me."

In that fun-filled atmosphere, Aarushi suddenly came to Simran, placed her tiny hands around her ears and whispered something. There was broad smile on the face of Simran and her eyes were brimming with joy. She carefully looked at Suman. Rani asked, "What secret is being shared between the two sisters?" Aarushi placed her finger on her lips suggesting Simran not to say anything.

"This is top secret. It will be known to everyone after five or six months. Till then, all must wait."

All were astonished. Rani shouted, "What a surprise? We did not know. Congratulations, Suman and Daljeet." Suman blushed, got up and went inside the kitchen. Simran tightly hugged Aarushi. "Thank you, Aashu. You have given me the happiest news of my life."

Turning to Aarushi, Rani said, "Aashu, do you know your Simran *didi* is getting married?"

Aarushi ran to Simran, clung to her and said, "*Didi*, I will dance in your marriage. Will you also dance with me?"

"Of course, I will also dance with you. All of us will dance with you." Lifting her in her lap, she resumed, "I will buy a *lehenga* for you. You will also be in full bridal dress."

Aarushi put her tiny hands around the neck of Simran and said, "I love you *didi*." Simran kissed her.

There was a wave of happiness and merriment all around. In those moments of intense joy, seriousness occasionally returned to the face of Simran. Some future fear had started agitating her mind. But by no stretch of imagination, she could even dream of the nefarious plan of crafty Rajeshwar Saxena, who was determined to dump in dust the innocent Simran.

□

9

Chain of tragedies in the life of Simran that started with her birth had occasional respite, but began to show their ugly face again. Short interludes of joy and happiness appeared intermittently, only to wither away soon. Gaurav had promised to tie the nuptial knot and was her dream-boy for a happy and prosperous married life. This dream was also finally shattered. Love and trust could not survive before the lure of gold. One betrayed trust, and destiny changed the course of lives of both. A luxurious but unhappy broken married life for a short period came to the lot of one and mistrust completely changed the course of life of the other, shattering forever her long-cherished aspiration of marital bliss.

Having successfully executed the first part of his treacherous plan, it was time for Rajeshwar Saxena to initiate the second part, sending Gaurav to America. Shrewd as he was, he carefully tried to hide his disgraceful plot up his sleeves. Believing in the sincerity of his father, innocent Gaurav could never understand the sinister motive of his despicable design. His mother also maintained a very optimistic look throughout. About a month after the departure of Ramesh Puri, Rajeshwar tried to exploit the emotions of Gaurav.

"Gaurav, you know as elder brother, I had always been very close to Rakhi. On his deathbed, my father had given her responsibility to me. Her husband is not keeping good health now and there is none to look after her and the family. She is crying all the time, and I want you to go to America to console her as I cannot take leave at this stage. The marriage may have to be postponed further by about a fortnight."

Rajeshwar was very clever and knew that shock in small doses was less painful, and periods of delay should be short to retain trust. He wanted Simran to get finally disgusted with the passage of time. He told Gaurav, "I have already informed Ramesh Puri about the changed programme, giving detailed reasons for the same. You may now talk to Simran and explain everything to her. By nature, she is so adjusting, so cooperative. I am sure, she will not mind, as she is now a part of our family."

"When have I to leave and what about my visa formalities?"

"Rakhi has made all preparations and has sent the documents to me along with your ticket. You will have to leave after four days."

Gaurav did not like the way his father had tried to hide everything from him, and annoyingly said, "Dad, it would have been better if you had told me earlier. I would have kept Simran posted with all the details. She is quite broad-minded but this smells lack of trust, when we have such close relations and are soon going to be husband and wife." Posing a very gloomy and dejected look, Rajeshwar Saxena did not say anything, but was inwardly happy that his secret plan had worked perfectly well so far.

Gaurav was highly apologetic and explained everything to Simran. She had full faith in his sincerity, but was not happy at the cold behaviour of his father, who was keeping his son also in the dark. Occasionally, negative thoughts began to haunt her, and some inner sense predicted a distressed future. Gaurav departed, and with him departed forever the peace and happiness of her life.

Rajeshwar Saxena was satisfied at the successful execution of the second part of his perfidious plan. The third and final part was to block Gaurav's return, and ensure his permanent stay in America. This was the most difficult part and he had no immediate solution for the same. About a week after Gaurav's departure, he rang up Ramesh Puri and requested him for further postponement of marriage, as Gaurav had to prolong his stay due to serious decline in the health of his brother-in-law.

The course of destiny is preordained and is unpredictable. Sometimes, it favours the devil, and dumps the pious. Fortune further favoured the plan of wily Rajeshwar, and Simran again became destiny's victim. Unfortunately for her and fortunately for Rajeshwar, Rakhi's husband did not survive. Both Rajeshwar and Lalita left for America without informing Simran. Two days after the demise, Rajeshwar rang up Ramesh Puri.

"Rameshji, I have to convey very sad news to you. Unfortunately, my brother-in-law died two days back, and we have come to America. As elder brother, I had promised to take full responsibility of his family in case of any unforeseen eventuality. We will stay here for about a month. I cannot take long leave due to service exigencies, and Gaurav may have to stay here little longer due to business and settlement of the family. I have told Gaurav to talk to Simran."

"It is really very sad. Man has no option but to bow before the will of God and bear the unbearable." Ramesh could not say anything more, as it was not the proper occasion to touch the subject of marriage.

Rajeshwar was inwardly happy that luck had favoured him in the automatic execution of the last and most difficult part of his plan. He told Gaurav to talk to Simran and explain the change in decision due to this sudden and unfortunate development. Gaurav was deeply saddened, but was helpless. He was confident that Simran would understand and realise the gravity of the problem, and cooperate with him in the time of their grief.

"Simran, you will be distressed to know that my uncle expired two days back. Mom and dad have come here and will stay here for about a month."

"Oh! It is so sad. I always prayed for his early recovery, but we are helpless before the will of God. We have no option, but to bear the tragic loss. May his soul rest in peace. Please convey my heart-felt condolences to all. I will talk to mom and dad. Tell me, if I can do anything at this moment of your family tragedy?"

"Thank you very much for all those words of sympathy. I cannot say more and shall talk to you later."

Helpless Simran had no choice but to wait for the return of Gaurav. Equally distressed, Gaurav had no intention to stay there any longer, and was in constant touch with his love. Long daily calls were the only consolation for both. He was getting restless to return to India and tie the knot with his soul-mate. The only person happy at the turn of the events was Rajeshwar Saxena, whose intention of separating Gaurav from Simran and creating a wedge between the two had worked perfectly well so far. Meanwhile, Rakhi was constantly pleading with her brother to let Gaurav stay in America and look after the business as single-handedly, she was unable to manage the vast empire.

To ensure Gaurav's permanent stay in America, Rajeshwar tried to emotionally blackmail his timid and obedient son. "Gaurav, the tragic developments have completely devastated the life of Rakhi and peace and stability of her small and happy family. In this hour of her need, I cannot desert her, and it is my moral and social responsibility to support her. So close to my retirement, I am not in a position to resign or take long leave. My only hope is pinned on you."

"Dad, I understand the situation but cannot stay here any longer. Like you, I have also my social and moral commitments in India."

The shrewd Rajeshwar feigned a depressing look and managed some fake tears in his eyes. "Circumstances have changed, and with them our decisions have also to change. Nobody had any idea of the death of Rakhi's husband."

"Dad, I have a suggestion. I may go back and come with Simran, after our marriage."

"I had discussed this proposal with Rakhi. It has legal complications. You are not a citizen of America and don't have even Green Card. Visa cannot be arranged for Simran. Option of bringing her at this stage is not possible."

"Can't aunty get her daughter married, whose husband may then look after the family and the business?" asked an annoyed Gaurav.

Rajeshwar was shocked at his son's convincing solution. Not able to think of a suitable reply, he said, "Arranging her marriage will take some time."

"Another viable proposition is that our marriage may be performed and Simran may stay in India, till aunty finds a suitable match for her daughter. In between, she can come here on tourist visa."

"I don't want to perform your marriage in a haste", said the irritated Rajeshwar.

"And in your delay, our happiness may be crucified?" retorted the infuriated Gaurav. Maintaining little calm, he resumed, "Dad, option of voluntary retirement is available. Why don't you avail that? This will not affect your pension, and your presence here will be of greater satisfaction to aunty also."

Rajeshwar was getting restless at the strong arguments of his intelligent son. With eyes blazing anger, he replied, "I have deeply thought of all possibilities. The only option is your further stay here to look after the business."

Poor Gaurav was helpless and asserted in frustration, "May be, but I cannot betray and desert Simran."

"And you can betray your parents, who have done so much for you in life?" said the agitated Rajeshwar. Exploiting his emotions further and creating a sense of greed in him, Rajeshwar calmed down and played his last card. "Gaurav, compare the standard of life in India and America. Prospects here are certainly brighter, and you will not be able to get in lifetime what you are getting here from day one. I love Simran and have nothing against her, but my main concern is your life." Without pointing to the family background and socially tarnished life of Simran, he simply said, "A bunch of personal values cannot earn even two simple meals, not to talk of comforts and pleasures available here. Remember, relations are like a ladder. You can go to the top with the help of your aunt. Look after her and in course of time, her whole business shall be in your grip, besides the business of the girl that she has chosen for you. It takes years to establish a business, that has fallen in your lap without any effort."

Joining her husband, Lalita pleaded, "Gaurav, consider all that your dad has said. We do not demand anything in return, for what we have done for you. It was our duty as parents. Your dad is more concerned about your future. You have seen Leena. She is so smart and beautiful. She is the only child of her parents, and her father is a big businessman. He commands great respect among the Indian community. Moreover, she also loves you and is ready to tie the knot. Destiny has opened the doors of a gold mine, and prosperity awaits you with open arms. Fortune knocks only once at your door and if not opened, leaves, never to come back again. Do not kick this golden opportunity. For our sake, and for your glorious future, settle down here. In course of time, we will also come here and join you."

Shedding some crocodile tears, Lalita tried to exploit the emotions of her son. Holding his hand, she pleaded further, "Gaurav, we cannot desert Rakhi and her young daughter at this stage. It is our moral duty to help her. Children also owe some responsibility towards their parents. If you do not stand by us at this time of our need and her distress, all of us will be ruined, and you may have to repent whole life. Our desire is to see you happily settled, before we close our eyes. If you don't need us, and want to desert us at the cost of someone else, throw us in the well or give us poison before you leave." Weeping and sobbing she left, leaving Gaurav to take a difficult decision of his life. He did not want to betray Simran and at the same time, could not run away from his moral responsibility towards his parents. Daily arguments, persuasions, wailings and tears finally won the race. Leena's charms, advances and enchanting life-comforts of the fairyland further mesmerised him. The emotionally weak Gaurav also yielded to the daily pressure of his aunt, and finally decided to stay.

When destiny deserts, everyone leaves. Solemn promises got crushed under the weight of gold. Treachery won against trust and glorious dreams of a poor noble soul were completely demolished. Distance further weakened the intensity of love and sincerity. Shadows of despair began to lengthen in the life of Simran. Every day, long calls became less frequent and finally almost ceased. She was intelligent enough to feel the change in Gaurav's behaviour.

Though no celebrations are normally held during the period of bereavement, Rajeshwar bypassed all social and religious compulsions, and decided to immediately perform Gaurav's marriage, to fully and finally seal his separation from Simran.

One evening, Ramesh Puri rang up Simran. "Simran, is Gaurav talking to you these days?"

"Very rarely. Whenever I call him, he says that he is busy and would talk to me later. Fed up with his indifferent, irritating behaviour and negative replies, I have also not called him for the last few days."

With tears in his eyes and voice fully choked, Ramesh said in hardly audible voice, "Simran, I want to tell you something, but promise that you will not weep and cry."

"Has Gaurav married?"

Simran's sudden reply left him stunned. "How do you know?"

"Your quivering voice and the word 'promise' were sufficient for my guess."

Ramesh Puri was completely speechless. With great difficulty, he gathered some strength and said, "Simran, Rajeshwar rang me up yesterday morning. He started saying that he had promised his sister's husband to look after his family, and to marry Gaurav to one of his nieces. To fulfil his last dying wish, they had arranged Gaurav's marriage, which was being solemnised in the evening. Look at the shameless fellow? He invited me for the marriage. Showing some fake and outward sympathy, he wished a bright future for you. In the whole conversation, there was not a word of apology for Gaurav's inability to marry you."

Maintaining her calm and controlling her emotions, Simran said softly "Uncle, life is a maze of twists and turns. With the passage of time, Gaurav's attitude on phone had started becoming cold. His words lacked the earlier warmth of love. He stopped mentioning about marriage and his return. Suspicion of change in his decision grew stronger in my mind. For sometime past, the contact had virtually ceased. His silence was a clear indication of some incoming storm. I also got disgusted with his untrustworthy behaviour and decided to snap all connections and relations with him. If relations begin to hurt, it is better to change course."

"Simran, I have a gut feeling that they had decided it much earlier. Their attitude towards marriage had been lukewarm. I had noticed this in our last meeting, when Rajeshwar requested for the postponement of marriage. In our simplicity and blind faith, we failed to judge their deceptive move. They have stabbed us at the back. In fact, life never teaches us straight. We learn through contrasts and contradictions. I feel Rajeshwar was against this marriage right from the very beginning. Had they been sincere, they could have at least solemnised the engagement ceremony before Gaurav's departure? On that day, I suspected coldness in his eyes but had faith in Gaurav's promise, whose eyes always reflected trust. Shrewd Rajeshwar very cleverly gained time in small doses to keep the hope alive in us. He might have hidden his evil intentions even from his son, but I blame Gaurav for having not taken a firm stand, as he had promised." With voice choked and eyes full of tears, he resumed after gaining some strength, "Simran, nothing has hurt me more in life than this betrayal of trust. I had always dreamt of a happily settled married life for you. I am devastated and all my aspirations are totally shattered." Taking a deep breath, he said, "Anyway, it is better to forget all this as a bad dream and move forward. More we think, more is the pain. In distress, we must maintain our calm. Let us gracefully accept His command with folded hands. Life must go on."

"Rani *maa* had exactly identical views about Rajeshwar uncle's cold behaviour. She had also started doubting the sincerity of Gaurav immediately after his departure. I remember, she said one day in a very lighter tone, 'Simmi, as mother, I should not say but try to hunt for some boyfriend in your profession. You may need one.' I did not understand her far-sightedness, and just brushed it aside as a light-hearted joke. Perhaps she had anticipated that Gaurav may not come back. I wonder at her deep understanding of human mind." Heaving a sigh, she continued, "Uncle, you know I had never forced myself on Gaurav. A straight denial would have been less painful and the intimate friendship would have also continued. Gaurav may not have a direct role in this drama, but the way his parents have behaved, is simply distressing and unacceptable. Earlier also, I had a feeling that Gaurav was mentally a weak person, and was not strong enough to oppose his father even on justified issues. They did not realise that they can break my bone, not my spirit. However, as you said, it is better to forget all this as a bad dream and move ahead. Tough times never stay. Life must continue."

Ramesh Puri wanted to be with Simran at this moment of her distress to console her, and to relieve her of her intense agony. Changing the topic he said, "Simran, I am planning to come to India, and shall let you know about my programme."

"That is very nice of you, uncle. Please come. I am feeling so lonely and need your presence. Rani *maa* is also not keeping good health and wants to meet you."

Love is a string of pleasant and unpleasant experiences. The clouds of uncertainty, if any, finally withered away with the confirmation of Ramesh. The fate of the once-promised trust of lifelong relations was permanently sealed. Once a love-mate, Gaurav betrayed her and finally deserted her for the glitter of gold and charms of a foreign land.

During her talk with Ramesh uncle, Simran tried to be normal, but inwardly, she was grievously hurt and sadly devastated. She did not want to reveal the pain of her heart to him in his old age. Plunged in grief, she dropped dead on the bed. Her eyes were dissolved in tears, and she violently cried the whole night. Events of the past began to flash before her eyes. Life had been spaced with hope and despair, joy and sorrow, and pleasure and pain. With the arrival of Gaurav in her life, she began to dream of a glorious future and a settled life of love and happiness. His sincerity during the court case further strengthened her trust in him. She thought that all her woes had finally come to an end. But the invisible hand of destiny, treachery of Rajeshwar Saxena and weak trust of Gaurav crushed all aspirations of innocent Simran. Her noble thoughts and deeds could not change her fate.

Simran had often dreamt of being a bride waiting for her love to come, and lift her long-drawn veil on the first night of marriage. Hands clutched around her knees, she would say, "Before you lift the veil, it is customary to give a gift to your newly wedded wife."

"But I have not brought anything. I promise I will certainly bring it tomorrow."

"Then you have no right to touch me tonight. You can lift my veil tomorrow, when you bring the gift."

"But wait of even a second is a killing torture. How can I wait for a day?"

"The fruit of patience is always sweeter."

"Let this moment stop for me to enjoy the enchanting sight. I am observing this captivating beauty for the first time in life. I did not know that my baby doll is so beautiful, so charming, so enticing. My patience is getting exhausted. I can't wait."

"I am the same Simran. The perception of the beholder has only changed."

"Behold beauty with the eye of the beholder. Everything may be same but the moment is different."

Itching to cling to her soul-mate and enjoy the unique once-in-life moment, she would say, "If not a gift, I want one promise from you on this solemn night."

"Tell me darling. My whole life is at your feet."

"Henceforth, I want to be legally and socially known as Simran Gaurav. 'Gaurav', the pride of Simran."

Surprised at her unusual request, Gaurav would say, "In that case, you have also to give me one promise."

"It is granted before you say."

"I want Time. All your time in life should be for me and me alone."

"This moment, the next, and the next till eternity shall be for you." With souls already merged into one, the two bodies would then also fuse and become one.

Pious aspirations of marriage just remained hollow dreams. Though not very keen for marriage, Gaurav had ignited the pleasures of marriage. His unexpected betrayal was the brutal blow that smashed all her glorious dreams. She was distressed at the cruelty of her tragic life. Happiness came in life in small measures, only to wither and leave her dejected. In life, people came, some gave unbearable pain, some intense love, but all departed one by one, leaving her lonely once again. Ramesh uncle had to leave to be with his children and grandchildren. Rani *maa* was her only consolation, as she had been the whole life. Unable to bear the shock of Gaurav's betrayal and Simran's devastation, she also suddenly left, leaving her weeping and crying to bear all sorrows. Loneliness was her sole companion again. Ramesh Puri came to India to be with her for some time in the hour of her grief.

"Simran, I know you are totally devastated because of Gaurav and his parents. Rani's sudden death has further blown you apart. But remember, you have passed through turbulent times and have faced such ordeals many times in your life. You are a mountain of strength, and with your maturity can courageously bear all that has happened. Do not hold on to distress and never be disheartened."

"Uncle, throughout my life, someone or the other has been there by my side as my support. I am strong enough to bear all problems, but unfortunately, I am now alone. Rani *maa*'s love and your strength are no more with me."

"Plants that grow under the shade of a banyan tree do not get their share of air and sunshine. You have to now get out of that shade to enjoy the sunshine. Chart your own course of life. You are strong and mature, and don't need any support or protection now."

"I am at the crossroads of life's pathway, from where I am unable to choose a direction."

"Simran, remember the will of Pooja. You might have not fully comprehended her words at that moment, but they were the essence of wisdom. You have to differentiate between right and wrong. Choose the right and follow the same. If at any time, the courage is shaken, follow the call of your conscience. You will never fail to get the right direction."

"Uncle, this is where one needs presence and guidance of elders."

"Age-related problems like difficulty in hearing and failing eyesight have crept in my life. I am struggling to live with these deficiencies, and may not be able to come here again." Waiting for a moment, he resumed, "What have you decided about your future? I mean about your marriage?"

"Uncle, every cloud has a silver lining. Gaurav's trust aroused the aspirations, that have been crucified by his mistrust. Instead of moaning over the loss, I want to explore gain in his deceit. I want to devote my life for the service of people, particularly women in distress. Life gives us so much, let us give something in return. Everyone lives for self; I shall live for others. People seek solace in maximising pleasures for self; I want to explore happiness in minimising misery of others. I want to be the voice of the voiceless, defence of the defenceless. Life is too small; I want to make it great. So far as marriage is concerned, it has never been a priority in my life. I shall not marry in life. I have carefully considered all aspects of my life and have come to this final decision after long self-deliberation. As my guardian, you may have different opinion, but on the issue of marriage, my decision is rock firm and shall not change."

"Simran, Pooja would have discussed more freely with you to convince you, but I also request you to reconsider your decision. You are broken at this moment, and have lost all faith in man and marriage. Daljeet and his family have already settled in Patiala, and loneliness will always be frustrating. You have a long life before you."

"Life has to be great and purposeful. Depth and not length should be its aim. I want to lead a fulfilling and meaningful life. Uncle, alone doesn't always mean sad, just as relationship doesn't always mean happy. Moreover, I am not alone and shall never be alone. I have a very large and ever-expanding family. I believe in *Vasudhaiva Kutumbakam.* The whole world is my family."

"It is difficult to beat you in arguments. I still hold that marriage may be essential for peaceful settlement in life." Drowned in some serious thought, Ramesh resumed, "Simran, if you don't want to marry, you come to America. This way, my worry of your loneliness here will also be solved, and you will live happily in a family."

"Uncle, I want to live and die in the land of my birth. You have done so much for me and I feel ashamed of disappointing you. Please do not feel bad, but I cannot desert my land and my people. My cherished mission is to serve them."

"Simran, this is your life and you have a right to live the way you want. But I must say, don't be rigid in your decisions. Resort to flexibility, as it opens a plethora of chances. Obstinacy is stagnation. Plant that can bend, survives the flurry of the tempest. If you hold on tightly to one view, mind shrinks. Fluidity of perception is essential, and even truth is relative and amenable to change. Life is in a constant state of flux. Change, if tomorrow the circumstances change."

"Uncle, I am grateful to you for all those words of wisdom. I will always keep them in mind. If there is a change, you will be the first to be informed."

"Simran, I always advised you to forget the past and move forward, but howsoever hard I may try, I myself cannot get rid of Gaurav's betrayal. He has not proved to be trustworthy, though he posed to be very sincere." Ramesh became little serious and said, "Simran, I do not wish, but some inner sense in me predicts that Gaurav may not enjoy a happy married life by betraying a girl of your qualities."

"Uncle, everyone enjoys or suffers as per his destiny. I wish the best for everyone, and will not blame anyone for my misfortunes. Everyone has the right to take decisions and choose the path of his life. His promises collapsed under the weight of circumstances, and his greed for wealth. Instead of being honest, he deceived me and kept the hope alive. I only wish he had trusted me and told me his decision. I would have gladly accepted the same. Such relations exist only on tongue and are not etched on heart. His betrayal and broken trust have certainly hurt me. The wise say, carry the burden of your life yourself; others carry only your dead body. I will follow my mission single-handedly. Gaurav is also a closed chapter, and with this has closed my life's decision on marriage."

"How do you want to pursue your life now?"

"Uncle, life is a ship without an anchor. It is ever moving. My views, mission and direction of life are crystal clear. Purpose of life defines our goals. It is not chosen by others; we choose it. I shall fight for the identity of distressed and deprived women. My passion is service of humanity with empathy and affection. I shall trade time, the most precious commodity that God has given us free, for the cause of the destitute, particularly the girls. I will invest my life in their cause, take up their cases, and fight for their justice and restoration. I want to create a revolution for the rehabilitation of women, devastated due to rape and other criminal offences. Name, fame, glory and wealth have no place in my life. I have no lust for money, and shall spend all my earnings for this cause." Reflecting for a moment, she resumed, "Uncle, recollect what aunty said when I came here? Her words still echo in my ears. 'Always think you are born for a mission.' Let me fulfil her dream. So far as my personal life is concerned, I will lead a life of complete austerity. Luxuries shall not be a part of my life. I want my mind to be still and focused within."

"I appreciate your sentiments and single-minded devotion to your noble cause. I know you are a girl of strong determination, and will have no peace unless you follow your mission. For success, one needs passion, which you possess. I fully endorse your views and would always be a source of strength for the fulfilment of your noble cause."

"Uncle, your words have further fortified my determination. Please do not worry about me. Look after your health, and enjoy your life with your grandchildren."

"Simran, some time back you asked me about my flat in Delhi. I discussed it with Rohit and Dolly. All of us have decided to donate it for your sacred mission, as Pooja's contribution to the Trust. I will sign all documents before my departure." Pooja's memory brought tears in Simran's eyes, and she buried her head in the lap of her uncle.

Ramesh Puri stayed with Simran for over a fortnight to restore her shaken confidence. Though not related, her happiness always meant a lot to him and Pooja. Both lived in her joy, and suffered in her sorrow. With Gaurav coming in her life, they were certain of her happy married life. Unfortunately, Gaurav betrayed her. Ramesh always felt that Gaurav should have not been emotionally so weak and should have shown some moral courage to convince his parents, rather than meekly succumb to their pressure. Perhaps, he was also blinded by the dazzling lights of America and was enchanted by its charms. Simran became a victim of his avarice and betrayal. It was, however, futile to blame anyone, for when destiny defies, all doors close. If dreams of all could turn into reality, crown would be on every head.

Normalcy slowly returned to the life of Simran. She renounced all luxuries and adopted a life of simplicity. She believed, more the luxuries, more the choices and more the pain; less the luxuries, less the choices and less the pain. She was an ardent believer in the philosophy of minimalism. Rani's life had created a deep impact on her thoughts. She used to say, looking at people above you creates frustration, looking at those below you, gives satisfaction. There are poor who get one bedsheet to cover their body during life and the same serves as coffin after that. With less desires in mind, she created more space for wisdom to grow. She invariably used public transport, whenever needed. Personally, her clothes were very simple. Her only jewellery used to be a pair of cheap artificial ear studs, a wrist watch and a *kara*, a steel bangle normally worn by Sikh men and women in the wrist. A part-time maid was employed for domestic work, whose young daughter was financially supported for education. One room of the flat was office of the Trust, and servant room was for the occasional stay of poor women clients, who could not afford a shelter. The flat had only very essential furniture, that was not costly at all. Books on law, religions and social issues decorated some wooden shelves. Her food used to be simple and home-cooked. She refused to visit restaurants whenever invited by her colleagues. Her friendship was also confined to only a few advocates, and that too for professional matters. Though she maintained her normal smile on her face, once hilarious and bubbly Simran was now absolutely reserved. She was free and friendly only with her clients-in-need.

Three years passed, and Simran was busy in courts fighting cases involving empowerment of women. She was known far and wide for her magnanimity, and women thronged to her for legal help, which she rendered free of cost. Many business houses also began to financially support her Trust. Her noble and selfless social work was being widely recognised and duly rewarded by national and international social agencies, which she accepted with great humility and without any ego or pride. Her greatest reward was, however, her inner satisfaction.

Simran was an early riser and would be ready, even if it was a holiday. It was Sunday and an off day for the maid. After her usual prayers, she had just finished breakfast prepared by her, when the door bell rang. She was little surprised at such an early visitor on a holiday. On opening the door she was shocked to see Gaurav. She hesitated for a moment to digest the sight, and then made way for him to come in.

Making himself little comfortable on a chair, Gaurav cleared his throat. With great hesitation and voice partially choked, he said, "Simranji, I am sorry to disturb you on a holiday without informing you."

Simran retained her normal calm and went to the kitchen to bring a glass of water. Gaurav was looking tense. His face was pale and bereft of the earlier glow. He had lost weight and looked ten years older than his age. Surprisingly, baldness was conspicuous and hair had also started graying. Feeling that he was struggling to speak, she said, "How are uncle and aunt?"

"Both are not maintaining good health and are sad and dejected because of me." '

"Why because of you?"

The volcano of Gaurav's suppressed thoughts suddenly exploded. "They do not want to live in unhealthy environment, where only ego and selfishness survive. Leena hated them and accused them for their low standard. Extremely arrogant, she was always shouting at my mother and treated my parents as domestic servants. She is a pampered child and her father has no control over her lifestyle. Her only hobby is spending money and enjoying with friends. She accused me for not having any business of my own and living on borrowed crumbs, like a beggar. Having been born and brought up in Indian traditions, I could not tolerate her indolence and disrespect to my parents. Clash of values has totally ruined my life. Family relations have collapsed. All of us have now moved to Delhi." Gaurav said all this in one breath.

Simran had completely lost touch with Gaurav and his parents after his marriage. She came to know of his wife's name also for the first time. She was stunned to know the shocking details of Gaurav's life and could not have imagined this even in her wildest dreams. She was absolutely speechless and did not react. Condition of old parents was her greatest concern, even though they were themselves responsible not only for their sufferings but for her agony also. After some time, Gaurav continued, "Leena aborted our child as she refused to bear the burden of child-rearing. She felt that it would disfigure her body, and would adversely affect her independent social life. I understand she had relations with a boyfriend and still maintained them. She had an abortion, when she was hardly sixteen and cannot conceive now. She, her parents and even my aunt had hidden her shady past from all of us. Fully aware of her character and behaviour, they exploited my innocence and dumped her on me. I know I do not deserve any sympathy, but I am telling you all this to lighten my heart." Gaurav tried his best to hide his tears, but the drops were too heavy for the delicate eyes to hold them longer. Simran was not in a position now to wipe them, and remained glued to her seat to patiently listen to the sad story of Gaurav and his parents.

Gaurav resumed, "Leena and I are separated now. My life is virtually ruined. I understood life when it had slipped from my hands. This is the reward of my sins, and I have reaped what I had sown. Totally heart-broken, I do not know what to do?"

"What about the business of your aunt?"

"My cousin sister was married to a distant cousin of Leena, and the business was now totally in the grip of her ambitious husband. My aunt was completely under the control of her dominant son-in-law, who became a prominent contributing factor in ruining our relations. I was like a labourer, not even a salesman. Aunt used me in need, and discarded all of us when her purpose was fulfilled. I could never understand the complex dynamics of these self-centred relations. Now there is nothing but darkness all around, with none to even console me in my distress." Simran suddenly remembered and wondered at the prediction of Ramesh uncle for the future of Gaurav after his marriage.

Just at that time, the bell rang and Simran saw a woman and a girl standing at the door. The girl in her teens was unable to walk, perhaps due to hunger or some other reasons, and the mother was sobbing with tears dried on her sunken face. They appeared to be in great distress. Simran could not ignore them, though she wanted to listen to the distressing tale of Gaurav.

"Mr. Saxena, I will have to devote some time to these women. They seem to be in some trouble and need my help. You can wait or come later."

Gaurav got up, folded his hands and left without saying a word. His eyes were still full of tears. He wanted to stay, but the sudden arrival of the two women deprived him to open his heart further, and reveal the real purpose of his visit, for which his parents had forced him to meet Simran.

Back home, Lalita wanted to know whether Simran was married. Gaurav told her that she was perhaps not married, though he was not very sure.

"Could you propose to her?" asked Lalita.

Gaurav was furious at her query and retorted "There was no time to talk about these things."

Little disappointed at some positive outcome of Gaurav's visit, she said, "We will go to her tomorrow evening and talk to her about marriage. I will apologise and am sure, as a noble soul, she will not disappoint me. Your dad can also come with me, though he may not be able to walk and speak properly."

Next day Lalita, accompanied by her husband, went to Simran's flat. Rajeshwar had survived a severe paralytic attack. He had difficulty in walking, and was not so coherent in his speech. Simran welcomed them and extended normal courtesies. She was shocked to see the condition of Gaurav's father. Both looked more than a dozen years older than their age. The glow and charm on their faces had completely withered. Once fair and charming, Lalita had gone miserably pale. Sunken eyes were telling the tale of their woes. Worry and tension was discernible on their wrinkled faces and seemed to have ruined their lives. As a kind-hearted person, sympathetic and helpful to the aged by nature, Simran showed all due respect to both and tried to know about their health. Lalita did most of the talking and was very apologetic throughout. She told Simran that Leena had always been insulting them and one night, in a violent outburst of emotions, she turned them out. Rajeshwar's sister also refused to give them shelter and help them in the hour of their need. He was unable to bear the shock and the result was the attack. They stayed with a friend for a few days and then left America. With some difficulty, Rajeshwar tried to say, "Simran, we always loved you and admired your noble qualities. Gaurav also loved you and wanted to be your life-partner. Unfortunately, due to the death of my sister's husband, we had to change the course of life of Gaurav much against our wish. My ambitious and selfish sister deceived us. She forced Gaurav to marry Leena and intentionally tried to hide her background. We fell in the trap of her sweet talk. She used us in need and refused to give us shelter even for one night. My own blood betrayed me. She has ruined the lives of all of us." With folded hands, he bowed down.

Simran intently listened to Rajeshwar's tale of distress. She maintained her mental cool, though inwardly she was amused at his lame excuses for changing the marriage decision. She was shocked that age and physical disabilities had absolutely no effect on his wily character, and basic habit of hiding the truth. Time and adversities had not dented his ego and pride. There were no signs of remorse visible in his eyes. To justify his deception, he was now conveniently shifting the whole blame on his sister. It was like a fool, who curses the mirror for the dirt on his own face.

Lalita tried to explain the real purpose of their visit. "Simran, destiny has totally ruined our life and that of Gaurav. He and Leena are separated, and we have left America. I will not mince words and say straight, the purpose of our visit. We request you with folded hands to pardon us, and accept Gaurav as your life-partner. He has repeatedly told us that he would only marry you, or never marry in life. He is completely ruined and needs your support. Lives of three of us are in your hands. You are a noble and kind-hearted soul. Please do not disappoint us. There is no one to look after us in old age. You are our only hope." Saying this, she started crying profusely and fell on the knees of Simran who tried to lift her. "Aunty, please don't do this. You are like a mother to me." Simran took the glass of water from the table and offered to her. Rajeshwar continued to sit with his hands still folded.

Simran did not know how to salvage this unexpected situation, suddenly created by Lalita. Though rock firm on her decision of marriage, she did not want to be discourteous to them. With utmost humility, she said, "Aunty, I had no idea about your life and was all along under the impression that all of you were enjoying a very comfortable and settled life in America. I am shocked to know all these details for the first time. Since you have suddenly put me in an awkward situation, I request you to please give me some time to think over all aspects of my life." Waiting for a few seconds, she resumed, "Aunty, you cannot put the hands of the clock back and undo what has happened. I request you to look after your health. By God's grace, everything will be all right and in course of time, all of you will enjoy a happy and peaceful life."

Both Rajeshwar and Lalita were satisfied with the discussion, and from the reaction of Simran, they were sure that her response would be positive. Simran had carefully replied in words so that they did not feel disheartened. She was, however, convinced in her mind that Rajeshwar was still twisting facts to dispel any doubt from her mind. She knew that he and he alone, had intentionally planned to desert her and arrange the marriage and settlement of Gaurav in America, much before his departure. She realised now that Lalita was aware of the nefarious plan of her wily husband, and fell a prey to the same. Weak Gaurav was tempted by the greed of gold, and all the three had their share in finally ruining her life. She had now lost trust in all of them, and was determined not to fall in their trap again.

Rajeshwar Saxena was extremely selfish and self-centred

by nature. Earlier, he had discarded Simran as a rotten egg and as a trampled flower. Self-interest now propelled him and his wife to embrace Simran with the same past that was the cause of her rejection earlier. They had now no fear of the society and its criticism for marrying their son to a rape victim. Abused and kicked by one, who had hidden facts of her sexual relations and even pregnancy before marriage, they tried to convince Simran of their sincerity. They did not respect her truth and realised the value of truth and honesty, when bitten by falsehood and deceit. Simran was a woman of firm determination, and her decision on marriage was not amenable to change. Still, she did not want to be a cause of distress and suffering to anyone, nor wanted return of pain and tragedy to her own life.

Saxenas revealed all details to Gaurav. They were virtually convinced that Simran had agreed to their proposal. This gave them some moments of happiness, and that was the purpose and aim of Simran. She realised that age and agony of the old deserved sympathy, and did not want to hurt them. Respect for the aged was her greatest concern, and their service her cherished mission. She had stopped saying words that would hurt anyone, even though she had to bear the pain. She had written off hatred and retaliation from the pages of her life. Humility had taught her to be respectful even to her sworn enemies. Her only mission in life was to spread as much happiness and love as possible.

Simran had requested Saxenas to give her time to think, but there was nothing to ponder over. She had already decided the future course of her life and had firmly conveyed the same to Ramesh uncle, her sincerest benefactor and mentor. Having suffered enough in life, she now wanted to live in peace, and not on false and broken trusts and promises. Earlier, after her suffering due to the betrayal of Gaurav, she had momentarily thought of renouncing the world, but decided against this, as that would be cowardice and abdication of her cherished social mission. She decided to live in the society, and serve the cause of the poor and downtrodden, especially women. Finally, she wanted to discover solace and tranquility in returning to society, whatever she had got.

Legal and social activities of Simran were mainly confined to *Karkardooma* court. On his return, Gaurav also started practicing in the same court. He had clearly told his parents that he would not marry anyone, except Simran and if she refused, he would devote his life to their service. With a guilty conscience, he was too timid to talk to her directly about marriage. He knew that Simran was a woman of great self-respect and would turn down his proposal. To explore chances of marriage, he started crossing her path more frequently to win over her heart in course of time. This created turmoil in the life of Simran. She thought that Saxenas would continue pressing her for marriage, and would be distressed at her brutal denial. Her nearness would be a cause of pain and going away from the path of their lives would minimise the same, and eventually diminish with the passage of time. This may also compel Gaurav to marry and be a source of peace and happiness to his parents. As an embodiment of sacrifice, she had always given priority to the happiness of others. She thought of leaving Delhi and moving to Jaipur, but after careful consideration, decided against this and changed her residence and place of practice to Rohini.

Simran did not want Gaurav or his parents to live on the false hope of any future relations. She was courageous enough to directly talk to Gaurav about her decision, but finally decided to write a letter to him to put a complete end to his hope of marriage, if any.

"Mr. Gaurav Saxena,

Events of last few years of your life have shocked me. If you peep deep into the past, you will recollect that I never forced myself on you and it was your considered decision to be my life-partner. Both your parents had approved our marriage, and conveyed the same to Ramesh uncle. Till your departure, you and your parents kept on promising marriage, and I was confident that all of you were sincere in your promise. As a result, I had installed your idol in my heart due to your promised love and trust. However, the professed love proved to be sheer pretence, for true love is never so weak to bend or break. You sacrificed love and noble qualities for the material world, but in the bargain lost everything.

Relations survive and thrive on trust and respect. If you had frankly refused the proposal, I would have gladly accepted the same and would have willingly gone out of your way. I vividly remember, Ramesh uncle and I having clearly told you, that if you ever decide against marriage, you should not deceive me and honestly tell me your decision. Your words, 'Greed of gold or any other temptation has no place in my life' and 'Love and sincerity are my primary concerns' still echo in my mind. You sacrificed your 'primary concerns' and decided to desert me for 'Greed of gold' and 'other temptation'. You said 'Simran is my life' but three of you dug my grave and you buried your 'life' alive in the grave. You promised trust but gave instead only mistrust. Pain caused by a wound gets healed, but pain caused by mistrust never heals. It remains buried in some corner of the heart. It may be forgotten with time, but not its perpetrator. I can never put behind your betrayal, howsoever hard I may try or you may convince.

Remember, you had sworn, 'You are my present; you are my future', but I remained neither your present nor your future. I remained only my past. Not making a promise is not painful, but making one and then breaking the same is disastrous. Intentional and deliberate pain had been caused to me by all three of you, but I particularly felt the stand taken by you in betraying me. Men in my life, barring Ramesh uncle, had been the cause of my sufferings. Your betrayal of trust has now completely shattered my heart and any remaining faith in the sincerity of man. Heart is like a glass. Once it breaks, it continues to break into smaller pieces, that can never be joined.

You aroused sweet aspirations in me, only to demolish them by false promises. With your departure, collapsed the world of my dreams. Your desertion created a void and state of zero-ness in my life. There was none to share my pain. Betrayed in love, timid retire from life, weak suffer in silence but the bold continue to live. I decided to live, create my own dreams and give them a fresh flight. Sometimes, small dreams remain just dreams, for God has reserved better and bigger ones for us. Now I don't see happiness in seeing dreams but in realising them.

You deprived me of love, trust, promise and everything, but could not snatch my mission and reason to live. I never wanted to waste time in stumbling through life. Life is not a sprint; it is a long distance marathon. It is a journey with no destination and must continue till His call. To fulfil my cherished ambition, I have decided not to wallow in the past, and want to fill the created emptiness with the pursuit of my pre-decided social mission. I always desired to live life for a satisfying purpose and for a more meaningful cause. In the desired path, I have dropped all thoughts, emotions and notions. I have now decided to resign to a more peaceful life and seek refuge in social emancipation. Destiny snatched everything from me to bestow the fulfilment of my most valued desire.

Having suffered your betrayal, I desired stability and did not want to be tossed further by the deceit and betrayal of man. When I look back, I feel that your betrayal proved to be a blessing in disguise. Pain opened windows of wisdom. The shackles that could have chained my mission were broken. Sometimes, loss is more profitable than gain. In losing you, I gained the strength of my mission. There was another silver lining. Love blinded by the charm of gold cannot survive, and if this had happened after marriage, my life and that of children would have been completely shattered.

Human mind is slave of objectivity, and fails to discover subjectivity. Your parents looked at rape and pregnancy and not their cause. They carefully gained time in small doses, though decision had perhaps been taken much earlier. All of you dumped me in dust and now want to embrace me for your selfish motive, with my presumed soiled soul and disgraced body. Selfishness always played a significant role in your motives, particularly of your father. Self-interest now viewed my alleged vices as virtues. Your parents could not tolerate truth, and strangulated it by the noose of lies. They suffered unbearable pain, when they discovered the deliberately hidden vices in the other girl after your marriage. The selfish known betrayed them and faithful unknown, they did not trust. Having been betrayed by everyone, including your aunt, they have now come to one, whom they betrayed. They have placed the proposal of marriage. I had already decided the course of my life after learning about your marriage. Let me say it straight, rather than betray and keep the hope alive, as you all did. Offer of marriage is not acceptable to me. My decision is final and irrevocable.

Trust terrifies me now; tears don't. I have left pleasure and pain far behind. Crossing path everyday in the course of our profession or any further nearness, not to talk of a relation, would simply cause nothing but pain and distress to all of you. This will keep the hope of further relations alive in you and your parents. I do not want to drag on that hope, and then betray as you did. I have suffered this pain and do not want your parents to suffer. To bring an end to this drama of hope, one had to leave the path of the other. I decided to change my course. I don't want to be chased by deceptive relations. Do not stroke the burnt wood. You won't find even a spark in the heap of ashes. Let me now blissfully live every moment of my life.

Your arrival scratched my past wounds. But with all the sufferings caused to me, I am not the person to retaliate. I have forgotten all the hatred, jealousy and pain given to me by my known and unknown. Deprived of love and happiness in life, my mission is to spread the same. My painful concern today is the suffering of your parents, and its deleterious effect on their physical and mental health at this advanced age. It is your duty to give them peace and happiness. Parents have a right to the love and care of their children, and children owe a responsibility to provide and ensure the same. Having suffered in my life, I can understand and feel the agony that they might be suffering from. By refusing the offer of marriage, I am not causing any suffering to anyone. The sufferers themselves suffer the reaction of their action.

Long back, I had conquered hatred and fear of fall. Now I have conquered mistrust. Pleasure and pain had played a seesaw game in my life, right from birth. After a long and peril-filled journey of life, I have overpowered them, and am now beyond the reach of any pain. I am alone, but not lonely. Pursuit of my mission and service of the people are always with me. I wish and pray for peace and happiness in the life of all.

Simran"

Life of a motherless child that started with hatred of her father, ended in the agonising mistrust of her love-mate. In the process, it was decorated with love and care by the unknown, that she, in turn, passed on in greater measures to everyone who came her way. Heart-wrenching tragedies were a part of her destiny and happiness occasionally peeped in small measures through the slits of her life-windows, only to wither soon, making way for greater pain. In the painful journey of life, she longed for love, but remained bereft of that. In the drama of her life, actors came in turns, played their part, and left the stage one by one with memories, bitter or sweet. Tragedy continued to be the harsh reality of her life. She fought to seek justice for others, but fate did not bestow the same on her. Even her noble thoughts and righteous deeds were often defied by the invisible hand of destiny, that she fought with sheer determination and strong will-power. Betrayed by the outside world, she finally sought peace within. Tranquility and eternal bliss ultimately came through the service of mankind, in search of enlightenment, and existence beyond the mind. She discovered herself.

□□□